Perfect Fit

Perfect Fit

carly phillips

BERKLEY BOOKS, NEW YORK

THE BERKLEY PUBLISHING GROUP
Published by the Penguin Group
Penguin Group (USA) Inc.
375 Hudson Street, New York, New York 10014, USA
Penguin Group (Canada), 90 Eglinton Avenue East, Suite 700, Toronto, Ontario M4P 2Y3, Canada
(a division of Pearson Penguin Canada Inc.) • Penguin Books Ltd., 80 Strand, London WC2R 0RL,
England • Penguin Ireland, 25 St. Stephen's Green, Dublin 2, Ireland (a division of Penguin
Books Ltd.) • Penguin Group (Australia), 707 Collins Street, Melbourne, Victoria 3008, Australia
(a division of Pearson Australia Group Pty. Ltd.) • Penguin Books India Pvt. Ltd., 11 Community
Centre, Panchsheel Park, New Delhi—110 017, India • Penguin Group (NZ), 67 Apollo Drive,
Rosedale, Auckland 0632, New Zealand (a division of Pearson New Zealand Ltd.) • Penguin Books
(South Africa), Rosebank Office Park, 181 Jan Smuts Avenue, Parktown North 2193,
South Africa • Penguin China, B7 Jiaming Center, 27 East Third Ring Road North, Chaoyang
District, Beijing 100020, China

Penguin Books Ltd., Registered Offices: 80 Strand, London WC2R 0RL, England

This is a work of fiction. Names, characters, places, and incidents either are the product of the author's
imagination or are used fictitiously, and any resemblance to actual persons, living or dead, business
establishments, events, or locales is entirely coincidental. The publisher does not have any control over
and does not assume any responsibility for author or third-party websites or their content.

PERFECT FIT

A Berkley Book / published by arrangement with the author

ISBN: 978-1-62090-963-8

BERKLEY®
Berkley Books are published by The Berkley Publishing Group,
a division of Penguin Group (USA) Inc.,
375 Hudson Street, New York, New York 10014.
BERKLEY® is a registered trademark of Penguin Group (USA) Inc.
The "B" design is a trademark of Penguin Group (USA) Inc.

PRINTED IN THE UNITED STATES OF AMERICA

I am so lucky to have the following people in my life:

If not for Janelle Denison, who reads my pages, rereads my pages, and talks me through my "I'm stuck" moments, I'm not sure there would BE a Serendipity! Leslie Kelly and Julie Leto, my plotting buddies and close friends, whose brains save me each and every time. I DO need a stinkin' plot and thank goodness you two are great at twists and turns and even better at being friends. And Shannon Short, who is my constant, who e-mails/talks me through things I cannot discuss here, but who understands this business as well as anyone and lets me vent and share the ups and downs . . . You have no idea how much I value you all! I can't imagine my life without each one of you in it and I hope I give back as much as you give to me.

A special shout out:

Writing can be a very solitary profession—unless you're an Internet junkie, like me. A special thank you to my #Sprint partners on Twitter—Marquita Valentine, @marquitaval; Lissa Matthews, @lissamatthews; Olivia Kelly, @oliviakelly_;and Andris Bear, @andrisbear—you were there for me at 9 A.M. for the writing of this book. You were invaluable in keeping me motivated, in my chair, turning out words in our thirty-minute shifts. We may not have met in person (yet) but I feel like I know you all. Thanks and I hope you're there for the next book, too!

A special thank you to Alexis Craig—@Dispatchvampire—whom I also met on Twitter and who allowed me to pick her brain about all things cop related. I hope I didn't drive you too crazy! Thanks to Kelli Bruns for the nursing info.

And locally, a very special thanks to Frank for answering my questions in e-mail form, not laughing (at least not when I could see or hear), and for having the utmost patience. Not to mention for taking care of my parents. I'm grateful!

Any and all police- and/or nurse/injury-related mistakes are solely my own!

One

Perfection was overrated, Mike Marsden thought, as he approached his childhood home. He arrived in time for dinner, just as he'd done every Sunday since his return to his hometown of Serendipity, New York, almost a month ago. Sunday evening meal at his parents' house was mandatory, and each of his siblings would be there. Nobody said no to Ella Marsden. And since Mike had been away for a half dozen years or so, his mother was especially glad to have him back, no matter how uncomfortable the notion of coming home made him.

He shoved his hands into the pockets of his leather jacket and looked up at the white clapboard house with blue trim and matching shutters. Small but well kept, the two-story home on a residential street was as perfect on the outside as it was on the inside. Same as it was when he'd left for Atlantic City all those years ago. Maybe that was why he was itching beneath his skin now. The idea of perfection made him antsy. It always had. And despite wanting to please his parents, Mike was the kid who'd always tried their patience.

Impulse control issues, his teachers called it. Mike blamed heredity. He couldn't stick with one thing very long, be it his small hometown, a relationship, or a monotonous job. Simon Marsden, Mike's adopted father and the man who'd raised him, had been the police chief of Serendipity. Mike's brother, Sam, had followed in his footsteps, becoming a homegrown cop like his dad. Their sister, Erin, was the assistant district attorney to Serendipity's D.A.

And Mike? He liked his life, choosing his career as a New York City undercover cop, where he'd carved out a name for himself by skating the rules instead of strictly following them. He made sure his job, his women, and even his friends were easy enough to walk away from when the impulse arose. Never again would there be a repeat of a woman misinterpreting his intentions or expecting too much. He'd run from that strangled feeling once before, ending up in Atlantic City. He wasn't about to repeat past mistakes or risk what he knew was a genetic inability to stick around.

Yet here he was, back in his small hometown, having taken over his father's job as chief of police while his dad fought cancer. The doctors said it was treatable, and Mike forced himself to believe it. Coming home was the least he could do for the man who'd both raised him and treated him no differently than his biological children—even if Mike hadn't always deserved it. The situation was temporary while Simon recovered, or Mike didn't think he'd have been able to say yes to the position.

He knocked once and let himself inside, the smell of his mother's pot roast seducing his senses and making his stomach grumble.

"Michael, is that you?" his mother called from her post in the kitchen. When he was a kid, he'd thought she had a sixth sense that told her which child walked in the door, but as an adult he realized they each had their own arrival time and his mother intuitively knew their routine.

"It's me," he yelled back, bending to give his parents'

new dog, a small white fluffball that resembled a dust mop, a pat on the head, still marveling that they'd named the furry thing Kojak.

"Well, come give me a hug," Ella called out, as if she hadn't seen him in ages. In reality, she'd stopped by the police station yesterday to say hello.

He grinned and his shoulders eased downward. The insecurities that always followed thoughts of perfection fled at the warmth in his mother's voice and the comforting smells of home.

"Come on, little man. Let's go say hi to Mom." He headed for the kitchen, Kojak by his side.

Along the way he passed the family room, where his father lay snoring in his recliner, football game on the big-screen television he and his siblings had bought them for Christmas last year. Knowing Simon needed his rest, Mike let him sleep.

"Hey, Mom," Mike said, entering the kitchen and giving her the requested hug before turning to the oversized pot on the stove. "Smells delicious." He lifted the lid only to have his mother smack his hand with her wooden spoon.

"Hey! No sampling." She waved her weapon in front of his face, a knowing smile lifting her lips.

Despite his father's illness, she'd managed to retain her cheery disposition, and if a few more lines creased her beautiful skin, it didn't affect her good looks at all. Wavy auburn hair curled naturally around her face, adding to her youthful appearance.

"Hey, family!" His sister Erin's voice sounded from the entryway.

"In here," Mike called back, then winced because his father was sleeping.

"Dad's snoring," Erin said, striding into the kitchen with a box in hand. "A hurricane couldn't wake him."

"That's because I gave him a painkiller a little while ago. His back was hurting," Ella said.

Mike pushed past the fear in his throat. The old man was strong. He would pull through. "What kind of cake did you bring?"

"Angel food. Dad's favorite."

Of course. Erin was always the good girl, doing the right thing without being asked. Mike could barely remember to get himself someplace on time, let alone bring something with him.

His sister placed the white bakery box on the counter. "Hi, Mom," she said, pecking her cheek. "Big brother." She grinned and pulled him into a hug.

"Hey, pest."

She nudged him in the ribs with her elbow. "Jerk."

"Squirt."

"Enough!" Ella yelled at them like they were naughty kids, and Erin laughed.

"It's just so easy to fall back into it." She shook her head and grinned. Erin was a true mixture of both parents. Their mother's once-dark hair was now auburn with reddish highlights, and Erin's was naturally so with Simon's hazel eyes. Eyes that now danced with laughter. "So where's Sam?" she asked.

"Your brother isn't here yet." Ella glanced at the clock on the oven and frowned. "He's late, and that's not like him. Is he working a shift today? Maybe he got held up." She looked to Mike for the answer, since he was now his brother's boss.

"Not that I know of, unless he switched with someone."

"Well, let's sit down in here for a little while and wait. Give your father some more time to sleep." Ella gestured to the Formica table and they all grabbed a seat, same chairs they'd each eaten in growing up.

"How's Dad doing?" Erin asked. "You mentioned back pain?"

Ella nodded. "The doctor said he might try radiation this

week instead of waiting until later on. It's supposed to shrink the tumor and help with the pain. But he's handling the chemo well enough. And his spirit is amazing," she said with obvious pride.

"What about you?" Mike asked his mother, reaching for her hand.

She immediately waved him off. "I'm fine, Michael. I'm not the one who's sick."

Mike shot his sister a knowing look. Their mother acted like Superwoman, stepping up and handling everything without complaint. Perfection personified, Mike thought. But he knew she had to be exhausted. He opened his mouth to argue that she needed rest too, but Erin shook her head, telling him to let it go.

Fine, he'd listen for now, but at some point his mother would have to give in and let someone else help her out for a change.

Suddenly the telephone rang, and Ella rose to answer it.

"Don't pressure her. She likes feeling needed," Erin whispered as their mother spoke on the phone. "I'm coming over to sit with Dad one day this week so she can go get her hair done. Sam promised to play chess with Dad one afternoon this week. She's getting breaks."

"Why didn't anyone ask me to help out?" he asked, too petulantly for his liking. The fact that he hadn't thought to relieve his mother had him feeling out of sorts and selfish. As usual, he'd fallen short compared to his siblings. So what else was new?

"We figured you had your hands full taking Dad's place and getting up to speed," Erin said.

"It's been a month. I'm as up as I'm going to get. The rest depends on everyone accepting how I want to do things." He'd have made time for his mother. He was about to say as much when Ella returned.

One look at her pale face and Mike shot to his feet.

"What's wrong?" he asked, placing a bracing arm around her shoulder.

Erin came around her other side. "Mom?"

"Sam's been in an accident."

Heart pounding hard in his chest, Mike eased his mother into the nearest chair. "What happened?"

"That was Cara," she said of Sam's partner. "His car crashed into a tree. He's at University Hospital now."

"Cara was with him?" Mike knew for a fact they weren't on duty today, but it wasn't surprising they were together. Those two made a mockery of the notion that men and women couldn't be just friends.

It was Mike who couldn't just be Cara's friend, not after an explosive one-night stand three months ago that he'd yet to get out of his head. "Are they both okay?"

"Cara sounded fine. Sam's being assessed," his mother said, still trembling.

Mike swallowed hard. His mother's fear wasn't an easy thing to deal with, not when she was usually so strong. But she'd been hit with too many things at once lately.

"I need to go to your brother, but I can't leave your father. I don't want to drag him out there and put him under all that stress, around sick people and germs . . ."

This was something he could do to help. "I'll head over to the hospital," Mike said, glancing at his sister.

She nodded. "And I'll stay here with you and Dad."

"No." Ella shook her head. "You go with your brother. You two should be together when you get news on Sam."

Mike immediately thought of a solution. "I'll tell you what. I'll call Aunt Louisa to come over," he said of his mother's sister who also lived in Serendipity a few streets away. "That way you and Dad won't be alone."

"I don't want to be a bother to her."

But Erin had already reached for the phone and begun dialing over their mother's objections.

A few minutes later, their aunt was on her way over while Mike and Erin headed for the hospital.

Officer Cara Hartley paced outside the emergency room, hoping for news on her partner and waiting for his family to arrive. She didn't know which members would come, given Sam's father's condition, but her gut told her his brother, Michael, would be one of them. As laid-back as he appeared, when it came to doing his job or caring for his family, the man was as take-charge alpha as they came.

He also liked control in the bedroom, something Cara knew only too well. She shivered at the reminder of one incredible night a few months ago when Mike had been home for the weekend visiting his father. He and Sam had shown up at Joe's Bar, they'd flirted, he'd bought her drinks, he'd walked her to her car, and the next thing she knew, she'd agreed to let him follow her home and take her—not just to bed but wherever he damn well pleased. He'd been phenomenal, bringing her to heights she'd only dreamed of and igniting a hunger that had fueled many fantasies in the months since.

"Dr. Nussbaum, please call extension fifty-three. Dr. Nussbaum, extension fifty-three." The voice over the hospital loudspeaker broke into Cara's heated thoughts.

Although those sensual memories had been a welcome distraction from worrying about Sam, the last thing she wanted to be thinking about was the man who was now her boss. He'd completely rocked her world, but he hadn't mentioned it since his return. Granted, she hadn't brought up the subject either, but his complete refusal to acknowledge her as more than one of his officers grated her female pride. Even the few times they were alone, Mike had been abrupt and all business.

When he arrived, she had no doubt he'd want to talk

about what she and Sam were doing on Route 80, heading back to Serendipity from the outskirts of town. They'd been looking into a cold case Mike had assigned to them and were just beginning to realize that the implications of their findings might affect Mike personally. She wouldn't share anything without Sam's permission. Not even with her boss. Hopefully he wouldn't push for information. If she had good news about Sam, maybe he wouldn't delve too deeply into where they'd been or why.

Suddenly the street doors swung wide and Cara caught sight of Mike, his dark hair longer than regulation for a cop, his leather jacket giving him a dangerous edge. During the week, he wore suits and ties when he had scheduled meetings, but Cara knew he preferred his beat-up leather and jeans to the stuffy boss clothing the job demanded.

Mike barreled through the lobby and headed straight for her, his sister right behind him.

"How's Sam?" Erin asked.

"What the hell happened?" Mike barked at Cara.

She straightened to her full height, which at five foot three wasn't much compared to his almost six feet. "We were in an accident, Chief."

"Any news on Sam?" Erin asked.

Cara shook her head. "Not yet, but he was conscious when the ambulance brought him in."

"I didn't have you two on the schedule today." Mike pinned her with a steady stare.

Cara looked into his chocolate brown eyes, wondering how they could have been so sexy all those months ago and so cold and forbidding now. "And if you'll notice, I'm not in uniform. Your brother and I were out for a ride. It's a gorgeous day," she said, hating the evasion that fell from her lips.

"Ease up," Erin said, punching Mike in the arm. "She's not on duty and she's as worried about Sam as we are. And lay off the formalities. Cara's like family."

Cara and Erin were the same age, and though they hadn't

been best friends in school, they'd been in the same general group of girls, while Sam, a year older, had been a friend; it wasn't until they both joined the force together that their friendship solidified and Cara became more a part of the Marsdens' inner circle. By then, Mike had been long gone.

Erin pulled Cara into an embrace. "I'm glad you're okay."

Cara managed a nod and hugged Erin back. "It was scary," she said, allowing herself to admit her fear for the first time. She stepped away from Erin. Suddenly cold, she wished she were wearing a heavier jacket.

"You're shaking." Erin said, breaking into her thoughts. "And your cheek is bruised."

"Air bag," Cara said softly.

"Were you checked out?" Mike asked, his tone deep and gravelly, sending shivers through her that had nothing to do with the earlier accident.

"The paramedics cleared me at the scene. It's just a delayed reaction, I guess."

Mike's frown deepened. "Let's sit." Without waiting for her to agree, he grasped her elbow and led her to a chair.

Because Cara's legs were truly unsteady, she let him have his way. Erin picked a chair across the aisle, while Mike chose a spot beside Cara. He sat next to her, so close the musky scent of his aftershave warmed her in ways she couldn't think about now.

"What happened?" Erin asked softly.

In a weird way it was a relief to go back to the accident and share the experience. "Sam was driving. He was fine one minute, and the next he doubled over in pain. I reached for the wheel, but I had no leverage and the car hit a tree."

She blew out a stream of air and steadied herself before continuing. "My air bag deployed. His didn't. Sam's head hit the steering wheel"—she winced as she recalled the awful sound—"and his side of the car took the brunt of the impact. I was able to call for an ambulance and here we are." She clenched her fists until her nails bit into her flesh.

"Easy," Mike said as his big, strong hand covered hers and he gently pried her fingernails away from her skin.

Her entire body reacted to his touch, awareness jolting through her like a sudden burst of electricity. Startled, she met his gaze and in that moment she *knew* he was as stunned as she.

Until he jerked his hand back and rose to his feet. "Where is a damned doctor with some news?"

Erin rose and put a hand on her brother's shoulder. "I'm sure we'll hear something soon." No sooner had she spoken than a familiar voice called out Cara's name.

"Alexa!" Relieved, Cara jumped up and turned to Dr. Alexa Collins, a beautiful woman with auburn hair now pulled back in a bun. She was not only one of Cara's closest friends but the doctor on call.

"How is he?" Sam's siblings asked at the same time.

"He's stable. He had an appendicitis attack while he was driving." She glanced at Cara. "Did he mention any pain during the day?"

She thought back and shook her head.

Alexa frowned. "Then he must have covered and ignored it. Appendicitis pain typically increases over a period of time. Stubborn man," she muttered, knowing Sam as well as Cara did. "Okay, well, he's in surgery to take care of the appendix, and barring any complications he should be fine. He's also got a concussion from impact with the steering wheel, but again, barring complications, nothing life threatening." She smiled at Erin, Michael, and Cara to put them at ease. "I'm going to go back in. As soon as he's in recovery, I'll let you know. You can see him later."

"Thank you," Erin breathed out in relief. "I'll go let Mom and Dad know." She rushed outside, probably to a place she could use her cell phone.

"Thanks, Alexa," Cara said.

The other woman smiled. "I can honestly say it's my

pleasure. It'll also be my pleasure to kick his ass for ignoring pain. And trust me, he had to have felt something earlier."

"I'll help you," Mike muttered. "Thanks for everything."

Alexa nodded. "I'll be back soon with news." She, too, took off, leaving Cara and Mike alone.

Most of her earlier shakiness had subsided, leaving Cara exhausted. "I'm going to get some coffee. Want some?" she asked the hulking, silent man beside her.

"No, thanks."

She shrugged. "Suit yourself," she said, more uncomfortable now that the mood between them had shifted from connected to awkward. But awkward was the way things had been since his return. She turned and headed for the door.

"Cara."

Surprised, she pivoted back toward him. "Yes?"

"Thank you. For calling 911 and making sure Sam got here quickly."

It was as much of an apology for his earlier rudeness as she was likely to get. If she hadn't been in the room with him that night three months ago, under him, over him, him deep inside her, his recent behavior would have convinced Cara that the most spectacular evening of her life had never happened. But it had, she thought, shivering as her body recalled the intimate connection. And that brief time together along with the flare of heat in his eyes today had convinced her she wasn't crazy. He'd been as affected as she was, whether he showed it or not.

It was his choice not to acknowledge it that proved he wanted nothing to do with her. Heck, he clearly didn't even want a repeat performance, which merely reinforced Sam's point. As he'd informed Cara before she'd left the bar with his brother, Mike viewed everything and everyone in life as temporary. He'd even reminded her of Tiffany Marks, the woman he'd dated before leaving for Atlantic City. Everyone in town knew she'd gone so far as to make inquiries into booking the only church in town for a wedding Mike had never planned on happening. Except Tiffany had been certain Mike was on the verge of popping the question, and she'd been heartbroken when he'd left.

When Cara had agreed to their one night, she'd been okay with that. She knew that while he didn't stick around, she was a small-town girl at heart, with small-town aspirations. She'd happily remain in Serendipity long after the big-city detective left his temporary job as chief of police behind. She had no doubt if she got involved with Mike again, she'd end up with a broken heart. But he wasn't asking her for anything.

Yet if he pressed, she'd be tempted. And what did that say about her? She shook her head to dislodge thoughts of a man who clearly wasn't interested. Cara wouldn't chase after a man any more than she'd let one take advantage of her. Her mother and father's unbalanced, unhealthy relationship set an example Cara refused to follow.

With that reality firmly in mind, she went for coffee.

Mike had faced down drug dealers and embezzlers with enough at stake to warrant killing him in order to keep their activities secret, and he hadn't been afraid. He'd be damned if he'd let one pint-sized police officer with ocean-blue eyes get under his skin. His brother would be okay, and that was what he needed to focus on, not the way Cara, the always-in-control cop, had nearly broken down, reminding him she was also soft and female. He already knew that all too well.

After seeing Cara at the hospital yesterday, Mike had promised himself that except for work, he'd steer clear. He'd even thought his self-imposed directive would be simple. But when he came to visit his brother the next morning, Cara was already there, having stopped by on her way to work. He heard her laughter from the hallway as he approached Sam's room.

Though he wanted to come back later, Mike wasn't a coward. He gripped the handle and let himself inside.

"Nice way to get some attention," Mike said to Sam, who was laid up in bed.

"I'm not stupid." His light-brown hair was messed and sticking up at odd angles, his face pale, yet he managed a grin.

"No, you're not. The nurses are lining up to take care of him," Cara said, catching Mike's gaze.

She rose to her feet. In her blue uniform, she looked every inch the professional.

"I was just leaving for work. I'll let you two visit." She gestured for Mike to take the chair she'd vacated by the side of the bed.

"Don't let me run you off," Mike said. "I'm sure your boss won't mind if you're a few minutes late for your shift."

Cara pursed her lips. "Oh, I don't know about that. He's quite the hard-ass sometimes."

Sam burst out laughing, then groaned and shut his eyes.

"I'm sorry." Cara leaned over and pressed her hand to his cheek. "Are you okay?"

He nodded. "Maybe you should go. I may burst my stitches if you stick around while he's here." Sam inclined his head toward Mike.

He frowned, not liking that Cara hadn't yet removed her hand from his brother's cheek. "I'm her boss," Mike reminded them. "Doesn't that warrant at least some respect?"

"Only when you're on duty, big brother." Sam swallowed what was sure to be another laugh.

Cara shook her head, her smile coming through as she finally pulled her hand away.

Apparently she'd taken his sister's words to heart and decided she could give him a hard time off duty. Her sassy mouth was one of the things he'd enjoyed about her when he'd visited a few months ago, and it could definitely get him in trouble again now.

"I'm going, I'm going," Cara muttered. "But I'll be back after my shift. You," she said, wagging a finger at Sam. "Behave and listen to your nurses."

"Bring me a burger from The Family Restaurant?" he asked.

Cara shook her head. "Not until the doctors say it's okay." She glanced at Mike, meeting his gaze with a wry smile, showing off two dimples in her cheeks.

Damn. How could she be professional, cute, and sexy all at the same time? He'd worked with many women over the years, and he'd never been affected like this. Never mixed business and pleasure on the job because that made a situation harder to walk away from.

"Who's her partner while I'm stuck here?" Sam asked.

One of the changes Mike intended to make within the department was eliminating partners. The way he viewed it, the force was small, as was the town. No need to tie up two officers together who could cover more areas separately. He'd planned to schedule a meeting with his officers next week, but now he'd wait a little while longer until Sam was up to speed.

"I paired her with Dare," Mike said, giving her a heads-up.

"Dare and I work well together, so thanks," she said, sounding surprised.

Did she really think he'd deliberately put her with someone more difficult after the day she'd had yesterday?

"Don't forget to save the fun stuff for me," Sam said, sounding suddenly intense.

Cara met Sam's gaze. "You know it," she said.

Which, to Mike, sounded like a promise. He glanced from his brother, who lay prone in his bed, to Cara. She stood by the door, massaging the muscles in her neck.

"Are you sure you're up to working today?" Mike asked. "No whiplash, pain, or trauma?"

"Nah. I'm tougher than I look. And definitely tougher than my partner." With a wink at Sam and a quick gaze at Mike, she ducked out the door, leaving the brothers alone.

"Sit," Sam said in a no-argument tone that belied the fact that Mike was the older brother and Sam was laid up in a hospital bed.

Not wanting to upset Sam in his condition, Mike lowered himself into the chair. Folding his arms across his chest, he leaned back. "What's up?"

"What's going on with you and Cara?" Sam asked.

"Nothing."

"You haven't discussed what happened between you two yet?" Sam asked, or rather croaked through his dry throat.

Mike handed his brother a cup of water from his tray. "It hasn't come up."

Sam drank and put his cup down. "You mean she hasn't brought it up, so you won't."

"Why the hell did you wait until you were lying in a hospital bed for this discussion? It's not like we couldn't have had this talk weeks ago." *Or preferably not at all*, Mike thought.

"Because you'll pay attention to me now." Sam smirked at that little bit of truth.

"It's none of your business," Mike tried reminding his brother. He shifted his gaze to the white hospital walls. Unless . . . A sudden thought came to him. "Did Cara say anything to you about us?" The word sounded awkward on his tongue.

"No. She knows not to expect anything from you," Sam muttered.

"Good." Mike exhaled the breath he hadn't realized he was holding.

The last thing he needed was a woman he'd slept with and who now worked for him having any expectations. He shuddered at the thought. It was taking all he had inside him to focus on staying in Serendipity, working at his father's job, and worrying about his old man.

"Good?" Sam clenched his fists at his side.

When it came to Cara, his brother's protective instincts came out like crazy. Another reason Mike knew he'd made a mistake sleeping with her.

Except it hadn't felt like a mistake at the time. And he wanted to do it again.

"Just because she knows doesn't mean you aren't making her feel like shit by ignoring what happened. Jesus, Mike, was it that bad?"

"No, it was that good. Now can we drop it?" Mike barked at his brother.

To his shock, Sam grinned. "Just one question first. What would you do to someone who treated Erin the way you're treating Cara?"

Mike preferred to think of his younger sister as a sweet innocent, not a twenty-seven-year-old woman. "I'd kick his ass," Mike said immediately.

Sam's knowing stare, full of meaning and, yeah, disappointment, stabbed Mike in the gut, and blood rushed to his cheeks in embarrassment. Shame quickly followed. Okay, so he and Cara had some talking to do.

And clearly Mike had walked right into his brother's trap. "I'm still not discussing Cara with you."

"Good, because I don't want details. I just wanted you to look at things the right way." Sam gestured to the water, and Mike poured him some more. "Besides, I figure you two can only ignore the obvious for so long before something gives."

Sam had a point. Which brought Mike full circle to his earlier thoughts. No matter how much he denied it or tried to pretend otherwise, the woman got to him in a way that made her more dangerous than any potential suspect or case. And now that he realized he could no longer ignore the past, putting it out for discussion would only make the feelings between them more real.

No, not feelings, he thought with a hard shake of his head. That word involved emotion. What he and Cara had shared was hot sex. Hotter than any he'd ever had—

"So how are you feeling?" Mike asked Sam, deliberately changing the subject.

His brother's wince said it all. "Like my head's about to explode, and my abdomen's bloated and hurts like a son of a bitch."

Mike nodded in understanding. "Rest. I'll tell everyone at the station to hold off visiting for a day or two."

Sam's eyes began to close. "I'd appreciate that. I'm getting kicked out in two days, so they can come by and visit me then."

"Do you need me to move in for a couple of days and help you out?" Mike asked.

Knowing his stay in town wasn't permanent, and never needing much space, he'd rented the empty room over Joe's Bar. Sam, like the true Marsden son, had already bought himself a small house in Serendipity, picket fence and all.

"Nah. Cara offered to let me take the spare room at her new condo."

Mike ignored the hot flush of jealousy creeping through his veins. It was as unwarranted as it was ridiculous. Sam and Cara were best friends and partners, but there was nothing sexual between them. And even if there was, Mike didn't plan to pick up where they'd left off, so what was his problem?

"That was nice of her to offer." Mike forced out the words.

"Yeah. I might take her up on it," Sam said, sounding groggier by the minute.

"Hey, did you click on your meds while I wasn't looking?" Mike gestured to the button attached to his brother's IV.

Sam nodded, a goofy grin on his face. "Yeah. Feeling no pain, my man."

Mike rolled his eyes. Time for him to go. He braced his hand on the bed and rose to his feet. "You get some sleep. I'll come by after work. Mom said to tell you they'll be here around lunchtime."

"Okay. They came late last night for a quick hello, but I was pretty out of it."

"Yeah, but they both slept better for seeing you."

Sam didn't reply. He was already passed out cold. Mike shook his head and walked out. First stop coffee shop, then he'd get lost in work. Later on today, he'd deal with Cara Hartley.

Two

The morning passed quickly. A beat-up Trans Am blew through the stop sign at the corner of Main Street, forcing Cara and Dare to pull over a teenage driver who carried only a permit and who wasn't supposed to be driving without a licensed adult in the car. His attitude didn't help his cause, nor did the fact that he should have been in school. They wrote up the ticket and gave the truant an escort to the high school before heading back to town and doing their basic drive-by.

"Man, I hope Tess doesn't end up like that punk," Dare said of his fifteen-year-old half sister.

"I'm sure having a cop for a brother will keep her from turning into Danica Patrick too soon," Cara said with a laugh. "Although knowing Tess, she'll find a way to keep you all up at night worrying."

Tess lived with Dare's oldest brother, Ethan, and his wife in the landmark mansion on the edge of town. Making things more interesting—and titillating for the more gossip-minded residents in town—his middle brother, Nash, was married to Tess's half sister. But whomever she lived with, they all worried about Tess, given her history before moving to Serendipity.

"I just hope Ethan doesn't buy her an over-the-top car," Dare said.

Cara shook her head at the thought. "Ethan has a level head." She caught Dare's look of disbelief. "Now. He has a level head now." The whole town remembered his past.

Ethan had left Serendipity at eighteen after their parents died at the hands of a drunk driver, abandoning his brothers to state welfare. He'd returned last year, wealthy beyond anyone's imagination and had made peace with his siblings, Dare included.

"Besides, he's got Faith in his life," Cara said of Ethan's wife. "I wouldn't worry if I were you. Tess is in good hands."

Dare grinned. "Yeah, she is. And so far she's staying out of trouble."

"Coffee?" Cara pointed to Cuppa Café, the town's only stop for a good caffeine fix.

"Yes."

Cara pulled into an empty spot on a side street, and together they walked into the coffee shop. Dare ordered a black coffee while Cara chose a nonfat latte. They paid for their drinks and Dare pulled open the door in time for Felicia Flynn, the town's newest mayor, to enter.

"Thank you, Officer Barron." With her jet-black hair, blue eyes, and tailored suits, she was striking in appearance.

"Ma'am," Dare said, with a nod of his head.

Felicia was the youngest mayor of Serendipity and the first female to hold the position. For that alone, Cara wanted to admire her. She'd run on an anticorruption platform, promising to weed out the old boys' network that had been in place in Serendipity since what seemed like the beginning of time. Another reason for Cara to like her.

"Officer Hartley, I've been hoping to talk to you."

Cara gritted her teeth and forced a smile. For all the woman's positives, she was a pit bull and a ball buster, making the liking and admiring Cara wanted to do too darned difficult.

"You owe me answers on a certain investigation," the mayor said, pointedly meeting Cara's gaze. "Are you avoiding me?"

Cara felt Dare's curious stare. She shook her head as she answered the mayor. "I had an unexpected emergency. My partner is in the hospital with a bout of appendicitis, a car accident, and a serious concussion. It's put us on hold," she explained, hoping the mayor bought the white lie about why she hadn't been in touch.

She and Sam *had* been avoiding Mayor Flynn and her tenacious please-the-people platform. Cara and Sam were looking into a cold case that was at least three decades old, involving ten thousand dollars in marked bills in the evidence room and ties to the motel on the border of Serendipity and Tomlin's Cove, known as the old Winkler place. From the time they were old enough to understand sex, the kids in Serendipity had heard about how the Winklers had once rented out rooms by the hour. Older kids heard they'd also supplied the women, but nobody had proof of the rumors. It was also suspected that the old boys' network in town had ignored any truth to the suspicions. Whatever went down there had long since ended, and, as Cara and Sam had confirmed, the place was deserted. The mayor just wanted all cold cases revisited and either solved or confirmed dead.

"When did the accident happen?" Mayor Flynn asked.

"Last evening," Cara said.

The mayor nodded, understanding and compassion in her usually cool gaze. "Please send your partner my best."

"I will. Thank you."

"But you get back to work on things." She shot Cara a pointed look. "I'll expect a report soon. Have a nice day." She turned and headed for the counter.

"Witch," Cara muttered under her breath. The woman made her sweat, which wasn't an easy feat.

"What was that all about?" Dare asked, following Cara out the door and into welcome cold winter air.

"She's got us investigating an old cold case, and she's just impatient," Cara said.

Though she trusted Dare implicitly, their digging had turned up some Marsden family skeletons. It just wasn't her story to tell.

"You want to drive?" Cara asked, tossing Dare the keys in order to distract him from the subject.

He grabbed them in midair. "Sure. But if you need help, you'll ask?"

She knew he referred to the mayor. "You bet," she said, grateful for Dare as her friend.

With Sam out of commission and the mayor breathing down her neck, she needed a plan. Which meant she needed her partner's permission to bring in a replacement. She didn't know who, but she'd have to talk to Sam.

Thankfully the rest of the day passed quickly, and at the end of their shift, Cara and Dare parted ways at the station. She didn't mind doing paperwork and sent him home to his wife. She still couldn't believe Dare was married, but she had to admit that Liza McKnight was the right woman for him. He'd always been Cara's happy-go-lucky friend, but before Liza, he'd had occasional shadows in his brown eyes he thought no one noticed. Cara was glad Liza had not only forced him to confront old demons but given him a bright future as well.

A part of her filled with envy at the notion of having someone to come home to at night. But the saner part of her remembered her parents and how difficult it was to choose that right person. Unless Cara was absolutely sure of any man, she was better off alone.

She shook her head and refocused on the paperwork in front of her when she felt a large shadow looming. The back of her neck tingled, and she looked up to see Mike standing beside her.

"Got a minute?" he asked.

"Umm . . . sure." She set her pen down on her desk and met his gaze.

"In private," he said.

Something about his tone made her insides quiver, but she dutifully rose to her feet. "Is this about a case?" she asked as she followed him to his office.

"It's personal."

She missed a step and tripped, catching herself before she barreled into him.

He paused at the door and gestured for her to enter. She stepped around him and into the small room reserved for the chief of police, catching a whiff of his masculine scent as she brushed past. He wore the same cologne, and the subtle musky scent settled deep in her bones, reminding her of *that* night.

He shut the door behind him and braced his hands against the wooden frame, leaning back against the wall.

Just being alone with him, Cara was already at a disadvantage, and for a woman who could hold her own with any criminal, that was saying a lot. "What's up, Chief?"

"Could you not call me that?" He visibly bristled at the title. "I can't say what I need to if you're putting the job between us."

She narrowed her gaze. As far as she knew, the job was between them and had been since his return. His status as her boss as well as whatever other barriers he'd erected kept her at a distance. Cara knew how to take a hint. She also knew how to pretend his aloof treatment didn't bother her. No man had utterly dismissed her like she'd meant nothing before. She didn't jump into one-night stands often, and though she'd known the score and could handle sex without messy emotions, her night with Mike had been *more*. Even if he refused to admit to it.

Unwilling to make whatever he had to say easy for him, she waited for him to speak, and the silence stretched uncomfortably between them.

"You asked me in here," she finally reminded him.

He exhaled hard. "When I came back and took this job, I didn't handle things between us as well as I could have."

His unexpected admission surprised her. "You didn't handle it at all."

A wry grin tugged at his lips. "Neither did you."

He had her there.

But he spoke before she could formulate a reply. "I'm the one who came back to town. I should have at least acknowledged that something happened between us." He looked at her with regret in his brown eyes and more than a hint of an apology in his expression.

"Something did," she whispered, suddenly seeing the man she'd taken to bed and not the police chief who barely noticed her.

His heated gaze swept over her, and an unmistakable arc of sexual awareness shimmered between them. She melted on the spot. But she wasn't naïve, nor would she take an apology of sorts as an opening.

Though she would admit to hoping he'd offer one. "Why are you bringing this up now?" she asked.

"Truth?"

She nodded. "Always."

He inclined his head. "Sam asked what I'd do to a guy who treated Erin the way I treated you."

Not the answer she'd been hoping for, and deep inside, hope withered. Mike hadn't suddenly decided to care about her feelings. He was merely making amends because her best friend had come to her rescue.

She straightened her shoulders, preparing to walk out with her head held high. "Don't worry. I knew the deal going in, so you can relax." She was proud that her voice didn't waver.

"Oh." He blinked, appearing surprised by her answer.

Well, what had he expected? Her undying gratitude that he'd stepped up as a man? Or for her to cling and beg him to give them another chance? Neither would happen. Not now and not if hell froze over, Cara thought.

"I'm glad we understand each other," he said gruffly.

She managed not to curl her hands into fists and show her real emotions. Feelings she wouldn't let surface until later, when she was alone.

"If we're finished, I have paperwork to complete." She started for the exit, but he still blocked it with his large frame.

Realizing he stood between Cara and her escape, he stepped aside and opened the door.

She was almost past his alluring scent and the tempting warmth of his body when she forced herself to pause. "Mike?"

"Yeah?"

"You can tell Sam he worried for nothing. I always knew you weren't the kind of guy to expect much from," she said, sweeping past him with as much dignity as she could muster.

Only when his door slammed shut with him inside did she allow her knees to buckle as she sank into the chair behind her desk. She'd get past this moment, she promised herself.

She'd get past Mike Marsden. On the job, she'd continue to be a good little officer and treat him with the respect he was due. But off duty? No more tiptoeing around him. She'd be herself, the only way she knew to put him and the entire night behind her once and for all.

I always knew you weren't the kind of guy to expect much from.

He knew what Cara meant with her cutting remark. Not only had he deserved it, he'd prided himself on that very thing. Unless the people involved were his immediate family, Mike made himself off limits. Like his biological father, Rex Bransom, Mike had taken off from Serendipity as soon as he got the chance, leaving his family and the police force he'd recently joined.

Also like his sperm donor, he'd hurt a woman in the process. At least Tiffany hadn't been pregnant, as Mike's mother had been with him. Mike was young then, barely twenty-two, and he hadn't known enough to lay out his feelings for Tiffany—or lack of them. To Mike, she'd been fun and he liked her well enough, but he sure as hell never planned on marrying her.

He shuddered at the thought, recalling how he'd used his escape from Tiffany as his ticket out of his small hometown, next stop Atlantic City, where he'd picked up again as a beat cop. He'd been bored, something obvious to his superior, who'd recognized his talent along with his tendency to skirt the rules, pulled some strings, and gotten him into the NYPD. There, life had been more exciting, keeping him hopping. Never bored, never tied down.

He loved his life. So why did Cara's words still bother him two full days later?

What bugged him even more was that he had to visit his brother at Cara's house, a place filled with memories even he couldn't shut off.

Parking his Ford F-150 in the driveway, he recalled following her home from Joe's and pulling up behind her sporty blue Jeep Cherokee. His hand on her back as they walked up the entry to the small condo. Her shutting the door behind them, flicking on the hall entry light. And then any gentlemanly qualities he possessed had flown out the window. Mike had always been a guy with a healthy sex drive, and his months undercover had been a long dry spell, but he was hard pressed to explain the chemistry that had his hands all over her immediately.

So what if her laughter in the bar had rung in his ears,

leaving him with a lightness inside him that he hadn't experienced in too long, if ever? And he'd seen sexy women in short skirts and cowboy boots before, but when Cara had leaned over a table to whisper something to a friend, Mike realized those tights she wore rose only thigh high. He'd broken into a sweat right then. Still, not enough of an explanation in his mind. Neither was what happened next.

Joe's Bar had never been known for dancing, but somehow Joe's fiancée, Annie Kane, had persuaded him to expand the bar and put in a dance floor. Mike had been nursing a beer with Sam when he caught sight of Cara in some guy's arms, his hands slipping downward from her waist to her ass. Mike was up in an instant, reaching her just as Cara gripped the man's wrist and threatened to break it if he didn't play nice. She hadn't needed Mike's help, but she'd gratefully let him cut in. Next thing he knew, *his* hands slipped from her waist beneath her shirt, his fingertips grazing the silken skin on her back. Except she didn't stop him.

When he asked, "Want to get out of here?" her softly whispered "Yes" slammed into him full force. She'd excused herself to say good-bye to Sam and Alexa and the other friends she'd been hanging out with. And the next few hours had completely blown his mind and had him leaving before she woke the next morning.

Was it any wonder he hesitated in front of her front door now?

Without warning, the front door opened wide and Cara greeted him. "Were you going to ring the bell? Or did you plan to stand outside all day?" she asked, a knowing smile on her face.

"I take it we're past the formality stage?" He followed her into the front entry.

"Unless you prefer we go back to the way things were, Chief? I could call you *sir*," she offered with a deliberately saucy smile.

He narrowed his gaze, determined not to let her provoke

him. "When we're off duty, informal is fine." He drew a long breath. "How's Sam?"

"I've never met a more annoying patient," she muttered.

"Which tells me he's recovering?"

She nodded. "He's in the den watching television. You know the way, so go on in." To her credit, though she blushed, probably remembering the last time he was here, she held his gaze and didn't flinch. "Can I get you something to drink? Soda? Water?" she asked.

He shook his head. "No, thanks."

A few minutes later, both he and Cara were seated near Sam, who looked a hell of a lot better here than in a hospital bed. "You're not green anymore," Mike said of his brother's coloring.

"I'm better. And I'm antsy."

"And it's only been forty-eight hours, so relax yourself. You're a couple of weeks away from being cleared to return to work, so chill."

Sam muttered a curse. "I've got things to do."

"Nothing that can't wait. Cara can hold her own with Dare. Once you're back, I'll give him a rookie to train as his new partner."

"Better him than me," Cara said, curling her bare feet beneath her on the oversized chair in which she sat.

Pink toes peeked out from beneath her navy-blue sweats, which rolled at the top. A faded gray T-shirt, imprinted with the SPD logo, had been cut off, revealing a tantalizing sliver of bare skin between the frayed edge and the waistband of her sweats.

"Mike, quit mooning over Cara and pay attention; this is important." Sam's voice broke into his musings.

Son of a bitch, his brother hadn't just caught him, he'd called him out. When Sam was better, Mike intended to beat the living crap out of him.

Cara's face blushed a cute shade of pink. Mike figured his was maroon by now. "What?" he snapped, knowing he couldn't admit or deny without getting himself in more trouble.

"We have a situation," Sam said, his tone of voice more telling than anything else that this was big.

Mike sat up straighter in his seat. "What's going on?" He looked from Sam to Cara.

She shook her head. "It has to come from Sam," she said.

"You know how the mayor gave you a list of unresolved cases, especially those that involved the old Winkler place, and told you to do something about it?" Sam asked.

"Yeah. And I put you two on it," he said to Sam and Cara.

"Right. Most of the open complaints about the Winkler place were tough to run down since nobody is willing to admit they visited that . . . umm, establishment."

Mike still didn't know where his brother was going with this. "I'm listening."

"And I'm getting there. It's not simple. Back in 1983, the cops pulled over a car on a random traffic stop. They found drugs, arrested the driver, and impounded the car. In the trunk they found ten grand in marked bills. The money and the drugs were locked in the evidence room until the feds could pick up the cash. Somehow it fell through the cracks, and the money's still sitting there."

Mike muttered a curse, and Cara laughed.

"Fast-forward some weeks," Sam continued. "A women's group began protesting the old Winkler Place."

"The Best Little Whorehouse in Serendipity," Mike said, using the nickname he'd learned as a kid.

"Right." Cara waved a hand toward Sam, indicating he should keep talking.

"The group clashed with the people at the motel, the cops raided the place, and what did they find? The same type of marked cash, at which point it goes into evidence too. The hooker activity dies down for a while, the moms forget about the Winkler place, a new administration comes in, and lo and behold, the money sits and nobody takes another look.

Over time, any activity at the Winkler place ended, and nobody was willing to discuss what really went down there."

Mike shook his head in disbelief. "Okay, well, let's say I get that we're in a small town with shitty record keeping. And I also get how that old boys' network kept further investigation from continuing. We're talking about what? Money laundering in addition to prostitution out there?"

"We don't know," Cara answered.

Mike raised his hands in frustration. "What do we know?"

Sam cleared his throat. "Well, we know that the only person currently on the force with possible ties to all this in the past—is Dad."

Mike gripped the sofa seat, about to jump up, when Cara held up a hand. "Hang on. We're not saying Simon did anything wrong."

"At least not yet," Sam added. "But the thing is, after Cara and I got up to speed on the history of this case, we went to the evidence room to see what we could dig up. It turns out that the original marked bills from the traffic stop were referenced—but now there are one thousand dollars' worth of bills that don't match up."

Mike leaned forward in his chair. "Did you ask Dad about the bills?"

Sam nodded. "Damn right I did."

"And what did he say?"

Sam frowned, and Mike's skin prickled with unease.

"He outright refused to discuss it, and believe me, I pushed hard. I'd planned to bring it up again, but he was diagnosed and went right into treatment. The time hasn't been right since."

Mike gritted his teeth. "So . . . where do we stand now?"

Sam looked from Cara to the walls, everywhere but at Mike.

"What aren't you telling me?" Mike asked, his underlying tone making it clear it wasn't a question but a demand for answers.

"Go on," Cara said to Sam. "He needs to know."

Sam blew out a breath before answering. "Dad's partner at the time of the incident was Rex Bransom."

Mike swore and glanced at the ceiling, pulling himself together. Though he probably should have seen this coming as soon as Sam grew more reluctant to tell the story, he felt blindsided anyway. "My biological father," he finally said.

Sam remained silent, giving Mike time to process the news.

His brother knew Mike's "real" father was a sore subject. As far as Mike was concerned, Rex Bransom was a man who hadn't wanted a family and who'd disappeared from his life when his mother was pregnant. Ella and Simon hadn't sugarcoated the truth—that Rex had bailed on his pregnant girlfriend—explaining that Rex had too many flaws and problems to stick around. But Rex had been Simon's best friend and partner, and when he'd taken off for parts unknown, Simon had stepped up, married Ella, and adopted Mike.

And they'd all had the perfect life without Rex Bransom involved in it. Deep down, Mike had always figured there was more to the story, but he hadn't pushed for answers. Probably because since leaving Serendipity, he knew first-hand how much like his real father he actually was. He couldn't bear to know more.

"Are you okay?" Sam asked.

Cara remained quiet, but he felt her perceptive gaze and sensed her pity, one emotion he did not want her feeling for him.

"I'm fine," he lied. Mike was happiest when not thinking of the man who'd given him life and probably the rest of his bad habits and behavior before abandoning him.

"Then you understand someone has to take over the investigation with Cara," Sam said, his point clear.

"Yeah. And because it involves Dad, that person is me." Mike leaned his head back and groaned.

"Hey, don't sound so happy about working with me," Cara said, probably hoping her tease would bring him out of the mood he'd sunk into.

"It's not about you," he said, and rose to his feet. Without sparing either of them a look, Mike headed for the front door.

"Give him time," Sam said to Cara, after his brother's departure. "Anything to do with his real father brings out the worst in him."

Cara bit the inside of her cheek, feeling sorry for Mike at the same time she knew he'd hate that particular emotion. "I didn't know he was adopted by Simon until we started this digging."

"It's never been a secret. My parents were always open with Mike and with us. They wanted him to know he was wanted and loved by both of them. And I've never seen a hint of anything different from my dad, so you had no reason to know." He shook his head. "Our dad. Simon's always been our dad."

"I get it. Family's never easy," she said, thinking of her own parents. "Speaking of family, my mother asked me to come to dinner tonight."

Sam blinked in surprise. He knew she was basically estranged from her family, or as much as she could be, living in the same small town.

"Did you say yes?" Sam asked.

She shook her head. "No, I said what I always say. Get rid of your extra baggage, and I'll be there in a heartbeat. I've even offered to help her do it. I'd take her to Havensbridge myself and help her get set up," she said of the women's shelter where she volunteered.

"What'd she say to that?" Sam asked.

"The usual. She ignored the comment and talked about something else."

He sighed. "I'm sorry."

"And sadly I'm used to it."

She rose to her feet. "I'll let you get some rest. I have some errands to run."

"Thanks. And thanks again for letting me stay here. I'll be gone by the end of the weekend. The doc said by Monday I can do more for myself."

"I don't mind the company," she said, with a smile.

"Hey, make sure you keep me in the loop on the investigation. Because my brother probably won't, and I know you're going to need a sounding board in dealing with him."

She forced a smile. "Don't worry about me; I can handle him. And don't go talking about me behind my back again, either. I appreciate you looking out for me, but I didn't need you squeezing a semi-apology out of your brother." Mindful that Sam was recuperating with stitches, Cara didn't lay into him the way she normally would have. Besides, she knew he'd meant well.

Sam didn't even wince at being caught. "Is that all he managed? A *semi*-apology?" he asked in disgust.

"Mind your own business," Cara reminded him.

"I'm sorry you have to work closely with him now." Sam's frown showed all the disgust he felt at being laid up.

"Like I told you, I can handle your brother." And she could.

As long as she figured out how to decipher the man's moods and the reasons behind them.

Their last time together, he'd been an open book, as eager to flirt and sleep with her as she'd been to do the same with him. But since his return, reading his usually somber mood was never easy. Cara was never sure if his disposition was related to being around her, being coerced into returning to town for an undetermined period of time, his job, his father's illness, or what.

Given that they'd be working together now, she'd have to figure it out because she couldn't work in a dark vacuum with a brooding man. Not when so much was at stake, including her sanity, considering she could not ignore him.

Three

Later that day, Cara pulled into Havensbridge, a women's shelter located twenty minutes from Serendipity, situated on an unpaved street almost hidden by trees. The house was immense, with a multitude of bedrooms, and had been left to Belinda Vanderbilt, a distant cousin of *the* Vanderbilts, many times removed. Belinda, now forty-two, had the good luck to have been born into money and the bad luck to have chosen the wrong man. After nearly losing her life at his hand, she'd run from her New York City luxury apartment and settled into the estate left to her by her great-aunt. After she'd been forced to shoot her ex-husband before he beat her to death, she decided no other woman should have to suffer the way she had.

Belinda turned her estate into a haven for abused women, and often their children, providing them with safe shelter and helping them get strong enough to survive on their own. She'd even gotten a degree in psychology so she could, along with trusted friends in the profession, provide counseling and care without alerting outsiders. The shelter had been in business for ten years.

Cara had been volunteering for the last two, her reasons for helping out here the same as the reasons she became a cop. She wanted the chance to make a difference in people's lives. It didn't take a psychiatrist to tell her she was over-compensating for not being able to change her mother's life. But Cara loved both her job and her work at Havensbridge and the women she met there.

Cara parked and headed for the front door, where she was greeted by Jane Baker, a corrections officer, who also volunteered here in her spare time. Cara's duties alternated between spending time with the women she'd referred or met here and guard duty, as Jane was doing tonight. Cara preferred one-on-one time with the women but was happy to stand in when they were short on security. Tonight she planned a short visit before meeting Alexa and her work friends at Joe's for drinks.

She paused to talk to Jane for a few minutes, then headed for the kitchen. Inside the large, homey-looking room, Cara found the person she'd come to see. Daniella was by herself preparing dinner.

"Hi," Cara said, not wanting to startle her.

"Hi!" The younger woman's sky-blue eyes lit up as she met Cara's gaze. "You came!"

"I said I would." Cara hopped up onto a stool near where Daniella was chopping peppers. "Where is everyone?" Cara knew the house had a few other women living there too.

"Lindsay's throwing her wash into the dryer, and Darla had a headache, so she's lying down. I hope I'm not taking you away from anything important," Daniella said, as she always did when Cara came over. She glanced at Cara with a shy smile.

"Nope. No place else to be," Cara said, and she picked up a knife and started helping Daniella by cleaning and cutting up carrots for the stir-fry she was obviously making.

For just this reason, Cara hadn't changed into the dressier clothes she'd wear later to Joe's. She wanted Daniella to believe she had no place better to be. And the truth was, Cara wasn't in any rush. As long as Daniella wanted to talk or needed an ear.

"How have you been the last few days?" Cara asked as she sliced.

Daniella had been there for only a week, and she was very much a work in progress—someone who intuitively knew she had to get out of an abusive situation but had a hard time believing that the emotional and verbal harm her ex-boyfriend inflicted would escalate into physical violence. It was often hardest to convince women that words and emotional battering did as much damage as a fist, or more.

"Not bad. It's hard being cut off from everyone back home, though." Daniella glanced at Cara, her long brown hair obscuring the side of her face.

"You haven't called anyone, have you?" Cara asked, aware of the catch in the other woman's voice.

"No. But I've thought about it," she admitted, dropping her knife to the counter.

Cara placed her hand over Daniella's. "It's hard in the beginning. All the women who've been here say the same thing, but once you make a plan, once you start looking forward to a healthy future, it's going to be worth it."

She blew out a shaky breath. "I hope so."

"I know so. What are you thinking? Have you and Belinda talked about possibilities?" Cara asked.

Daniella nodded. "I still have my paralegal license, but I haven't worked in two years."

No, as Cara knew, she'd stayed home because her boyfriend wanted her at his beck and call, and at first things had been great. She'd felt needed and wanted. Then slowly he'd begun isolating her from not just old coworkers, but friends, then family. Once he was the sole person in her life, his anger at little things showed itself more often. Which was how Cara met her the first time, after the neighbors called about the noise next door. Ultimately, after her now-ex raised his hand and slapped her once, Cara persuaded her to leave. But Daniella wasn't sure of her decision because she was so fragile and alone.

"All you need to do is brush up on your skills, maybe take a refresher course. Belinda has contacts everywhere. You can move out of state—"

"But my family is here," she said, tears shimmering in her eyes.

Cara drew a deep breath, understanding the need to be around family and friends. "I was going to say, or you can take out the restraining order you haven't wanted to get and look for a more local job. Nothing too close to your ex, but somewhere nearby." She squeezed the other woman's hand. "The good news is you don't need to make any decisions right now."

"I know. But I'm not smart enough to—"

"Hey! None of that," Cara said, more harshly than she meant to. Nothing angered her more than the insidious way some men managed to invade a woman's mind and mess with her self-esteem.

Was it personal for her? Yes. Her own father had done his share of that both to her and to Cara's mother, using his drinking as an excuse. Cara had learned early how to stay out of the house for as long as possible, getting involved in sports and after-school activities. When she wasn't doing school-related things, she'd hide out at her friend Melissa's house. Luckily for her, Melissa's mom didn't mind. But Cara hated leaving her own mom at home, and as a teen she'd been overwhelmed with guilt for all the hours she spent out of the house. As an adult, Cara understood that her mother made her own decisions—but understanding and accepting were two different things. In other words, the guilt remained.

Melissa, meanwhile, had moved out of state, but they'd stayed in touch.

Forcing herself to focus on Daniella, Cara deliberately softened her expression and her tone. "What did the therapist tell you to do when Bob's voice gets into your head?"

"Positive affirmations. I'm a smart, capable woman," Daniella said, not sounding as if she believed it.

Cara nodded. "Exactly. Just keep repeating that to yourself, because it's true."

"Sorry I took so long!" A petite redhead interrupted the awkward moment as she joined them in the kitchen. "I had so many things to fold. But I'm back!"

"Hi, Lindsay," Cara said, greeting the other woman with a smile.

"Hi, Cara. What's shaking?"

"Not much. You?"

"I have a job interview tomorrow," Lindsay said, beaming with excitement.

"Fantastic! Congratulations."

The young woman was a bundle of positive energy these days, and Cara hoped her enthusiasm for life and change would rub off on Daniella. Cara truly worried that Daniella's depression would lead her straight back to her ex, something she didn't want to see happen.

"Thanks. Are you staying for dinner?" Lindsay asked.

Cara shook her head. Now that Daniella had company, Cara decided it was the perfect time to leave. "I can't tonight, but I'll see you soon."

"Thanks, Cara. I mean it," Daniella said.

"And I meant what I said. You're amazing. Remember that." She hugged Daniella and then Lindsay, who vibrated with excitement over her upcoming interview.

She'd make a quick stop at her place to change clothes and head on over to Joe's. After being with Daniella, Cara was in the dumps and needed something to change her mood. Maybe some good old-fashioned dancing and a couple of drinks would do the trick.

Déjà vu was a potent aphrodisiac, Mike thought as he entered Joe's Bar. The music, something he still wasn't used to, vibrated around him, the dance floor already full. Normally he'd be meeting up with his brother, but with Sam out of commission, Mike was here alone. He could have called up an old friend or two with whom he'd reconnected since his return, but he wasn't in the mood for idle talk.

He was in a mood, and it wasn't a good one. He hadn't wanted to go upstairs to the tiny apartment and stare at the four walls or the TV while he was still mulling over all he'd learned from Sam and Cara about the mayor's investigation. Until he knew what they'd find out about Rex or Simon, he couldn't begin to wrap his mind around the possible implications. No matter what, he and Cara would have to proceed with caution and keep things low-key. Something he'd have to discuss with her. But for tonight, he needed downtime.

So here he was, at Joe's Bar, where instead of peace he found himself remembering a hot night with a beautiful woman he couldn't have again.

Swell.

He headed straight for the bar, figuring if nothing else he could shoot the shit with Joe. As he approached, he was surprised to find Cara sitting alone, staring into her almost-empty cocktail glass, probably waiting for friends.

Every instinct inside him screamed at him to turn around and head on upstairs and away from temptation. Ever the risk taker, Mike continued toward her only to realize the guy to her left was making a play, something that seemed to happen to Cara regularly, and Mike didn't want to examine the feeling gnawing at him too closely.

He'd placed an arm behind her chair and sidled up close.

Mike's stomach twisted with what he would have liked to think was hunger. He knew better and didn't like the possessive feeling one bit. The knowledge that she could get to him on any level filled him with frustration.

The guy leaned in and whispered in Cara's ear.

She immediately stiffened and pushed her chair back to get away from him. "What part of get lost don't you understand?" she asked the man Mike didn't recognize.

The rejection was all Mike needed to see in order to ease the painful cramping in his gut.

"I just want to buy you a drink, sweet thing." The other man smiled, more than a hint of arrogance in his grin.

Cara cocked her head to one side. "I already said *no thank you* twice. Get lost or I'll show you I'm nobody's sweet thing."

Mike stifled a laugh. She hadn't realized he was watching, and he wasn't ready to call attention to himself just yet. Cara was a handful on a good day. She could more than take care of herself, something he definitely admired about her.

She was off duty, but like him, he'd lay odds she carried a piece somewhere on her. The night they'd spent together, they'd each had to unstrap their guns before things got going.

The persistent guy still looked at Cara as if trying to determine whether she was serious or playing hard to get. Given the swing of her leg, encased in steel-toed cowboy boots, the man really ought to take a hint.

Before she could kick him in the nuts, Mike decided to step in. "The lady is with me. Take a hike." Mike came up beside Cara on her free side, deliberately looming large and close.

She glanced up at him in surprise.

"I'm not poaching on your woman, Chief," the man said, obviously recognizing Mike. "She didn't say she was taken."

"But she *did* say *no*," Cara muttered. With a scowl, the other man left. "Idiot."

"You can say that again. Waiting for friends?" Mike asked.

She shook her head. That she was alone surprised him. Unlike Mike, Cara was a people person.

"Alexa had an emergency and I wasn't in the mood for small talk." She gestured to a table where a group of people from the station were hanging out. "What about you?" she asked, as she finished her drink.

"Same. Sam's out of commission and I wasn't in the mood for people either." He hooked his leg around a suddenly free bar stool and settled in beside her. "What are you drinking?"

"A Manhattan."

He cocked an eyebrow. Strong with a hint of sweetness, just like her, though he opted not to point that out. Instead he gestured to Joe to refill Cara's drink and give him his usual. "So what's got you needing a strong drink?"

Cara pivoted in her chair until their knees touched. "What is this?" She pointed back and forth between them.

"What are you talking about?"

"Me. You. Real conversation. Are you sure you're feeling okay?" She settled her blue eyes on him as she turned the tables.

He'd prodded her much the same way when he'd shown up at her house to visit his brother, so maybe he deserved it, Mike thought. He hadn't exactly been a decent guy since his return.

"Since we have to work closely together now, it makes sense, doesn't it?" He didn't want to give away too much of what he was feeling. Hell, he couldn't define it for himself, let alone verbalize his emotions.

She narrowed her gaze, studying him. "I suppose."

"Here you go. A Manhattan for you." Joe placed a new cocktail glass in front of Cara. "And a whiskey neat for the chief," he said with a grin.

"Thanks," Mike said.

"How's Annie doing?" Cara asked Joe.

The bartender's eyes lit up at the mention of his fiancée. "She's great. We're great. You got the wedding invitation, right?" he asked.

She smiled brightly. "You bet. I RSVP'd right away."

Mike merely nodded.

Joe waved in dismissal. "I don't pay attention to things like that. Who's coming is Annie's job. I just want to marry the woman."

Cara's pleased laugh expressed how she felt about that sentiment. "Well, I'll be there. I wouldn't miss it."

"And not a minute too soon," Joe said.

A happy couple, Mike thought, and took a drink, enjoying the first burn as the liquor slid down his throat.

"I knew you two would be good for each other." Cara smiled, and warmth seeped through Mike's veins.

He tried to tell himself it was the alcohol hitting his system and not her megawatt grin.

"Is Annie feeling well too?" Cara asked.

"No MS episodes for a while now," Joe said, then glanced toward the sound of his name. "Gotta go. I'm being summoned at the other end of the bar."

"Put it all on my tab," Mike called out to the bartender before he made his escape.

"That's not necessary," Cara said.

He'd expected her protest. "Maybe not, but I'm doing it anyway."

She shrugged. "Thank you."

"You're welcome. Now . . . what's wrong?" he asked, bringing the subject back to where they were before Joe had interrupted.

She frowned at him, and he discovered—or should he say rediscovered—her dimples. "I had a rough day." She took a long sip of her drink. "No, that's wrong. I have it good. Someone else is going through a bad time."

The pain in her voice bothered him. "Anyone I know?"

She shook her head. "I volunteer at Havensbridge."

"The women's shelter." At her surprised look, he said, "I know we refer domestic violence victims there."

"One of the women . . . she's so demoralized, and I'm afraid she won't hold out long enough to get help, that she'll go back to her ex."

He met her gaze. "You can't make her choices for her." Despite knowing better, he placed his hand over hers on the bar.

Cara visibly stiffened, but he didn't remove his hand. "All you can do is give her your advice."

"Sometimes words aren't enough. I ought to know."

It was a small enough town that Mike knew that her parents didn't have the best marriage. Her father wasn't the nicest person around, especially when he'd been drinking. What Mike didn't know was whether Cara had ever been on the receiving end of his abuse. The thought made Mike want to hit something or someone himself.

"Cara?"

"Hmm?"

He wanted to ask if her father had ever hurt her. More, he wanted to protect her from anyone else harming her either. But she didn't need his help any more than Mike knew what to do with these crazy feelings she inspired.

"Do you want to dance?" he heard himself ask instead. *Not bright, buddy,* Mike thought to himself.

She paused a beat before answering. "Why not," she said at last.

They wound their way through the morass of people and onto the crowded dance floor, the jukebox playing Adele. No sooner had they reached a comfortable spot than another slow, crooning song came on, and Mike had to wonder why the universe liked to toy with him this way. Still, he'd asked her to dance, and Lord knew he wanted her in his arms, so he held out his hand.

She placed her smaller palm in his.

He thought he'd been prepared for the crackle of electricity, but the zing that went through him was stronger than he'd remembered or anticipated. He pulled her into his embrace, hoping like hell he could control his body's reaction because in this tight space, with her flush against him, there was no way she wouldn't notice.

She got to him.

Cara didn't talk, and neither did he. Somehow the ease with which she fit into his arms and the relaxed way they swayed to the music spoke for them.

He ought to feel that uncomfortable itching sensation now, like the one he'd always used to experience when Tiffany tried to make plans in advance, or like the one he got when he approached his parents' house and he felt like home and expectations were closing in on him. Yet he experienced none of those things, only the feeling of comfort along with the ever-present arousal she inspired.

Cara sighed then. A small sound shuddered through her body and as she laid her head against his chest, something he'd been holding tight inside him seemed to ease. Her hair smelled fruity and delicious, and déjà vu returned full force.

Last time, she'd been as eager to leave the bar as he. As willing to indulge in hot, needy sex without discussion or questions of what the act might mean. And she'd satisfied the needs not just of his body but of something more. So much so that he hadn't slept with a woman since. He'd tried not to think about that, but now he couldn't focus on anything else. He had the one woman he wanted in his arms. Again.

He wondered what she'd say to picking up where they'd left off. A no-strings affair, one with a definite ending when he left town. But Cara knew that about him already. She'd said as much herself, and though her jab about knowing not to expect much from him grated, it was the truth.

The one thing he didn't question was his sudden

turnaround. It was as clear as his need for her and his admission that for now, no one else would do.

Cara had lost her mind. There was no other explanation for the fact that in Mike's arms, she'd found peace from her thoughts, or that she wasn't running from the heavy desire pulsing through her body.

Mike's large hand splayed against the thick fabric of her shirt, hot against her back. With a grateful sigh, she leaned her head against his chest and listened to the rapid beating of his heart.

His fingertips dipped slightly lower, into the top band of her jeans, and pressed her lower body against his. She couldn't miss the hard length of his erection or the silent question. Yes, her breasts were heavy, dampness settled between her thighs, and she wanted him more than her next breath. But how could she go there again and walk away whole?

But maybe a better question was, how could she walk away now?

"Cara?" he asked, his voice a gruff, low rumble.

She tipped her head back and met his gaze. "Yes." She knew exactly what she was saying.

His impossibly brown eyes darkened even more. "Are you sure?"

She nodded.

He leaned close and whispered in her ear. "Go up the back and I'll meet you outside my apartment in a few minutes."

Leave separately, she thought. This time he was paying more attention to propriety, which was so un-Mike-like.

"Okay," she said, and slid out of his arms. Anticipation swept over her and she savored the feeling, heading for the restrooms first.

She paused by the mirror, surprised by the flush in her

cheeks and the glassy eyes looking back at her. She hoped nobody else noticed what a fevered state she'd been in, or sneaking out back wouldn't mean much at all.

When she hit the fresh air, it was cold outside, and she'd left her jacket and purse in the Jeep, so Cara was glad Mike caught up with her almost as soon as she reached his place.

He unlocked the door, then slid his hand into hers and pulled her inside.

A glance around at the sparse apartment gave her a stark reminder of his constant state of impermanence. The man didn't need a home base. Just a bed in which to sleep. She'd do well to remember that, and the knowledge helped shore up her defenses, which had slipped while he held her so tightly on the dance floor.

He tossed the keys onto a small table. "I'm glad you didn't say no."

She swallowed hard. "We were good together." He made her feel more than any man ever had. And today, Daniella's situation had reminded her that what she and Mike had was rare. Great sex and an open, honest understanding of their situation.

"We were combustible," he said.

Even his voice was arousing, but somehow she managed to keep her wits about her. "I just expect one thing," she said, forcing herself to turn and face him. "It's a deal breaker."

He folded his arms across his chest. "What is it?" he asked, clearly wary.

The poor man was worried she wanted commitment. She actually felt sorry for him. His unwillingness to open himself up to anyone meant he'd miss out on so much in life. She wondered why, coming from such a warm loving family, Mike ran from the same. Cara's parents' marriage was far from ideal, yet she refused to give up on the idea that maybe there was a man out there she could trust.

She doubted it, but she refused to let go of that kernel of

hope. Mike had already given it up. But now wasn't the time to go there.

She stepped closer, her hands on the top of her blouse. She slipped one button out of the loop, then worked on another. "I just want you to promise me that things between us won't be awkward tomorrow. That you won't go back to defensive mode and treat me like . . ."

She was going to say *dirt*, but she realized that hadn't been his intent. "Like you're afraid I'm going to ask for forever."

He actually paled. "You think you know me that well?" he asked, his gaze more on the swell of her breasts pushing upward from the cups of her bra.

"I know I do." She let another button slip through. "But you should know something about me."

"What's that?" he asked, his voice a harsh croak as her hands hit the last button and her blouse hung open wide.

"I only want what you'll willingly give."

Apparently her words appeased him because a sexy smile lifted the corners of his mouth and he reached up, grabbing her wrists, stopping her from slipping off her shirt.

This was the Mike she remembered, calm and in control. The man who fired her blood and stirred her arousal. His dark gaze bore into hers as he slowly lowered his head, leaving no doubt that he intended to kiss her. But instead of his lips landing on her mouth, he turned his head and pressed his cheek against hers. His razor stubble rubbed against her skin and felt warm and good, making her want to cuddle closer.

Before she could act, he latched onto her earlobe, nibbling and suckling until she felt the pull straight down to her toes. He never did what she expected or anticipated. That was also the man she remembered.

The man she still wanted.

He slid his lips from her ear to her jaw, grazing her skin as he slowly worked his way to her lips. By the time he settled his hot mouth over hers, she was shaking with need. And he'd barely touched her. He knew the power of their attraction, understood how to heighten the anticipation, and she loved every second.

He'd worked his tongue lazily inside her mouth and proceeded to devour her. His tongue tangled, sliding against the roof of her mouth, the sides, leaving no part of her untouched. Suddenly his hands came to her hips and he lifted her, carrying her to the kitchen counter, which in this small apartment wasn't far away.

Once he placed her down, he settled himself between her legs, braced his hands on either side of the counter and leaned in for another kiss. One that was too quick.

"How is it you can be so tough on the outside and yet so damn sweet?" he asked.

His words poked at the barriers she had to keep erected against him, but he made it so hard. Thankfully he kissed her again, devouring her before she could formulate a reply.

He surrounded her, a hot male who smelled good and promised delicious things with his sexy gaze and heated kiss. Liking everything about what he was doing, she wrapped her legs around his waist, locking him in place, and he rewarded her with a groan of approval. And when she threaded her fingers through the silken strands of his hair, his groan deepened, reverberating through her.

He broke the kiss, his breathing rough, then reached for her shirt. He slipped it off her shoulders, trapping her arms at her sides, finally revealing her to his hungry gaze.

Thank goodness she wore a lacy bra and panties when she wasn't on duty or else this would be a lot more awkward, she thought, unable to suppress a smile.

"What's so funny?" he asked.

"Just thinking it's a good thing I wore something sexy," she said, being completely honest.

He fingered the lacy fabric of her bra with roughened fingers. "That you did," he said as he drew one fingertip down her abdomen, stopping at her navel.

He leaned in, breathed deep, and pressed a hot kiss to her stomach. Her entire body quivered with need as moisture flooded her panties.

"You taste sweet too," he murmured, leaving her with an aching yearning for him to fill her, hot, hard, and fast.

"Michael," she murmured, arching her back and lifting her hips in an effort to tell him what she needed.

"Soon." The gruff word was a definite promise.

Suddenly the sound of a phone ringing interrupted the heated moment. "That's mine," she said, unable to hide her disappointment.

"Don't move." He reached behind her and pulled out the cell phone she'd tucked in her pants pocket and handed it to her.

She glanced at the screen. "It's the station," she said to Mike, surprised she'd be called now when she was off duty. She freed her hands, hit a button and put the phone to her ear. "Hello?"

"Cara, it's Andy, the night dispatcher. I thought you'd want to know a call came in from your parents' neighbors."

All the warmth in Cara's body dissipated, and a chill took over. "What did they say?"

"They reported shouting and the sound of something hitting the walls. I sent a car to check it out," Andy said.

She nodded, feeling Mike's concerned gaze, knowing he'd been standing so close he'd heard every word the dispatcher uttered.

"Thanks for the heads-up. I'll meet the car over there." She disconnected the call.

Nauseated and embarrassed, she couldn't look Mike in the eye. "Sorry. Gotta go," she said, pushing herself off the counter as she hopped to the floor.

"I'll go with you." She heard the steel in his voice and knew it wasn't an offer.

"No!" She jerked her head toward him. "I mean, no thanks. There's no need." She didn't want him to see her father at his drunken worst. Bad enough he could read the report later and feel sorry for her.

Four

From the determined look on Cara's face, Mike knew better than to offer to drive or go with her on the call. He knew embarrassment when he saw it, and Cara didn't want him to witness her parents' issues. Too bad. She might be a tough thing when it came to the job, but she had her vulnerabilities and he'd seen those tonight when she'd talked about the woman at Havensbridge. She might not want him there, but she needed him.

He waited until she'd buttoned her blouse and practically run out the door before grabbing the keys to his truck and heading out. At the very least, the cold night air and the drive to her parents' place would give him time to cool down. He was still erect from their encounter. When he inhaled, he could smell the luscious scent of her body and remember the feel of her soft skin as he breathed her in deep.

He drove with the window open, the rush of cold air blasting him and tamping down on the heat still flushing him from the inside. By the time he pulled up to the garden apartment complex address he'd gotten from dispatch, his officers were back by their car, one talking to Cara, the other writing up the incident.

She watched Mike climb out of his truck, a scowl on her pretty face. *What the hell are you doing here?* He could hear her thoughts as if she were broadcasting them out loud, but because he was her superior and there were other officers present, she held back and he admired her restraint. Found it sexy, even as he had no doubt she'd let him have it in private.

"Hey, Chief," Rob Sumter said.

Mike nodded.

"Any arrests?" he asked, not meeting Cara's gaze. He didn't have to. Her glare bore holes right through him.

Rob shook his head. "Mrs. Hartley declined to press charges," he said, without looking at Cara. "We'll just write up the incident so it's on record."

"Thanks, Rob."

The other man inclined his head and joined his partner in their squad car. A few silent minutes later, they drove away, leaving Mike and Cara where they'd started. Alone.

"I thought I told you not to come." Cara's eyes flashed angry fire.

"Since when do I do what I'm told?" he asked, stepping closer.

He didn't miss the shiver that rippled through her. Unable to stop himself, he pulled her close. "What happened?"

Stiff at first, she surprised him, letting herself relax into his embrace. "My father was drunk and started ranting at my mother. Apparently he threw dishes at the wall, and the neighbors didn't appreciate the noise. That and they were worried for my mother's safety."

"Is she okay?"

Cara shrugged. "According to Rob."

Mike paused. "You didn't talk to her?"

She shook her head, still burrowing into him. "I can't. I've told her I won't see her again unless she leaves him."

Mike was considering his reply carefully when without warning, Cara pulled out of his grasp. "I need to go."

"Wait," Mike said. It wasn't a request. He'd laid down the order like he expected her to follow. He wasn't sure if she'd listen, but he was determined to try. He didn't dig into why it was so important she not run off alone right now.

She turned back to face him. "What?" Her teeth chattered and she wrapped her arms around herself for warmth.

"Where's your jacket?"

She blinked at him, startled. "In my Jeep. Is that what you wanted to know?"

He stifled a laugh. "No." He shrugged his leather jacket off and wrapped it around her shoulders. "Let's go."

"Where?" she asked, digging in her heels, literally refusing to walk another step.

"You're freezing and upset. We're going to get a cup of coffee and talk, and then you can get in your car and drive home."

"Bossy," she muttered, as she pulled his jacket tighter around herself for warmth.

Okay, so she wasn't bolting, and relief gripped him. He grabbed her hand and led her down the street from where her parents lived, then around the corner to Lynette's. The small diner on the corner was a favorite of locals and cops assigned here.

He opened the door, allowing her to step ahead of him inside. At this hour it was fairly empty, and they walked to the back, slipping into a booth. Instead of sitting across the table, Mike slid in right beside her, intentionally crowding into her personal space.

"What are you doing?" she asked, still defensive, probably from embarrassment.

He couldn't hold back a grin. "Using you for body heat."

She shot him a disbelieving stare.

"What? You have my jacket and it's January, remember?" That and he just wanted to be close to her.

He hadn't gotten over the heat they'd generated in his apartment, and though he wouldn't make a sexual overture when she was vulnerable, he still wanted her. And his body demanded he stay close. A part of him he didn't recognize wanted to take care of her now that she was upset, but again he refused to look at that too closely.

"What are you doing here so late?" Lynette, the diner owner, a heavyset woman in her midfifties, came over with a pot of coffee in her hand.

"Just warming up," Mike said to her.

"Cara, honey, want some coffee?" she asked.

Mike wasn't surprised Lynette knew Cara by name, what with her having grown up in the neighborhood and being given shifts here.

"Can I get tea? Something decaf?" Cara asked. "I'll never sleep if I have caffeine."

"Sure thing. Plain old decaffeinated or chamomile?"

"Chamomile sounds great, Lynette. Thanks."

"What about you, Mr. Police Chief? Coffee?"

Mike nodded. "Thanks."

A few minutes later, they each had their drinks and Lynette had disappeared into the back.

Cara wrapped her hand around her cup, closed her eyes, and sighed, clearly savoring the warmth, making Mike glad he'd pushed the issue and brought her here.

After giving her a few minutes of silence, he broached conversation. "So."

Her eyes popped open. "What?" she asked warily. "Do you want to know how often my father drinks? Loses his temper? Throws things? Hits people?"

Instead of making him angry, her defensive tone melted his heart. "I don't want to know anything you don't want to tell me, Cara. I just wanted to give you a few minutes to calm down before you drove home."

"Oh." Her eyelashes fluttered down. "I'm sorry. I'm just—"

"Embarrassed," he finished for her.

"Yeah."

"Well, there's no need to be. I'm not judging you by your father's actions or your mother's behavior," he assured her.

"What about judging me for not going in and checking on my mother?" She held herself tight and stiff, backing herself into the corner, as far from him as she could get.

Which wasn't far. He stretched his arm behind the seat, reaching her hair. Grateful to have some part of her to touch, he wound a strand around his fingers. "Why would I judge you for that?"

She exhaled a long breath, and some of the starch left her shoulders. "I've done all I can for her. If I go in, if I beg her to leave, if I make him angrier, all I'm doing is enabling the entire screwed-up situation." Frustrated tears filled her eyes, and she wiped them away with the back of her hand.

He knew better than to comment about those. "There's no need to defend yourself to me. You're talking to someone whose genetics are questionable at best," he said, bringing up the subject he abhorred. "My real father walked out, never to be heard from again."

Mike sure as hell wasn't enough to make the man want to stick around. Nor was he enough for the rest of his family. He'd always figured they were better off without him there.

"And pretty soon you and I are about to investigate something that my gut tells me will end badly for my whole family. So don't expect me to pass judgment. I'm here, I'll listen, but I'm sure as hell not going to look down on you for any choices you make." He paused, then admitted, "Frankly, I think you're doing the right thing."

"Really?" She looked up at him, her eyes so moist and big, and he realized how fragile she was deep down inside.

"Yeah, really." Then, not giving her a choice, he pulled her back beside him. "It takes more guts to stay away knowing someone's hurting. But sometimes there's nothing you can do."

She nodded. "That's just it. I can't help her unless she wants help. I can't fix the situation unless she changes it."

"Was it always like this?" he asked, hoping the one question didn't send her into full retreat.

"It's always been a roller coaster. The lows depended on whether he was holding down a job. If things were good, he'd manage his liquor. If something went wrong, it was everyone else's fault and he'd dive into the booze. The more he drank, the louder and uglier it became at home."

Now that Cara knew Mike wasn't judging, she seemed more willing to open up to him, for which he was grateful. But one question hovered in his mind, begging to be voiced, one he wasn't sure she'd want him to ask.

He shouldn't. And yet he couldn't not. "Did he . . . did your father ever . . ."

"Hit me?" She finished the question for him.

"Yeah." His voice sounded harsh, gruff to his own ears.

"No."

Mike released the breath he'd been holding.

"But not because he didn't want to. It was the one thing my mother managed to control, at least when I was younger. She said she'd have stabbed him if he touched me, and I think he believed her. But she couldn't do it for herself. He said she deserved it, and she came to believe it." Cara shook her head. "And as I got older, I stayed out of the house as often as possible."

She stared at the table, and yet he knew what she was thinking.

"Don't feel guilty for taking care of yourself," he said quietly. "That was your parents' job. Your mom obviously did the best she could for you, if not for herself. And your dad failed as a parent. So did mine. I'm just lucky I had Simon." Even if he'd never live up to the man and his legacy, Mike thought.

"How did you know what I was thinking?" Cara asked.

Because he was coming to know and understand *her*. But

that wasn't something he wanted to share. "Lucky guess." He forced an easy grin. "Feeling better?"

"I didn't even touch my tea, but yeah, I am. Thanks for being a *friend*."

He didn't miss her emphasis on the word *friend*, and he didn't understand why the distinction bothered him so much. They'd been frantic for each other earlier, but that was just sex. Wasn't it?

Mike paid, and, to his surprise, Cara didn't argue. He walked her to her car, pausing by the Jeep, unwilling to part ways with her just yet. Though he knew they'd have to get together to discuss strategy on looking into the cold case and Simon's involvement, it wasn't something he wanted to bring up now.

"What are you doing tomorrow night?" he found himself asking instead.

She blinked up at him, her eyes wide-open windows to her soul. "Nothing special. Why?"

"I thought you might like to come to my parents' house for dinner." Had he really just asked her to join him at a family event?

She worried her bottom lip, making him want to lean in for a long taste. Not the time, he thought. She'd gone back to skittish.

"Are you sure your parents wouldn't mind?" she asked, bringing his thoughts back to where they belonged.

He raised an eyebrow. "Are you kidding? My mother loves to cook, and we both know she adores you."

Cara flushed. "She's sweet. But aren't Sunday nights for *family*?"

Was it his imagination or did he hear longing in her voice with that word?

"You're like family to them." Not that he felt the least bit familial toward her, which made him wonder why he wasn't letting her off the hook for this dinner gracefully.

"Well, if you're sure." She looked up at him with grateful blue eyes, and he had his answer.

She wanted to join him as much as he wanted her there. "I am," he said gruffly.

She nodded her thanks. "I'll call your mom and see what I can bring."

Mike already knew Ella would just tell Cara to bring herself. "Come by their house around five."

"Okay." Her smile lit up something inside him. She reached for her door handle.

"Cara."

She pivoted back to face him.

Unable to stop himself, he lifted his hand and stroked his knuckles down her cheek. "Get a good night's sleep," he said gruffly.

At his touch, her cheeks turned a rosy red that had nothing to do with the cold air. "I will. Night, Mike." She ducked her head, opened the door, and climbed inside.

He waited until she started the truck and pulled away from the curb. *What a complicated woman*, he thought, watching as she drove away.

There was much more to Cara Hartley than he'd realized before. And he was drawn to the many facets of her personality: the strong cop, the vulnerable woman, and everything in between. She aroused warm and protective feelings he didn't recognize. Ones that would normally send him running. Hell, as much as he'd liked going out with Tiffany back in the day, her constant phone calls and neediness nearly choked the life out of him. She'd always told him she relied and counted on him, but Mike didn't want to be needed that way. By anyone.

Just like his old man, Mike thought in disgust. Which was why with every job and woman, Mike made a point of being up front with his intentions. Even Mike's sergeant in New York knew that when a case ended, if Mike felt the need to go—he would. Luckily the variety of assignments in the city kept him interested. The women? Not so much. But Mike wasn't bolting from Cara, despite the bouts of awareness that told him he *should* be panicking.

He couldn't. Because Cara had a grip on Mike that wasn't letting go. Which meant he was in it for the duration.

Besides, there was no downside, he reasoned. When Simon recovered, Mike would step down as chief of police; he would leave town as he'd planned all along.

Cara always felt a mix of admiration, gratitude, and envy when she visited the Marsden house. She appreciated the sense of family they shared and wished with all her heart she had the same for herself. But she'd long since stopped pining for things she couldn't have. Instead she appreciated the fact that they included her on occasion. Today felt different because she wasn't coming at Sam's request, but Mike's. She didn't know why he'd asked her or what it meant, but she'd promised herself she'd take the invitation at face value. Dinner with a family she'd always felt close to, that was all.

She rang the doorbell and Ella Marsden greeted her almost immediately. "Cara! I'm so glad you could make it," she said, opening the screen door to let her inside.

"I appreciate you having me on such short notice." Cara stepped into the foyer.

"Nonsense. We love having you. Now what's that?" Ella asked, glancing at the foil-covered pan Cara was holding.

"Lasagna. I thought you and Simon could freeze it and eat it on a day when you aren't up to cooking." When Cara had called, Ella insisted Cara didn't need to bring anything tonight, not dessert or side dishes. As usual, she had it handled.

That was fine, but Cara knew how tired the older woman had to be, taking care of and worrying about her husband. Flowers seemed like a useless thank-you, so Cara had gone shopping early that morning for the ingredients and made the dish when she got home.

She held out the pan for Ella to take.

"Thank you." Ella accepted the food and tipped her head, indicating that Cara should follow her into the kitchen. She passed through the family room where Simon dozed in his recliner and caught a glimpse of the wall of family photos, pausing for a closer look.

She had to smile at the variations on the family photo that changed over the years as the kids grew up. Sam and Erin were lighter in coloring than Mike, both resembling their mother and Simon. For the first time, Cara wondered what Mike's real father looked like, whether his hair was as dark as his son's, his eyes like delicious hot chocolate.

"Cara?" Ella called.

"Coming!" Cara headed for the kitchen, a smile still on her face. "I was just looking at the pictures on the wall."

Ella smiled too, but Cara noticed the strain around her eyes and mouth, small lines that hadn't been there last time she'd seen her. "They make me happy too. Let's sit. The boys aren't here yet, and Erin said she's running late."

Cara joined Ella at the table, declining her offer of a soft drink.

"So how are you?" the older woman asked.

"I'm good. Busy, which I like. Between work and volunteering at Havensbridge, I don't have much downtime."

Ella nodded. "I'm thinking of doing some volunteer work myself once Simon's back to himself. Maybe driving cancer patients to the hospital for treatment or reading to the children who are inpatient there."

"That's sweet," Cara said. "What do the doctors tell you about Simon?"

"That he's progressing nicely. He tolerates the treatments well, and he's been able to have them consistently. They hope he'll be in remission soon. And once he's finished with this part of the treatment, he should start to feel stronger and want to do more."

"I'm glad," Cara said.

They talked for a few more minutes about small things before Ella cleared her throat, looking suddenly serious. "Cara, honey . . ."

"Yes?"

"When Michael called and told me you were coming for dinner, he mentioned the incident at your parents' last night."

Everything inside Cara ran cold. Since driving away from her parents' apartment, she'd deliberately not let herself think about them. She didn't want anyone else thinking about it either. Knowing. Judging.

Mike obviously was doing one or more of the above. "So he invited me out of pity, then," she said without thinking.

Ella's frown told her she didn't agree. "You know better than that. You're comfortable here and we love having you, and I'm sure you can use being around people who think of you as family at a time like this." The older woman paused, not breaking eye contact. "Although, family's more Sam's way of thinking about you than Michael's."

Cara knew she blushed a deep red, and she couldn't think of a witty reply.

"I think Michael just wanted you here," Ella mused.

Cara shook her head. This conversation was getting awkward on every end. "I don't know what to say to any of this."

Ella patted her hand. "I just wanted you to know that if you need someone to talk to about your parents, I'm here. And if you're worried I might not approve of you and Michael, well, you'd be wrong."

Cara's eyes opened wide. "Mike and I aren't . . . we're not—"

"No worries, dear. We're all grown-ups." Ella winked at her, and Cara prayed for strength.

"Right. Well, thank you for the offer to talk about my parents." Wow. Her family had suddenly become the easier conversation, Cara thought, still reeling from Ella's frank words.

"I mean it, honey. It can't be easy for you," Ella said, in a purely motherly way that put Cara at ease.

"Thank you. I appreciate it, but there's nothing to say. My mother made her choice to stay years ago. And I made mine not to see her unless she leaves him." She waited for Ella to condemn her for her choices, but instead she nodded in understanding.

"I'm sure it wasn't an easy decision." Like Mike, Ella and her compassion and understanding made Cara feel more secure and at ease about her course of action than she'd been before. Maybe it did help to share, to have someone to talk to.

"It was a hellish choice," Cara admitted. "But anything short of sticking to it will only enable an ugly situation or make me so angry I get physically ill." She glanced down, embarrassed.

"Oh, honey, there's no shame in taking care of you. That was their job, and for whatever reason they fell short." Ella leaned in close, reassuring as only a wise, loving parent could.

"That's what Mike said." Cara managed to meet Ella's gaze.

"I knew I raised that boy right."

Cara nodded at that. Mike was a really decent guy.

"But you still feel guilty," Ella said, not dropping the subject.

Cara sighed. "I alternate between feeling like an awful daughter for taking care of myself and a self-righteous one for not understanding where my mother's coming from. I volunteer with women just like her, and I understand her world isn't simple."

"And yet you beat yourself up over something you can't control," Ella said, covering Cara's hand with her own.

The warmth she offered caused a lump to form in Cara's throat.

"I, of all people, know what it's like to doubt myself and my choices," Ella said softly.

"You do?" Cara would have thought Ella Marsden was so certain in every decision she made.

"Oh, Cara. You must know the story of how I ended up married to Simon, right?"

Cara didn't know which part of the story Ella was referring to. "I know you were involved with someone before Simon," she said delicately.

"I got pregnant and he left me," Ella said bluntly.

Not expecting such frank talk, Cara blinked in surprise.

"Simon was my best friend and he stepped up immediately to take care of me—as in he offered to marry me and adopt the baby as his."

"And that wasn't an easy decision to make?" Cara asked.

"No, it wasn't." Ella glanced down. "It didn't seem fair."

Cara's heart clenched at the other woman's honesty. "You loved Mike's real father a lot, didn't you?"

Ella nodded. "At one time, but he wasn't the man I thought."

And Simon was, Cara thought.

"But Simon? It's true and real. A love born of shared lives and children and appreciation for what a good, solid man he is. I love the life we've shared."

Cara smiled. The Marsdens had always been an example to look up to, a couple to be envious of and to emulate. "So no regrets?" Cara asked.

"No regrets," Ella answered immediately. "But lately I've had cause to wonder . . ." She trailed off with a shake of her head. "Never mind."

"No, it's okay, you can tell me," Cara assured her. Ella had been so sweet about Cara's own parents, so understanding, Cara wanted to return the favor by letting the other woman unburden herself.

Ella turned her wide eyes on Cara. "I've been corresponding with Mike's real father," she whispered.

"What?!" Cara knew that as far as Mike was concerned, nobody had heard from his father since he abandoned a pregnant Ella.

"A few weeks ago, he found me on Facebook. He friended me out of the blue. I accepted before I could think about it, and apparently that's what he wanted. Once I accepted, he was able to see the family pictures I posted. It let him know how we all were, that Mike had grown up to look just like him." Her voice was so low, Cara could barely hear.

"And you haven't told Simon." Cara stated the obvious.

Ella shook her head. "He was midtreatment, and even if he hadn't been . . ." Her entire body trembled. "He'd be so angry. To show up after all these years and ask questions about *Simon's* family. I don't even know if I'd have told him if he were healthy, but luckily I didn't have to make that choice."

"Yet." Again, Cara opted for the obvious.

An unexpected smile lifted Ella's lips. "Nothing gets by you."

"Occupational hazard." Cara grinned.

"Well, I don't have to decide whether to tell Simon now."

"What about Mike?" The words came out of Cara's mouth before she'd even had the thought in her head. If Mike knew his mother was in contact with his errant father . . . she shuddered at the notion.

She shook her head.

"He needs to know!" Cara said, certain Mike would be furious if kept in the dark.

"He can't! Mike struggles so much about his father, and he'd be so angry at me for even answering him." Ella reached for and grabbed Cara's hand. "Please, promise me. I know it's a huge burden to put on you, and I hadn't thought it through. I just needed someone to confide in and you offered . . ." Eyes wide, voice trembling, she squeezed Cara's hand tighter. "Please."

"Okay," Cara said, not wanting her any more upset.

"Or Sam. Or Erin."

Cara closed her eyes. "No one," she promised, sensing she'd live to regret it.

Ella released her grip and relaxed back into her chair. "Thank you."

Cara met her gaze and nodded.

"I'm sorry. It started as me wanting to assure you that you aren't alone in being conflicted and ended with you as keeper of my secret."

"It's okay." Cara managed a smile.

Ella rose and pulled her into a grateful hug before stepping back.

"Just a word of warning, though?" Cara felt compelled to add. "Secrets tend to come out."

Ella nodded. "I know. I just need Simon to be healthy before I bring this out in the open. The subject of Rex is complicated for everyone."

Cara studied Mike's mother, the flush in her cheeks, and wondered just what it was she and Rex Bransom talked about in their private e-mails. And whether those conflicted feelings Ella mentioned extended into the present.

"Mom!? I'm here, and Mike's right behind me!" Sam's voice shook Cara out of her musings.

A door slammed shut behind him.

Ella glanced at Cara and mouthed *Thank you* before pivoting toward the door. "In here!" she called to her son.

Cara braced herself for dealing with Mike, pushing aside the explosive secret she now had to keep from him.

Five

A few seconds and the heavy sound of footsteps later, Mike stood in the entryway of his mother's kitchen. He hadn't shaved today, and the stubble gave him a rugged, sexy look. Sexier look, Cara amended. The man oozed a confidence and sensuality that made her knees weak.

"Hi, Mom," he said, striding into the kitchen. "Cara." His dark gaze settled on hers.

"Hi, honey," Ella said.

"Hi," Cara said softly, attempting to hide the pure rush of pleasure she took in seeing him.

But it was the spark of satisfaction in his expression at finding her here that lit her up inside. He obviously hadn't been sure she'd come and was pleased that she had.

He stopped by his mother and kissed her cheek.

"Where's your brother?" Ella asked.

"Dad's awake, so Sam settled in the family room." Mike caught sight of the bread basket, lifted the foil covering, and snagged a piece of bread, popping it into his mouth.

"Enough of that or we won't have any left for dinner,"

Ella chided him, but the indulgent smile on her face told another story.

"So what have you two women been talking about?" Mike asked, his perceptive stare flickering back and forth between them.

"Not you." Erin joined them, taking Cara by surprise. She'd been so absorbed in staring at Mike that she hadn't heard Erin come in.

"Hey, all!" Erin greeted everyone with a smile before bumping her hip against her brother's, a bit too hard.

Mike flicked his fingers against her cheek in retaliation.

"Don't start," Ella warned, and both siblings tucked their hands into their jacket pockets like naughty children.

Cara grinned. She hadn't seen Mike and his family together in a nonstressful situation in years, and she found herself mesmerized by the easygoing side of Mike Marsden that she never saw at work. Even when they were alone together, he was always intense and focused, yet she liked this playful part of his nature and vowed to bring it out in him more often.

The entire family gathered in the den before dinner and everyone's focus was on Simon, making certain he was comfortable and feeling well. It was just as obvious that he didn't want to be the center of everyone's attention and concern. Despite the fact that he looked frailer than he had before his treatment, his will to live and zest for life were as evident as his love for his family.

He grilled each child about what was going on in their lives, despite the fact that both Sam and Mike visited their father often. Sam had spent a lot of his recuperation time here the past week watching television and playing chess and just keeping Simon company. And Cara had no doubt that Erin had done the same, making Simon's *interrogation*, as they all called it, unnecessary, just an expected part of their family day. No wonder Ella had fallen in love with him.

Cara wondered what it would have been like to grow up with such a warm, interested father and immediately pushed the thought aside. She couldn't change the past, and dwelling on it only made her unhappy, a mood that had no place in this house with this family.

Dinner consisted of Ella Marsden's apricot chicken, mashed potatoes, and green beans, and Cara couldn't believe how delicious the meal was. "This is amazing," Cara said, after finishing everything on her plate. "I'd love to have the recipe." She might live alone, but Cara loved to cook.

Mike glanced at her, surprised.

"What? You think I live on takeout?" she asked with a grin.

"I do," he muttered.

"That's because you didn't live in Serendipity," Erin said. "Mom cooks extra for Sam and me. I freeze it and always have a home-cooked meal."

"It wouldn't hurt you to learn yourself," Ella said, probably not for the first time, judging by her daughter's roll of her eyes.

"No time," Erin said. "But you have a willing cohort in Cara." She waved her hand, clearly happy not to learn her mother's cooking skills.

Ella refocused her attention, a happy smile on her face. "So I do. And I'd love to share. I've actually transferred all my recipes into the computer, so if you give me your e-mail I can send it to you," Ella offered.

"Look at my mom, becoming all computer savvy," Sam said. "I'm impressed."

Erin leaned over and hugged Ella. "I've taught her everything I know."

"Says the self-professed computer geek," Mike teased his sister.

Erin shrugged. "I can't help it. Someone in this family had to learn their way around computers and routers. You two had no interest, so it defaulted to me if we wanted to get online."

"Things change," Mike said. "I've been looking into ways to upgrade our system at work without it costing too much. We're too antiquated even for a small town."

Cara liked the way Mike referred to the station in such a personal way, the word *we* indicating he considered himself a part of the force.

"I don't understand why we can't leave things as is," Simon muttered. "Paper, pencil, and an old-fashioned filing system worked fine for years."

Sam gave Mike a knowing look. "The system's so good that we have discrepancies and issues dating back years," Mike said.

"Can you pass the green beans, Cara?" Simon asked her, obviously changing the subject.

Beside her she felt Mike stiffen, obviously annoyed at his father's stubborn, old-fashioned ways.

"Sure," Cara said, lifting the serving dish and handing it to Simon.

They ate in silence for a few minutes, until Erin chimed in. "Did you know Mom's on Twitter?" she asked, obviously still thinking about their technology conversation. "And Facebook."

Cara gripped her fork tighter.

Mike chuckled.

Sam burst out laughing. "Really? Mom, come on."

"What? I think it's good for her to learn computers and keep up with technology." Erin defended her mother.

Cara didn't dare sneak a glance at Ella, afraid Mike would catch her concern.

Forging on as if nothing was wrong seemed like the best bet, Cara decided. "I have a Facebook page. It's fun."

"I agree," Erin said. "When you live in a small town, so many people stick around, you think you see them all the time. But sometimes you'll hear from someone from your past and end up taking a trip down memory lane." Her voice grew soft, making Cara wonder just whom Erin had heard from on the social network.

This time Cara did glance at Ella, who'd gone pale.

"I know what you mean," Cara said, determined to keep conversation away from Ella. "I like catching up with old friends and finding out what's going on in their lives."

"Did you find any old boyfriends?" Sam asked her. "Like Adam Stone or Kevin Manning?"

Cara wrinkled her nose and shot him an annoyed look. Why did he need to go there? "Maybe they *found* me."

"Did they?" Mike asked, his voice suddenly dark and dangerous.

A shiver raced through her at the sound.

"Well?" he bit out when she didn't answer right away.

She tried to figure out the emotion behind his tone. Jealousy? Was it possible? If so, she no longer minded Sam's bringing up her past, if it meant Mike showed some interesting emotion.

"Let's see. Kevin dropped me a private note, and Adam posted on my wall," Cara said.

A low rumble sounded from Mike's throat.

"Did either of them ever marry? Or are they still pining over you?" Sam asked, chuckling as if the idea were absurd.

"Hey! I'm pineworthy."

Sam grinned. "Didn't say you weren't. So anyone else hear from an old flame?" he continued, clearly in a mood to cause trouble.

"Do we really need all this talk about old flames?" Ella asked, her voice rising in distress.

Oh damn, Cara thought as all of Ella's children shot her a worried look.

Simon seemed out of it, lost in his own thoughts, or exhausted and not paying attention.

"Mom?" Sam asked, clearly concerned.

"Are you okay?" Mike leaned forward, as if he could reach his mother across the table.

Ella rose from her seat. "I'm fine. If everyone's finished I'll start cleaning up. Give me a few minutes and I'll get dessert on the table." She gathered a few plates and rushed out of the room.

"Now that was odd," Erin said.

"I'll say," Mike muttered.

Sam nodded.

"Umm, I'll help clean up," Cara said, wanting to check on Ella.

"That's okay. I've got it." Erin rose to her feet. "You're our guest. I'll try and talk to Mom, see if she's okay."

There was no way Cara could object to Erin's being alone with her mother without causing more curiosity. "Yell if you need me?"

"Thanks," Erin said.

Sam turned to his father. "Dad, let's go watch some television." He helped his father stand up from the chair, and the two men left the room.

Cara turned to Mike, assuming he'd be worried about his mom. Instead she was surprised to find him staring at *her* with his usual intensity.

Gone was the lighthearted man who joked with his sister, and the predatory look in his eyes made Cara so hot she squirmed in her seat.

"What?" she asked into the silence.

"Let's go."

"Where?"

"Somewhere we can be alone for a few minutes." He held out his hand to her.

No way could she refuse.

She placed her palm against his. He gripped her hand and led her down a short hall to what must be his old bedroom. No sooner had she entered than he shut the door, turned, picked Cara up, and bounced her onto his bed.

"Now tell me about those old boyfriends."

From his position above her, Mike stared into Cara's wide eyes and waited for an answer, his heart beating too rapidly in his chest.

"Are you going to tell me about old girlfriends?" she shot back.

Spunk. She had it in spades. He liked it even as she created a shitstorm of trouble in his head.

"Adam? Kevin?" The names sounded like sandpaper on his tongue.

Cara evenly met his gaze. "Tiffany?"

He groaned. Turnabout was fair play, and he deserved the pointed question. "Last I heard through the grapevine, meaning my mother, she moved out of state and got married."

"Regrets?" Cara asked.

He raised his head. "You don't do anything halfway," he muttered.

"Neither do you."

He grinned.

She didn't.

"Not one damned regret."

"Now, why the grilling? What's gotten into you?" she asked. "Seriously."

Good question. One he'd been asking himself over and over. Unfortunately, he knew the answer. "*You've* gotten into me." He leaned in close, bracing one knee on the mattress, his arm on the headboard behind her. "You make me crazy."

A dimple puckered her cheek, and he could tell she'd liked the admission. "Okay, since you came clean, I will too. I heard from two old boyfriends."

Their bodies were so close, he could only feel and breathe her in. "And?"

"Both married. Neither interested me beyond some memories anyway. Why do you care?"

Damned if he knew. He'd never asked any woman about

who else she was seeing. He hadn't cared. "Because while we're together, you're mine."

Her breath came out in a whoosh of air. "We're together?"

"We're not?" he asked, his words a definite dare.

Mike knew he was being unreasonable, an arrogant ass, making demands without any discussion at all, but she brought out the caveman in him.

She studied him long and hard, making him wonder if she'd just slap him and storm out. He'd deserve it if she did.

Instead she reached out and slid her hand around his neck, pulling him closer. "You're going to break my heart," she murmured.

And there it was. The lightning bolt of panic crashed over him hard. Yet oddly, he didn't pull away. "No hearts involved," he said instead.

"Right." A flicker of *something*, suspiciously like hurt, crossed her face before she covered her emotions.

He didn't like that she hid her thoughts from him, never mind that he'd all but instructed her to do so. Her tongue slid over her lush, pink lips, and the single stroke broke his control. He crushed his mouth to hers and kissed her for all he was worth. Kissed her to take away her pain from last night, to soothe the hurt he'd probably just inflicted with his careless but necessary words, but mostly to assure himself she was on board.

His.

For now.

To his relief, she reciprocated, opening to him and letting him inside. His tongue stroked and glided, tangled with hers, and suddenly everything was right inside him once more. No more anger or jealousy or mixed-up emotions he didn't recognize, understand, or know what to do with. He groaned and came down on top of her, unable to hold his weight up anymore and needing to feel her solid and real beneath him.

She threaded her fingers through his hair and held on, holding her own thrust for thrust of their tongues and bodies until the call of his mother's voice brought him back to reality.

It wasn't easy, but he dragged himself off her and flopped to his side, placing an arm above his head. "Dessert's probably on the table," he said, willing his overheated body to calm down.

"I thought *that* was dessert."

He chuckled, amazed at her ability to go with the flow no matter the circumstances.

"But we shouldn't be doing this here anyway." She scrambled off the bed and paused at the small mirror, wiping beneath her eyes and fixing her tousled hair.

"I should go back first," she said. "If anyone asks, I'll tell them I was in the bathroom."

As if his family wouldn't figure out what they'd been doing in here? But Mike didn't want to upset Cara by pointing that out. "I'll be out in a few." As soon as he wouldn't embarrass himself, Mike thought.

After Mike's ridiculously possessive behavior at his parents' house, he and Cara managed not to cross paths for the next few days. Mike used the time to get himself under control and look into the cold case and the cash left in the evidence room for all these years. He wasn't kidding when he said they needed to upgrade the computer system. The one they had was shit, and in this day and age, that wasn't acceptable.

For now, he had to go with handwritten notes and people's memories, and the only person in Serendipity who knew about the case wasn't talking. He tapped his pen against the desk, thinking about various ways to approach this case. Why hadn't the feds stepped in and taken the money? That was one key issue. If they had, the cash wouldn't have been in the evidence locker for anyone to tamper with.

He frowned and thought some more. Finally it clicked. He had a contact in the Federal Bureau of Narcotics from his undercover ops in the city who'd have access to any database. Too bad she wouldn't help unless he went to see her in person, which meant a trip to New York. The drive to Manhattan would take only an hour.

Mike had just hung up the phone after arranging a meeting later that afternoon when the sound of familiar laughter drifted through his open office door. His gut clenched at the too-tempting, feminine sound. Mike rose to his feet and walked to the door, pausing to take in the scene in the squad room. A group of officers stood together, all men with the exception of Cara, who was still laughing at something one of the guys had said. Then she turned to Rafael Marcos and patted his cheek, a saucy grin on her face.

Mike wanted to be where the action was, not holed up in an office, and he strode out to join them. As soon as they noticed him, all laughter stopped, and everyone, including his brother, who was still on desk duty, went their separate ways and got back to work.

Mike frowned. Was that what his presence did to people? Was he that much of a hard-ass boss? He didn't think his father operated that way, and as much as he wanted to make his mark while in Serendipity, a stifling workplace wasn't something he desired. It wasn't a healthy atmosphere for his cops—or for him.

"I didn't see you on the schedule today," Mike said to Cara, still silently mulling over his dilemma.

She looked up at him. "I'm not. But I didn't have plans and thought it would be a good time to get some paperwork done." Her tone was stiff and formal, completely appropriate for work.

Damned if he didn't hate it anyway. "When you're finished, what do you say about a trip to New York to do a little digging into your cold case?"

Her eyes lit up at the idea. "What kind of digging?"

"I have a contact I want to hit up for some information."

"Sweet." She rubbed her hands together in excitement. "I'm in!" She glanced at her watch. "Give me an hour?"

"You got it."

She shot him a quick smile before reimmersing herself in work, ignoring him completely.

It grated on him, how easy she found it to put up barriers here at the station, ignoring the chemistry that sizzled between them when they were alone. Hell, just looking at her, he felt it now. He remembered how she'd looked lying in his old bed, all tousled and well kissed and open. To him.

If he couldn't hold it together at work, he really had a problem. Maybe he just needed to get her out of his system. After all, he hadn't had sex with her since his return. All this teasing and foreplay had him on edge. He needed to get her alone, and though that hadn't been the plan when he'd asked her to go to Manhattan, it was definitely his agenda now. New York City was his turf, and he knew just where to take her for some long overdue alone time, no interruptions.

By the time they came back to Serendipity, Mike had no doubt he'd be satisfied and have had his fill. No more jealousy, no more emotional thoughts crashing into his brain. He'd be his cool, calm, collected self once more.

Since Cara had planned to do some paperwork and head home, she'd worn jeans to the station. When she met Mike at his truck, she discovered he'd changed into denim too, so she didn't have to worry about being underdressed for whatever meeting they were going to have.

Unfortunately, the worn, faded denim lovingly hugged Mike's muscular thighs and tight ass. She sighed, knowing she was doomed to be distracted during this work-related trip.

"Ready?" he asked, as he slipped his sunglasses onto his face. Leather jacket, jeans, and aviators were a potent combination on this man.

"Yep." She pulled her own sunglasses out of her bag and plopped them on, hoping he wouldn't notice her staring.

He opened the passenger door for her, and she was struck by what a gentlemanly thing it was for him to do. She settled into her seat, buckling in. He joined her around the other side, and soon they were on their way.

Since leaving his parents' house on Sunday, she'd been on edge and off-kilter. Her mind fluctuated from his intense heated words, *While we're together, you're mine*, to his emotional withdrawal and colder reply of *No hearts involved*.

She shivered, and he glanced her way.

"Are you cold?" he asked, turning up the heat without waiting for an answer.

"Yes. That'll help." The lie slipped easily off her tongue as she glanced at him.

Though it was overcast and looked like snow, the glare forced them both to keep their sunglasses on, and she had a hard time reading him behind the lenses. Still, she didn't doubt that he desired her. Their sexual chemistry was off the charts, and she'd be stupid to deny herself something she wanted so badly. But she needed to hold on to the stark truth that for Mike, this thing between them was all about sex. And Cara had never been much good doing sex without emotion.

She bit the inside of her cheek and decided to put all those feelings into a little box, shut the lid, and push them aside to deal with when this relationship was over or Mike left town, whichever came first. She was good at compartmentalizing and shutting down emotions she didn't want to deal with. She'd had an entire lifetime so far to develop the skill.

"So tell me about this contact," she said to Mike.

"Someone I know from my undercover days. I'm hoping

I can be convincing enough to get my friend to dig into the database without raising a red flag. Last thing I need is to put this case on anyone else's radar," he muttered.

"Do you really think Simon knows what happened to those bills?" she asked, unable to reconcile the upstanding police chief and man she knew with someone who'd hold back crucial information on any case.

"Can you think of another reason he'd go silent on me or Sam?"

He had a point. "I guess not."

The rest of the ride passed in surprisingly comfortable silence. As they drove into the heart of Manhattan, Cara sat up higher in her seat to look out the window. Tall buildings and so many people bundled in their winter coats, some walking their dogs, their kids, and even babies in covered strollers.

"I can't imagine living here," she said, when they stopped at a traffic light.

"It's constant activity."

A car horn blared in the distance, followed by the wail of a siren—ambulance or police, she couldn't be certain. "How do you sleep at night?"

"You get used to it."

"I don't think I could."

"Maybe one day you'll get to find out."

She leaned her head against the cool window. "Doubtful. The few times I've been here I couldn't wait to get away from the crowds and all the activity."

"You're kidding?"

"Nope. Small-town girl, remember?" She turned to look at his surprised expression and raised a hand in a wave.

His answering low, sexy chuckle echoed throughout the car. "We're here." He turned into a parking garage in the middle of the busy street and pulled down a long, steep ramp, ending where a man waited to take his truck.

She hopped out and met Mike around the back of the vehicle.

"Ready to brave the big bad city?" he asked.

She rolled her eyes. "I'm not a farmer girl, for God's sake." And she had her mini Glock holstered behind her.

His small laugh turned into a bigger one. Next thing she knew, he'd grabbed her hand and walked up the steep incline to street level. "The place we're going isn't too far. Just around the corner."

She nodded and kept pace with him, surprised he hadn't let go of her hand. A definite spike of awareness settled low in her stomach at the prolonged contact, heating her from the inside out and helping ward off the cold winter wind. Serendipity was just as chilly, but the wind swirling between the high buildings lent a bite to the air, and she was grateful when he paused in front of what looked like a bar and grill.

He pulled open the door, holding it for her to step ahead of him. Inside, the place was small and dark, with low lighting and what appeared to be wooden booths lining the walls, but there was a warmth to the overall look.

"Mikey!" A booming voice greeted them, taking Cara off guard. She'd have thought their contact would be someone quieter, maybe sitting back in a booth somewhere waiting to talk. Instead a large man with salt-and-pepper hair and a large paunch strode up to Mike, a big grin on his face.

"Bill Carlson, you old son of a bitch. How have you been?" Mike slapped the big burly man on the shoulder, but Bill apparently wasn't satisfied because he pulled Mike into a brotherly hug.

"I'm good," the man said. "Damn good."

Mike stepped back and looked the man over. "Owning this place agrees with you. I think you're eating too much of your own food."

The other man, who had to be a good two decades older than Mike, merely grinned. "It's not just the bar, it's the woman. I married Lucy, and she makes sure there's a home-cooked meal for me whenever I walk in the door." He patted his round stomach.

Mike's eyes opened wide. "You tied the knot? I thought you said, and I quote, 'No damned woman will shackle me in this lifetime.' "

The big man shook his head and laughed. "Live and learn, buddy. Live and learn. So who's this pretty lady?"

Cara blushed at the description, but she was equally curious to know how Mike knew the man, since he seemed so happy to see him.

"Cara Hartley, meet Bill Carlson. Bill was a detective before he got soft and retired," Mike said, with a teasing glint in his eye.

Cara noticed he'd opted not to give Bill a description of who Cara was to him, and she tried not to let it bother her. Better no description than one she wouldn't want to hear.

"Soft happens to all of us, buddy," Bill said before turning his attention back to Cara. "Nice to meet you, Ms. Hartley."

She shook his extended hand. "Call me Cara," she said. "And it's nice to meet you too."

Bill glanced at Mike and cocked his head to the side. "I didn't know you were bringing company," Bill said quietly, but not so softly that Cara couldn't hear.

Mike shrugged. "Didn't seem important."

"Keep telling yourself that." Bill stepped back, his gaze sweeping over them. "Last booth on the right. It's big enough for three. I'll be in the back if you need me." He paused and glanced at Cara. "Pleasure to meet you," he said, before turning and heading back through the double doors leading to the kitchen.

Cara drew a deep breath. "Do you want me to wait here?" She wasn't oblivious to the fact that his contact wasn't expecting her and probably wouldn't be happy Mike had brought her along.

"No." Without another word of explanation, Mike started for the back, and Cara followed.

They reached the back booth where Mike's contact was sitting, and *she* was stunning. A knockout from her long, brown hair accented with beautiful blond highlights, tanned skin, and perfect features, to the way she didn't just wear her leather jacket and purple scarf—she owned it.

Cara's mouth went dry as Bill's words suddenly made sense. And Cara was suddenly aware that her dark green, puffy down jacket made her look like the Michelin man in comparison.

"Mike!" the woman said, gliding out of the booth and plastering herself against him like so much more than an old friend.

Cara gritted her teeth and promised herself she wouldn't give in to insecurity. Petty jealousy? Yeah, she'd allow herself that. What she wouldn't allow? For Mike to see how this affected her. She wondered if he and this woman had been lovers. Or did this woman just wish they were?

To Mike's credit, he grasped the other woman's forearms and pried her off him. "Always good to see you too. We have some questions for you."

"We?" She flipped her hair over her shoulders as she became aware of Cara's presence for the first time.

"Cara Hartley is a police officer in Serendipity. We're working on a case, and we need your brand of expertise," Mike said, gesturing to the booth, obviously ready to sit. "Cara, this is Lauren Nannariello."

"When you said you needed to see me, I didn't realize this was business." Lauren raised her chin a notch and slid back into the booth. "But then you've mixed business with pleasure before," she said in a deeper voice, and patted the seat next to her.

So they *had* been lovers. No more wondering there, Cara thought, a sick feeling in her stomach. Well, he'd made it clear a few nights ago he was with Cara now. And Cara wasn't the type of girl who let another woman hit on her man. How Mike responded to this would be interesting, but hey. He was the one who'd brought her here without giving her a heads-up on the situation.

"Mike?" Cara asked in her nicest but strongest voice.

He turned.

She slid into the bench opposite Lauren, looked Mike in the eye, and patted the seat beside *her*.

He shot her a look filled with regret and slid into the seat next to his contact.

The rational, cop part of Cara understood he needed to do whatever would get the information. The female part of her resented the fact that he'd brought her here to deal with this, and she'd make him pay for that bit of insensitivity later.

Six

Snow came down hard as Mike walked beside Cara down the city street. Her silence gave him time to think, and he wanted to kick himself in the ass. Just because he hadn't thought about Lauren as more than a *contact* hadn't meant she would feel the same way. The minute she'd greeted him, he knew he was in trouble.

Somehow he managed to get through the awkward conversation and come out on top. He'd explained to Lauren what he needed and asked her to do some digging into the FBN's computers to find out why the cash hadn't been picked up from the evidence locker back in 1983. Miraculously he was also successful at fending off Lauren's wandering hands beneath the table.

After Lauren agreed to help, Cara excused herself and went to the ladies' room, leaving him alone with the other woman, at which point Lauren demanded an explanation for his disinterest. Apparently hooking up on occasion meant more to her than to him. Mike hadn't managed her expectations well, and he was sure he'd done the same to Cara.

Though Lauren was pissed, she was still willing to help him—for old times' sake.

He and Cara left the restaurant and walked into heavy snow. Instead of taking her out for dinner, he decided they needed time alone first and headed to his place—another surprise he'd sprung on her. He'd seen the shock in her eyes when he told her his place was around the corner. And she hadn't said a word since. Clearly he was batting one thousand today, and he braced himself for her anger when they got inside.

He lived in a decent neighborhood in a one bedroom rent-stabilized apartment that he sublet for a great price. They walked through the lobby and the old battered mailboxes with some names hanging off, and up one flight of stairs.

He opened the door and let Cara step in ahead of him before locking up behind them. Without asking, she slipped off her shoes, and he did the same.

"Home sweet home," he said, tossing his keys onto the shelf in the small entryway.

Cara glanced at him quickly before walking inside and looking around. "Very nice," she murmured.

"I can't take the credit. My mother and sister insisted on helping." With them taking over and helping him buy furniture, everything had a warm, homey feel, with a primarily brown and beige color scheme and navy accents. Pictures of his family were scattered around the main living room, also courtesy of the women in his life. The ones who mattered, anyway.

Cara turned to him, an unexpected smile on her face. "They have good taste." She unzipped her jacket and he stepped forward to take it, still waiting for the fallout of his earlier stupidity.

"I didn't realize you had an apartment here, though I guess I should have. New York is your home, after all."

The tightness in his throat that he usually associated with

visiting his parents' house suddenly rose here. "Right now Serendipity is home. It just didn't make sense to give up a low rental when—"

"You plan on returning as soon as you can. I know." She looked away and headed for the windows to check out the view.

He came up behind her, standing close as she looked at the high-rise across the street. "Can we just get it over with?" he asked tightly, wanting to know what she was thinking.

"Get what over with?"

She spun around to face him, and he braced his hands on her hips . . . just because he wanted to touch her.

"Lauren," he said.

"Your contact?" Cara asked innocently.

Too innocently, and he narrowed his gaze. "You're mad I didn't tell you about her?"

"That you didn't tell me Lauren was a woman? It might have been nice to be prepared." She tilted her head to one side, her blue eyes bright.

But he couldn't read her. Damn that cop training.

"Or do you think I'm upset that you're obviously involved with her and didn't think to mention it? Yeah, that would have been good to know too." She held herself tight but didn't step out of his grasp.

No anger. Yet. Mike's heart beat harder in his chest. Lauren had come close to slapping him when he told her he was involved with Cara and had shown up with her without giving his ex-lover a heads-up.

Mike glanced at Cara, whose level of anger he still couldn't gauge. Perhaps he ought to put his hand over his groin. Just in case.

"Or maybe it was the fact that she was drop-dead gorgeous that I'd have liked to know?"

Mike winced, knowing that Lauren looked nothing like the computer geek she actually was. "I didn't think about it ahead of time because we're not currently involved."

Cara raised an eyebrow. He was certain many suspects had shriveled under that steely gaze.

"Come on. Her greeting left no doubt. And I'm not that stupid."

He couldn't help but grin at that. "No, but I am. We had an understanding. That's all it was. She scratched an itch."

Cara shook her head and tried unsuccessfully not to groan. "You are such a man."

"And yet you aren't yelling, screaming, or pitching a fit. Why is that?" The woman confounded him.

And wasn't that why he liked her so much?

"Because turnabout is fair play and while we're together, you're mine," she said, repeating his words back to him.

He burst out laughing, but it wasn't funny. She was one in a million and he wasn't ready to let her go.

Apparently she agreed because she *finally* wrapped her arms around his neck and pulled him flush against her. Those lush curves were a perfect cushion for the harder planes of his body and the even harder ridge of his aching erection.

"Do we have an understanding?" she asked.

"Seems only fair."

She blinked, looking into his eyes. "Did you and Lauren have that understanding?" she asked.

As he threaded his fingers through her hair, he could honestly say, "No. Lauren and I were an occasional, when-it-was-convenient thing."

"And what about me? Am I just . . . scratching an itch?"

God, he was an ass.

"No, you are most definitely not just scratching an itch." He shifted his hips, and a soft moan escaped her lips.

"Now that we've got that settled, can we get on with our night?" He'd more than satisfied her curiosity, and she liked his answers.

She smiled. "I'd like that. Very much."

Cara's body hummed with sexual need as Mike held out

his hand. One last glance out the big window overlooking the city showed her that the light flurries the weatherman had predicted had turned into more of a full-blown storm, and they might not get back to Serendipity tonight. She wondered if she cared.

She should. So many red flags had been waved in her face today, she knew she ought to heed them. From the day Mike left Serendipity when everyone knew he couldn't get away from Tiffany's expectations fast enough, to the present, the warning signs were clear. He had affairs with no emotional connection. He'd failed to warn her she'd be meeting a woman he'd slept with. He kept the lease on his apartment, though he had no idea how long he'd be in Serendipity. All were signs that he was a restless man who moved through life without thought to how his actions affected the people who cared about him. She knew better than to think he didn't care in return. He just didn't know how to deal with relationships.

If he'd said Lauren meant something to him or that Cara was just a quick fling, she'd have been gone in an instant. But in her gut, the same gut she trusted to keep her alive on the job, she knew he wasn't feeding her a line to get her into bed.

Cara got it. She knew who he was and desired him anyway. Which meant she had to accept him. As is.

So here she was in his bedroom. In her jeans and long-sleeved T-shirt, she was nothing like the glamorous woman he could have had. Yet he devoured her with an expression that told her he wanted to pounce.

"Changing your mind?" Mike asked, bringing her out of her thoughts. He still held out a hand, waiting.

A grin tipped the edges of her mouth. "Not a chance."

In an instant the energy around her changed. First she'd anticipated. Now she was awash in sensation. Mike met and held her gaze, every step he took deliberate and calculated.

"Clothes off." His eyes gleamed with desire aimed solely at her, and every fiber of her being tingled.

"Yours too." She wasn't letting him call the shots like he had the first time. She wanted to be an equal participant in this, someone he'd never forget.

He pulled off his shirt.

Never breaking eye contact, she did the same. While she couldn't tear her gaze from his muscled body, he stared at her chest and the lace bra, which was a lot sexier than her clothing choice had been. Thank God. His pants followed and he took his boxer briefs off with them, exposing his thick erection for her viewing pleasure.

She licked her lips and was happy with the low growl she received in response. She wriggled out of her jeans, removing her panties along with them until only her bra remained. And when she stood to face him, she found he'd stepped closer, his body heat tempting her to crawl into his skin.

Meeting her gaze, he cupped the back of her head in his hand. "I don't know what it is you do to me, but trust me, Cara, this is much more than scratching some itch."

A muscle ticked in his jaw, and she knew the admission cost him. But she wouldn't make him suffer for it. Instead she leaned into him, inhaling his sexy, masculine scent.

"I'm done talking," she said, and ran her tongue along his hair-roughened chest, eliciting a low groan.

He picked her up and tossed her onto the bed, leaning over her, skin touching skin as she stared into his gorgeous eyes. She braced herself for his next assault, figuring he'd take things hard and fast, but as usual, Mike never did what she expected.

He leaned in for a kiss that was slow and beautiful in its intensity, shattering her expectations and everything she'd anticipated from this affair. He kissed her as if it meant not just something but everything. And he kissed her as if he could do it all night and to hell with the sex she knew would come.

There wasn't a part of her mouth left untouched, and every lick and nibble, taste and thrust of his tongue inflamed the already burning fire between them. Cara was coming out of her skin, every exposed body part needing *something* more. But the further she writhed beneath him, the harder he held her down in one place, pressing into her with his taut, hard body.

The man did like his control, she thought, twisting her hips against him in search of relief.

"You know, the harder you try, the longer I'm going to make you wait," he said, his voice edged with a gruff tone that turned her on.

She grinned. "And you know you're a pain in the—"

He cut off her words with another hard kiss before moving downward with his oh-so-talented mouth, until he reached her bra, pushing the cup beneath one breast, and began to suckle on her already distended nipple. He spent a while there, alternating between breasts, until desire spun out of control, the pull stretching straight to her core, and she arched her hips upward so his erection rubbed against the place she needed pressure most.

He rolled to the side so he could lay his hand across her belly, teasing but not coming near where she needed him to touch her.

"Your skin's so soft," he murmured, both his tone and the words so un-Mike-like that something unraveled inside her. Something soft and emotional and very scary.

Before she could reply, he eased his hand between her legs and cupped her sex in his palm. "I'm going to take care of you," he promised, and proceeded to do so, his mouth trailing a path down her hip, laving the skin along her panty line, and finally, *finally* settling his mouth *there*.

Cara sighed in pure relief as he slid his tongue along the sensitive seam and took her higher than she'd ever been before. He licked, teased, nibbled, and when he set his attention to that sensitive spot, she immediately came apart, her orgasm hitting hard and fast, shattering her with its intensity. Mike didn't seem content to let her come down on her own either. He kept his tongue on her tight nub until he'd wrung every last tremor from her body.

She'd barely opened her eyes when she heard the wrinkle of a condom and suddenly he was over her, entering her, thrusting deep inside her and taking her completely.

She liked sex with Mike because he owned the act and she found it incredibly arousing. So much so that within seconds, she felt the slow build begin again.

He slid out and back in, and she spiraled higher. "Damn, you're good," she said, and was met with a sexy male grin.

"I do aim to please."

"And you do it well," she said, happy to keep things light despite the emotions threatening every time he moved inside her.

"Wrap your legs around me," he instructed.

She did and he plunged back into her, over and over, hitting the sweet spot that had her seeing stars, lights, and all sorts of other things as yet another orgasm swept through her quickly, taking her by surprise.

He kissed her through her release before picking up his own rhythm. Cara held on to his hard muscles and slick skin, feeling every ridge and swell of his thick erection deep inside her. And when he came, her body responded with another mini shock of orgasm rushing through her.

Cara blinked, surprised when she realized she'd fallen asleep in Mike's bed. She stretched a hand out, but no Mike. The sheets were cool. A glance at the clock on the nightstand told her it was nine P.M., and her rumbling stomach reminded her she'd skipped dinner. She stepped into the bathroom, doing her best to freshen up before heading out to look for Mike.

She found him in the den watching television, a large

pizza box on the coffee table. No formalities for him, she thought, amused with his easygoing, bachelor-like behavior.

With his focus on a basketball game, she took a private moment to study him. Wearing a pair of navy sweats and nothing else, he was the epitome of a masculine, sexy male, and she couldn't contain a smile. She vividly recalled his body heat over hers, the feel of those muscles against her skin and the power of him inside her.

She swallowed a moan and decided it was time to make her presence known. "Hey," she said, clearing her throat at the husky sound in her voice.

He glanced up and a grin lifted his mouth, assuring her there'd be no awkwardness between them.

"I can't believe you let me sleep this late."

"We couldn't head back home anyway." He gestured to the window, where big, fat snowflakes were still falling. "I let the station know we were in the city looking into some things and would be in later tomorrow."

She winced, then nodded slowly, not knowing how people at work would take her trip with their new chief of police. After all, Serendipity wasn't a hotbed of crime that necessitated investigations in Manhattan. Still, occasional cases, such as the one they were working on, did come up, so maybe nobody would think anything of their little venture.

"Don't worry, I didn't say anything that would let them infer it was anything but business," he said, reading her mind—or the expression on her face.

She managed a smile. "I appreciate that."

"Ashamed of me?" he asked, lightly, but a flicker of *something* crossed his handsome face.

Was it her imagination or did she glimpse a flash of insecurity before he'd covered it with a cocky grin?

"Of course not," she said, in case there'd been any seriousness in the question. "I just don't want trouble for myself now or after you're gone."

She loved her job and her relationship with her colleagues. If anyone thought she was sleeping with Mike or getting special favors, some of the more senior members and detectives might not treat her so well. Then again, Serendipity was a small town and relationships happened everywhere. She'd probably be fine. But since he was leaving, the longer she kept their relationship private, the better she'd feel.

Mike nodded in understanding. It made sense. Yet it bothered him that she wanted to keep things between them under wraps—which made sense to him but it pricked at his pride anyway.

"Hungry?" he asked, pushing the thought away.

Her eyes opened wide and she nodded. "Starving." She pulled her hair off her shoulders and twisted it into a funky bun that somehow held itself in place.

His gaze fell to the T-shirt she wore, the same one she'd traveled to town in, her bare legs peeking out beneath. She was petite yet solid, her thighs muscular and calves taut from keeping herself in shape, yet the rest of her was soft and womanly, from the curves of her hips up to her fully rounded breasts. She was nothing like the long, leggy women he'd dated before, Lauren included, and Mike had to admit he preferred Cara's lush body and the way she fit against him.

He patted the seat beside him. "Join me? I waited for you," he said, lifting the top of the pizza box.

She stepped closer, glanced inside the box, and grinned. "Half pepperoni, half plain."

"I wasn't sure what you liked."

"Both. Can I get us some drinks?"

"There's Coke and beer in the fridge."

She turned and walked to the kitchen, returning with a Budweiser in each hand.

"Good choice." Another thing he liked about Cara. No

pretense, no fussiness. She liked a beer as much as the next guy, he thought with a laugh.

"What?" she asked as she sat down next to him, criss-crossing her legs.

Damn. She'd put her panties back on, Mike thought, realizing he'd been hoping she'd be commando beneath the shirt.

"Hey, cut that out." She rearranged her position so she was sitting in a more ladylike way, her legs dangling from the couch and crossed primly at the ankles.

He rolled his eyes. "Get comfortable. Sit back the way you were," he said, wanting his visual back. Whether or not he could actually see anything, he didn't want her acting shy and prissy around him.

Instead of listening, she reached for the beer bottles, which she'd already opened, and handed him one. He took a long pull and set it down on the table. Then he stood, reaching for the waistband on his sweats.

"What are you doing?" she asked, almost spitting out the beer in her mouth in an effort to swallow and stop him at the same time.

"Taking off my pants."

"For God's sake, *why*?" Her cheeks turned pink in an adorable blush.

"I figured if I got more comfortable, then you would too."

"Fine!" She bent her knees and crossed her legs once more, this time her shirt riding up high enough to show him the small triangle covering her and a nice expanse of pale skin on either side. "Now cut it out and sit down. I'm not eating naked."

He laughed and flopped back onto the couch before digging in and handing them each a slice of pizza.

"Who's winning?" she asked.

"Knicks were," he said, but he'd long since stopped caring about what was on the screen. He tried to remember another woman who'd distracted him from sports. And couldn't.

They ate in occasional silence, talking in between, comfortable in a way he really enjoyed. He didn't even mind the fact that they were in his small apartment, a place he usually reserved for private time away from the job and any undercover assignment he'd been on.

"How are things going at Havensbridge? How's the girl you were worried about?" Mike asked her.

Cara blinked in surprise. "You remembered about that?"

"It was important to you. So yeah, I remembered."

Pleasure flashed across her face, her rosy glow reminding him when she'd come apart around him in bed. He shifted, his erection growing harder, and he wasn't ready for her to notice. Soon, but just not yet.

"She's fragile," Cara said of Daniella. "And lonely. She even admitted she's picked up the phone a few times to call her ex, but she didn't."

The sadness and worry in Cara's voice pricked at Mike's heart. "All you can do is trust she'll do what's best for her."

"You can't trust people to do that," Cara said, glancing down, and they both knew she was referring to her mother.

Mike didn't reply. There wasn't anything he could say to reassure her. Sometimes life sucked and you had to make the best of it and go on. They finished eating in silence.

Cara crumpled her napkin and leaned back against the sofa with a loud sigh. "I am so going to have to work this off tomorrow."

His gaze traveled from her still-crossed legs to her full breasts, watching as her nipples hardened beneath his hungry stare, before he met her gaze.

"Why not work it off tonight instead?" he asked.

At his suggestion, her eyes darkened to a deep blue color. "How about dessert instead?" she asked coyly.

Before he could reply, she'd unfolded her legs and stood.

"Lose the sweats," she said, hands perched on her hips as she gave *him* an order.

This was a new Cara. She usually let him call the shots, but now *she* was in charge and damn, it was hot.

His lips twitched as he tried not to grin. "I thought you didn't want to eat naked."

"What I want to eat *now* I can't enjoy unless you're naked." She impatiently tapped her bare foot against the rug. "Well? You're wasting time. Lose. The. Pants."

Mike's breath escaped on a whoosh of air. All the blood in his body traveled south immediately.

He rose and dropped his sweats to the floor. Dazed by the loss of blood to his head, when she pushed his shoulders, he easily fell onto the couch and Cara lowered herself to the floor beside him. She edged between his thighs. Then she grasped his erection, wrapping her smaller hand around his aching shaft. Slowly, she drew her palm up and down, up and down, mimicking sex, pulling him in deeper. And when she covered the head with her thumb, rubbing moisture over the top, sensation shot straight to his balls.

He groaned and fell back against the cushion. He barely caught his breath when she slid his erection into her mouth, enclosing him in rich, moist heat. He had to see, to watch. Forcing his eyes open, he looked down to see her run her tongue up and down the length of his shaft. He threaded his hand through her hair, absorbing the silken feel, the shallow movements of her head as she licked him, tasted him. Each time she reached the top, she paused to suck at the crown before drawing him in deeper once more.

Her wet mouth and the friction of her hand built sensation on sensation. He couldn't not move. Couldn't take it and began pumping his hips upward, thrusting himself against the back of her throat. She managed to keep up and soon he was boiling, ready to explode. But he wasn't about to come alone.

He tapped the side of her cheek with his hand and she released him with a slow, teasing withdrawal that had him shaking in his seat. She glanced up at him with wide eyes, glazed with desire. No doubt she'd enjoyed the giving, and that more than anything fired him up.

"Get over here," he said on a low growl.

To his surprise, she didn't argue. She levered herself up to the couch. With one swift pull, he tore off her underwear and tossed it to the floor.

"That's the only pair I have here!"

"We'll figure something out later. Now come." He patted his thighs.

She raised an eyebrow. "Condom, Mike." Her voice sizzled with the same heat he was feeling.

"Shit." He never forgot protection. Not knowing how he was conceived, the position pregnancy had left his mother in. The bedroom felt like it was miles away.

"But I'm on the pill," Cara said, so quietly he almost hadn't heard.

Relief rushed through him.

"I'm safe," he promised her.

Her eyes lit up at his meaning.

"Me too. There's been no one since y—"

He didn't want to hear the end of the sentence, so he lifted her by the waist and brought her over his lap as she grabbed his shaft, placing it at her opening. Even with the light connection, he knew she was wet. Ready. Probably aching, he thought, just as he was.

Once she'd positioned her knees on either side of his thighs, he released her hips and thrust up at the same time she slammed down onto him.

"Oh God," she moaned, the sound seeming to tear from deep inside her.

He knew what she meant. He felt her everywhere. "Ride me, baby."

Her eyelids flew open. "Don't call me—"

"Baby. Yeah, I've heard." And he'd find out why another time.

Now he reached for her, sliding his hand over her shoulder to her neck, feeling her pulse hammering beneath her skin. "Ride me, Cara."

He kissed her quickly and then she was off, lifting herself up and down, milking him in slick heat, her wet sheath contracting around him with each slide up and release. She clenched him tightly, taking him higher with every slide. When their bodies met once more, she twisted her hips, clearly searching for pressure he was only too happy to give.

He slid his hands between them and found the right spot. The slightest touch and she shook violently. A loving pinch and she lit up, exploding around him.

"Oh God, oh God, Michael."

He thrust his hips upward, slamming home, lost to thought, to reason, to anything but the incredible sensations crashing into him harder and faster until he felt his release explode inside her body.

Seven

At his sister's request, Mike headed into The Family Restaurant, located on the edge of Serendipity, for lunch and a chat. Sam, he knew, had also been summoned. Mike made his way into the dinerlike restaurant, which had been in the Donovan family for generations. Macy Donovan, the hostess, a pretty woman with light blue eyes and dark hair, smiled at his entry and gestured toward his siblings seated in the back.

On the way, he passed tables of people he'd known forever and nodded in greeting, stopping at the Barron brothers' table, where Ethan, the oldest; Nash, their middle brother; and Dare, his officer and the youngest sibling, were eating burgers.

"Hey," Mike said, encompassing them all with a sweep of his gaze.

Ethan rose. "Good to see you, Mike."

"Same." He slapped his old acquaintance on the back.

Mike and Ethan were the same age, having gone to school together, and Dare and Sam, though a couple of years apart in age, were also now close. Back in the day, Ethan ran with a troublemaking crowd, smoking, drinking, and generally raising hell until he'd gotten himself arrested, his parents died, and he'd subsequently bailed on his brothers and Serendipity for ten years. Mike's high school friends had been tamer but no more interested in education than Ethan's. They'd both gotten out of town and had that in common. Ethan returned to town a year or so ago, now a millionaire who developed weapons software the government paid big money to acquire.

"How's Faith?"

Ethan's always-hard expression mellowed. "Good, man."

"Heard you were a dad," Mike said, as shocked now as he was when he'd heard the news. He shook his head. "Ethan Barron, a father."

Both his brothers grinned. "Can you believe it?" Nash, the lawyer, asked.

"Don't know why you're talking. You've got twins," Dare said to Nash with a chuckle.

"Jesus." Mike broke out in a sweat but had to admit Nash looked as happy as his older brother. And Ethan, well, he appeared calmer and more grounded than he ever had. "I'm happy for you."

"Thanks."

"Congratulate Faith for me, okay?"

"Why don't you come for dinner one night and do it in person?" Ethan said.

"Uh—"

"Bring a date. I'll have Faith give you a call and set it up."

Mike managed a nod. "Sounds good," he said, even if dinner with the newly minted family man had Mike itching inside the damned suit he had to wear for work.

"I'll let you get back to your lunch," Mike muttered, and headed toward his siblings, his mind on Ethan's last suggestion. *Bring a date.*

It was a week after he'd gotten home from New York City

with Cara, and Mike knew that request would be make-or-break. They'd seen each other this week at work, and, as if by mutual agreement, they hadn't changed how they treated each other at work. No verbal or physical acknowledgment of the fact that they now had a relationship. But that didn't stop the covert looks he gave her when nobody was looking or the heated ones she returned when she thought the same. He couldn't help but admire the curvy body beneath the uniform or stop focusing on those bright blue eyes beneath the fringe of bangs.

Neither had had time to get together during the past week, but he'd called her at night, texted her on occasion, and found himself thinking about her at odd moments. Things he'd never bothered to do with a female before her.

Yeah, she'd gotten to him.

But going out on a real date with another couple, even at their house, meant going public, and he had no idea how Cara would feel about that. She'd made it clear she didn't want trouble at work now or after he was gone. He understood. Yet he, the guy who didn't do relationships, wanted people to know she belonged with him, and Ethan had given him an excuse to ask.

Sam mentioned they were going to Joe's tonight—Sam, Cara, Dare and Liza, and the rest of their group of friends. Mike knew firsthand what happened when Cara went to Joe's. Some guy ended up noticing and propositioning her, and that was something he wanted to avoid. Which meant it was time to talk.

"Hey, you're late," Erin said, tapping on her watch.

Her voice brought him out of his own head and back to his surroundings.

"We ordered for you," she continued.

"No problem." Mike didn't care what he ate as long as he did. He was starving. "A phone call ran long and I stopped to catch up with Ethan Barron." Mike settled in a chair next to Sam.

He glanced at his siblings. Since it was the middle of the week and a workday, Mike wore a suit. He'd spent the morning in meetings with the mayor—wasn't she a pain in the ass—and then with other town officials who'd requested a face-to-face. Sam, who'd come back to work on Monday, was in uniform, back on patrol; Erin was also dressed professionally in a skirt and blouse.

"Not that I mind meeting you guys, but you sounded upset," Mike said to his sister.

Erin's hazel eyes met his. "It's about Mom."

"Mom?" Sam and Mike asked at the same time.

"Not Dad? I thought you'd be concerned about Dad," Sam said.

Mike agreed.

"Except Dad's doing well enough, all things considered. Mom's jumpy."

"Erin, honey, wouldn't you be if you were her?" Sam asked. "Look at all she's been through with Dad."

"It's more," she said firmly.

"I think you're overreacting," Sam said.

Mike frowned at his brother. Erin was one of the most compassionate and insightful people he knew. If she said something was wrong with their mother beyond the obvious, he believed her.

"What makes you think there's more?" Mike asked her.

"After she overreacted to the whole Facebook conversation last week at dinner, I tried to talk to her. She clammed up. Didn't say she was fine, didn't say she was overreacting, she just pursed her lips and said, 'I don't want to talk about it.' That's not Mom. At least, not how Mom is with me."

"That's true." Ella was close to Erin and never shut her out. She rarely shut anyone out.

"Sam?" Erin asked. "You're going to hang with Dad tonight, right?"

He nodded. "Can you talk to her? Or at least just keep

an eye out and tell me if you notice anything . . .
different?"

"Sure," he said, giving in, though from his tone of voice
Mike could tell he thought Erin was nuts.

"How do you think everyone took the changes that I want
to implement at the station?" Mike asked Sam.

Erin raised an eyebrow. "You mean changing everyone
from partnering up to singles except on the night shift?"

"Word spread as far as the D.A.'s office?" Mike asked.

Erin shrugged. "We have to have something interesting
to talk about."

"Makes downtime more boring, but everyone's okay with
it," Sam said. "Especially since we got guys retiring in June
and you'll be able to add shifts to the rookies' schedules."

Mike nodded. "Good."

Before they could change subjects, the waitress came
with their meals and they all got distracted, important subjects off the table.

No sooner had he arrived back at his office when his cell
rang. A quick glance told him Lauren was calling. Hopefully
she had information on the open case. Something that would
put his father out of the running on any issues that cropped
up. But Mike's gut told him he wouldn't get so lucky.

In the week since she'd been home from the city,
Cara's life had returned to normal. Normal meant she
worked, she visited Havensbridge when she could, and she
didn't see Mike unless they were at work. When they acted
completely professional at all times.

Unless she thought no one was paying attention. Then
she studied him, her mind taking her back to that night in
Manhattan, and she wanted nothing more than to be with
him that way again. But she was busy, so busy she barely
had time to think. Until tonight when she was off for another

two days. First Joe's, and then she hoped she'd see Mike. Her place or his, she didn't care.

Lost in thought, she was startled when Mike's assistant called out that she was wanted in his office. She glanced around the room. Everyone was either busy at their desks or changing shifts, so there were a lot of people coming and going, and nobody seemed surprised that the chief had summoned her.

She headed for the private room in the back corner, pausing in the doorway for a calming breath. Hard to be calm when Mike sat at his desk, wearing a charcoal-gray suit and a deep lavender tie, looking sexy as ever.

Then his dark eyes lit on her. "Come in and shut the door behind you."

Cara did as he asked and remained standing, not comfortable that he needed a word now. Here. "Something you need, Chief?"

"Have a seat," he said, in a serious voice that made her stomach pitch uncomfortably.

She gripped the sides of her chair. "What's wrong?"

He muttered something under his breath. "You think something has to be wrong for me to talk to you?"

"Well . . . We're at work. So I figured it's work related and something's up." They hadn't discussed the case they were working on, and she'd figured he hadn't had any word from his contact yet.

His cell rang and he frowned. "Hang on." He glanced at it and held up one finger. "I've been expecting this," he said, and took the call.

"Good to hear from you," Mike said, looking pleased. He paused, obviously listening. "You two sure work fast." His deep laugh rippled through Cara, bringing back memories of the two of them having fun together in New York, laughing, having sex . . .

"I'd love to," Mike said into the phone. He listened, then,

"Sure." Some more listening, and he replied, "Am I bringing someone?" He met Cara's gaze and held on tight. "Yeah, I am."

Her stomach knotted with the intensity she saw there.

"Thanks. See you then and looking forward to it." He hung up and shoved his phone back into his pocket. "Sorry about that."

Cara shrugged off the apology.

He rose and came around his desk, propping himself on the edge, close to her chair, and leaned forward. "As it happens, I have news on the case we were working on. Lauren called."

Cara leaned forward in her seat. "What did she find out?"

"Nothing helpful. All she knows is that at the time the Serendipity Police Department turned the information into the feds, six months had passed since the driver of the car with the drugs and the cash had been arrested there and released on bail."

"How did that happen?" Cara asked. "Who gave bail to a guy with a carload of drugs and money in the trunk?"

"Judge Marshall Baine."

Cara turned the name over in her head. "I don't recognize the name," she said at last.

"He's retired now. But the guy must've skipped and nobody did anything about it. By the time anyone in Serendipity realized and contacted the feds, the perp had been hauled into jail in the Bronx for transporting cocaine over state lines. He was all too willing to make a deal in order to save his own ass and turn his suppliers over to the cops."

"In other words, the feds had no interest in pursuing a small-town case," Cara muttered.

"Exactly. Then somehow, the case went cold here, nobody dealt with it, and the money remained in the evidence locker in Serendipity."

"So we talk to the guy who was arrested back then and see what he remembers," Cara said, rubbing her hands together in anticipation. It was rare she got her hands on an old case that involved digging into the past. Despite its possible connection to Mike's father, she found it fascinating.

"Can't." Mike burst her bubble of excitement. "He was doing twenty-five to life and was shanked by another inmate five years ago."

"Damn."

"Yeah."

"But there is someone who might be able to help us. We can talk to the judge who gave the guy bail," Mike said.

"Okay, cool. I'm up for that."

He nodded, eyes laughing at her response. "I figured you would be." He grew silent, and Cara could tell there was something more.

"What is it?" she asked.

Mike met her gaze. "Sam asked to be let back in on the case since he's back on the job."

Cara enjoyed working with Mike, and though it was Sam's case originally, she hoped she wouldn't lose that one intense work connection she and Mike shared. "What did you tell him?"

"That since it involved my real father, I would appreciate him letting me handle things."

Mike's real father.

Cara had deliberately put Ella Marsden's confidence out of her mind, not wanting to think about the fact that she had information about Mike's father that she couldn't share. From the minute she'd found out Ella was in contact with Rex Bransom, she'd wished she'd never had that moment alone with his mother.

Cara glanced away, afraid her guilt would be reflected in her expression and he'd realize something was bothering her. "Is Sam okay with that?" she managed to ask.

"As long as I keep him in the loop, yeah. He is. He gets it," Mike said, his voice low. "He knows how hard it's been on me."

"What is?"

He didn't answer immediately. In fact he remained silent so long she wondered if he would. "My father left before I was born. He didn't want me." He didn't look at her while he spoke, but shadows filled his eyes and pain crossed his face.

Cara swallowed her surprise at the admission.

She reached out and tentatively placed a hand on his thigh. "You grew up with parents who loved you. Real parents in the true sense of the word, and they didn't run when things got tough. They stuck it out. That had everything to do with you and the man you are now."

He let out a harsh laugh. "And who is that? A man who can't stay in one place for very long? Who is nothing like either of those loving, giving people?"

God. She'd never have thought the overly confident Michael Marsden had insecurities that ran deep. Or that he'd admit to them.

"You're very much like those loving people, Mike. And just because you can't be the steadying permanent force they are, you give in your own way. Simon is sick and you're here, for as long as he needs you to be, taking over his job, making sure things run smoothly until he returns. Would your so-called real father have done that?" she asked. And she'd continue to defend him to himself until he believed it as much as she did.

He burst out laughing, and that easily, the darkness was gone. "And *that's* why you're more than some damn itch," he said, his sexy, chocolate-colored gaze meeting hers.

Her stomach curled sweetly at the compliment, and she just smiled in return. "Glad to help."

"By the way, that was Faith Harrington on the phone earlier," he said, completely changing the subject. "I ran into Ethan this afternoon and they asked me to come to the house for a cocktail Saturday night and then we'll go out for dinner. Come with me?"

"What?" she breathed out, certain she'd heard him wrong.

"You and me, going with Ethan and Faith for dinner. You know Ethan, Dare's brother?"

Cara nodded. She also knew Faith. Sort of. Although close in age, Cara and Faith hadn't run in the same high school crowd, Faith being one of the rich girls.

"You look nervous."

Cara lifted her chin. "It's just a lot to think about. And handle," she admitted.

"They're good people," Mike assured her. "Faith is nothing like her parents."

Everyone in town knew the story of the Harringtons, the former owners of the house on the hill. The richest, smuggest, most arrogant people in Serendipity had fallen hard and fast when Martin Harrington had been convicted of running a massive Ponzi scheme that ruined many people's lives. Ethan had bought the house at auction when he'd returned a few years ago; reconciled with his estranged brothers after a long, difficult journey; and married Faith Harrington.

"Dare adores his sister-in-law," Cara said. "And I like what I've seen of her." Especially how she protected Tess as if the teen were her own sister. "But . . ."

"What?" Mike leaned closer.

She supposed she'd have to broach the crux of the issue, no matter how uncomfortable it made her. "Are you ready to go out in public together?" They hadn't discussed this before, and she was shocked he was suggesting it now.

"Yes." He didn't hesitate. "Are you?"

Was she? Going public wasn't a work issue. She'd already decided the guys here knew her well enough not to assume she was after special favors. And everyone knew Mike's position here in Serendipity was temporary—he'd pretty much reinforced that five minutes ago when he'd compared himself to his father. She was just scared that the more public the relationship, the harder the fall when he left.

"Cara?" Mike's voice brought her out of her thoughts. "I'm here and I'm willing to push out of my comfort zone with you. Are you willing to do the same?" He eyed her warily, and she knew this was important to him.

Between his admission about his father and the fact that he was making an effort, she could do no less. "I'll go with you," she said, before she could back out.

He leaned forward and pressed a quick kiss to her lips before easing back, a genuinely pleased smile on his face. "Good. I'll pick you up at seven."

"Okay," she said.

Except she didn't have anything to wear to the house on the hill, and that was trivial compared to her real worry. Once they went out together in Serendipity, she'd have memories of him everywhere in town long after he was gone.

If there was ever a time to let loose and have fun, tonight was it. Cara was off for the next two days, she'd visited Daniella and the women at Havensbridge and everything was calm, no talk of changing minds or calling abusive exes, and on a personal note, she wanted to forget she had a public date with Mike on Saturday night.

Tonight was Eighties Night at Joe's, and Cara had plans to meet Sam and Alexa for drinks. Alexa had invited Dare and his wife, Liza, and they all grabbed a table; the two guys sat side by side, as did the women, so they could talk.

Cara had gotten to know Liza when she was having some personal problems last year, and she liked her a lot. Though she didn't have a lot of friends, Liza had expanded her social circle and included Cara, and they had fun together; over time, they'd begun to confide in each other. Now Liza and Alexa were Cara's closest girlfriends.

They dressed like the movie *Flashdance*: cut sweatshirts hanging over their shoulders with big hair, chunky jewelry, and heavy makeup. Bubblegum band music alternating with heavy techno and New Wave synthesizer sounds blasted on the jukebox, and Cara was on her second Long Island Iced Tea and happily feeling the buzz when she felt a strong hand on her bare shoulder.

She glanced up and into Mike's warm gaze, and before she could register what was happening, he leaned down and kissed her hello—smack on the lips. Not a short peck, either. A long, happy-to-see-you, tongues-included kiss that left her dazed and out of breath, her body pulsing with sudden need.

"I'm going to sit with the guys," he said, as if the hello had been perfectly natural and expected.

Cara centered herself and had just refocused on her surroundings when both of her friends leaned in close.

"What was that about?" Alexa asked.

"Holding out on us?" Liza said at the same time.

Cara raised her hands to her flushed cheeks. She'd been keeping everything about Mike to herself, including the fling a few months ago. Only Sam had known about that. Somehow they'd sneaked out of the bar and nobody asked her any questions.

Tonight, however, was another story, and Cara knew her friends wouldn't accept any hedging. "Mike and I had a one-night stand last time he was in town. When he came home this time, neither of us mentioned it again; I thought it was over, but it's not."

She blurted out all about dinner with his family, the overnight trip to Manhattan, and his most recent invitation to dinner Saturday night.

"I guess when he said he wanted to go public, he meant it," Cara said, still dazed enough to be in shock.

"That was hot," Alexa muttered, fanning herself.

"You can say that again." Cara decided she deserved another big sip of her drink and treated herself to a healthy gulp.

"Easy, that's strong stuff." Liza's brother was an alcoholic who'd completed three months as an inpatient at a treatment facility. As a result, she was always their designated driver if needed or, at the very least, their voice of reason.

Since Cara rarely indulged this much because of her own family history, she totally understood where Liza was coming from.

Still, Cara didn't mind nursing a drink when the occasion warranted. She tipped her head to the side, toward where Mike sat, knowing he'd made this just such an occasion.

"You look flushed," Liza said.

"Are you okay?" Alexa asked in her doctor voice.

"I'm in shock," she admitted. "He totally took me off guard. I mean, I can't remember the last time I was in a relationship that was so public." Cara was fussy about men and figured she had good reason. She'd had an exclusive dating situation in the past and a couple of hookups with nice enough guys, but this thing with Mike was different.

He was different.

Her heart pounded hard in her chest, and she crossed her legs tight in an effort to rid her body of the aftereffects of the kiss. Unfortunately, the act had the opposite result.

She suppressed a shiver and focused on her friends. "I'm fine." He'd just defined their status publicly, and she'd have to adjust as well as keep her heart locked up tight. Not an easy thing to do, but she'd known that going in.

"What about you guys? How are things going?" Between Alexa's schedule at the hospital and her own private office hours and Liza's at her architectural firm, they didn't manage to catch up often enough. "Liza?"

Liza brushed her bangs out of her eyes and sighed. "I'm happy," she admitted. "Happily married, my brother's managed to stay sober so far, and I'm really really scared it'll all fall apart any minute."

Cara reached out and squeezed her friend's hand. "Totally normal reaction coming from you. My advice? Push away the fear and enjoy every minute. You deserve it. You and Dare both do."

"She's right," Alexa said. "You've been through enough. The bad stuff is behind you. Don't look for trouble where there is none."

Liza nodded. "I know. You're both right." She tipped her head to the side and glanced at her husband, who was deep in conversation with his friends. "It's all good." She smiled. "What about you, Alexa?"

She stirred the straw in her drink. "All work, no play," she said.

"I figured that. The question is why?" Liza asked.

Cara studied her pretty friend. Though Alexa had gone out of state to med school, she'd returned home to Serendipity, and though she occasionally dated, she'd never been seriously involved. At least not that Cara knew of. She worked part time for her father, also a doctor, and put in many more hours at the ER. Her looks weren't the issue; with her auburn hair and green eyes, men were definitely attracted. She had brains and an amazing personality. But Alexa kept men at a distance and always put her work first.

"I just haven't met the right guy." She shrugged like it was a simple answer.

Cara suspected there was something more.

"Well, take it from me and now Cara. You never know when the right guy will come along," Liza said with a grin.

"Oh, no. Mike's not the right guy. Not that way." Cara shook her head, realizing that was stupid when the room grew fuzzy.

"What do you mean?" Liza asked.

"He's not permanent. Not like Dare," Cara whispered. "He's here for as long as his dad is out of commission. He's got an apartment in Manhattan to return to, and he's made it clear he isn't into long relationships."

No hearts involved, he'd said, and Cara wouldn't forget it.

"But you never know, right?" Liza asked hopefully.

"Don't you remember Tiffany Marks?" Cara spoke softly. "The minute she got serious, he left town. Normal people break up. He took off the minute she hinted at an engagement. And everyone thought they'd end up together."

"Maybe that was all Tiffany's doing," Liza said. "I don't remember hearing that it was Mike looking at churches and reception halls."

"And she didn't have a ring on her finger, so maybe it was all in her head?" Alexa suggested.

Cara shook her head. "He left town. Went to Atlantic City. Settled in Manhattan. Still has an apartment there. So I know what I'm talking about." Cara exhaled a long breath. "And I can't let myself think any other way unless I want my heart seriously broken."

"But—" Liza started to speak, but Alexa shot her a warning look even Cara couldn't miss.

"Okay, I'll let it go," Liza muttered. "I just want you to be as happy as I am. So take note. The man can't take his eyes off you," she said, obviously unable to heed her own words.

Cara's entire body heated up at her friend's statement. She turned her head and yep, she caught Mike watching her, a sizzling look in his eyes she could not mistake. He held her gaze, a mesmerizing smile lifting his lips.

"That was even hotter," Alexa said, following her pronouncement by lifting her glass. "Well, darn. Empty."

"I've got the next round," Cara said, even though she didn't want another one herself.

She rose from her seat before either friend could argue and made her way through the crowd to the bar. Despite its being busy, Joe refilled her order quickly and placed the drinks on the counter.

Before Cara could turn, Sam came up behind her. "Hey."

"Hey." He wedged in beside her. "We're friends, right?"

Cara bit the inside of her cheek. She thought she knew

where this private conversation was going, and she didn't want to get into it. "Of course we are."

"And you trust me."

She nodded.

"Then tell me you know what you're doing."

She swallowed hard. "Mike's your brother."

"Yeah, he is. And I know him better than anyone."

"Which is why I can't talk to you about this." She picked up the two glasses, but Sam boxed her in, not letting her pass. "I care about you, Cara, and as much as I love my brother, I know him. He won't hurt you on purpose, but—"

"I *know.*" Cara met Sam's gaze and tried to reassure him even though her stomach was twisting at both his words and the reality. "He hasn't made any promises, okay? I'm in this with my eyes wide open."

"Getting into my business?" Mike asked, coming up behind Sam.

Uh-oh. "No, everything's fine. Sam came to help me carry drinks back to the table." Cara, not wanting to cause conflict between the brothers, shoved one glass at Sam. "Right?"

"Right," he muttered, and took the second drink from Cara as well.

Mike stepped aside to let Sam pass, eyeing him warily the entire time. "I heard the tail end of the conversation and he wasn't here to help with drinks."

"He's just looking out for me."

"By warning you away?"

"By making sure I know what I'm getting myself into, and I do. Come on, Mike. You made a public statement with that kiss. Did you really think everyone would let it slide?"

His eyes darkened. "I didn't think. I did what I wanted."

Unable to help herself, she ran her hand along his stubbled jaw. "And you live with the consequences," she told him, liking the feel of his scruffy day-old beard.

"Is this one of those consequences?" he asked, grabbing her wrist and rubbing his thumb along the inside pulse point.

She swallowed hard. "It is." At their sexual banter, her heart tapped out a rapid beat inside her chest.

"Did you mean what you told Sam about your eyes being wide open?"

She managed a nod. Given a choice between this and not having anything with Mike at all, she'd take this. And deal later.

"Good." He visibly relaxed, but he didn't stop swirling circles on her wrist with his thumb and she felt the pull inside her, causing her breath to catch, her nipples to harden, and pure need to pulse between her thighs. "Ready to go back to the table?"

She thought he would have suggested they head upstairs. "Sure," she said, over her disappointment.

He eased his fingers down and grasped her hand in his. "Don't worry, honey, we'll go upstairs later."

"Honey?" She repeated the word.

"I need an endearment, and *baby* isn't going to work."

"Oh." He wanted an endearment. For her.

Her mouth went dry. He had her wired and on edge, ready to pull him out the back and to his apartment right this second.

He placed his free hand on the small of her back and steered her toward their table. For the rest of the night, Cara heard nothing else except a low buzz of her friends talking and the hum of anticipation in the air as she waited for the time when she could head upstairs and be alone with Mike.

Eight

Mike liked Cara in uniform. He liked her in jeans and a beat-up faded tee. He liked the cut-off pink sweatshirt that bared one shoulder, her long ponytail hanging down her back, swinging as she walked. Her hips were swinging as well, and as his gaze traveled lower, he decided he really liked her ass.

So why hadn't he taken her up on the invitation in her eyes to ditch the bar and go upstairs? Because as much as he enjoyed those things, he loved watching her laugh with her friends that much more.

Apparently he was in deep.

Sam didn't mention anything about the scene earlier. He also hadn't spoken to Mike directly ever since. Whatever Mike had with Cara was none of his brother's business, and Mike didn't plan on bringing it up either.

Eventually, Alexa yawned and said she was ready to turn in. Liza did the same, which led to Dare pronouncing their night over. He took his wife home, Alexa walked out with them, Sam left with barely a good-bye, and Mike turned to Cara.

"Ready?" He rose and extended a hand.

She grinned and stood up. He was happy to see that her buzz had worn off; she was steady on her feet and, from the look in her eyes, as eager to get upstairs as he was.

For the first time, they didn't sneak out separately. Instead he took her hand and led her to the back entrance. Mike didn't give a damn who saw them, and apparently she'd come to terms with her issues about being seen together in public. By morning, word would spread through Serendipity, and though he now had a responsibility to a woman he'd never willingly sought out before, this was Cara. And he didn't mind.

After his messed-up relationship in this small town, Mike had learned a lesson. He wasn't cut out for anything serious because, as he realized not long after his departure from home, he had his biological father's blood running through his veins. He'd proven it with Tiffany and let no woman afterward get close enough to make demands or have expectations. None made him want to give those things.

Cara did.

It didn't miss his notice that he'd willingly gone into a relationship with Cara. He was okay with that because if he wanted to move on before his time in Serendipity was over, she was prepared. He'd handle her with care. He wouldn't deliberately hurt her, and he wasn't worried anyway because he didn't see that happening any time soon.

The cold wind hit them as soon as they left the warmth of Joe's and stepped outside. Before he could give her his jacket or ask where hers was, she ran with him up the back stairs. He had his key in hand and let them inside quickly, shutting and locking the door behind him.

He shrugged out of his coat and hung it on a hook in the hall. A second later, Cara launched herself into his arms and plastered her shivering body against his.

She felt good and right and he wrapped his arms around her tight.

"Cold," she said, teeth chattering.

"I'll warm you. Where was your coat?"

"I left it in Alexa's car. It's such a hassle to have it with me at Joe's."

He grasped her beneath her arms. "Jump," he said.

She did as he asked and wrapped her legs around his waist, allowing him to fully embrace her. Then he sealed his mouth to hers.

He kissed her hard, while backing her up to the nearest wall so he could anchor her in place and free up his hands. He never broke the kiss as he lifted her shirt and pulled it over her head, then freed her luscious breasts from the confines of her bra. Only then did he move, licking a warm path down her cheek, her neck, and her chest, ending when he pulled her taut nipple into his mouth. He alternated long strokes of his tongue with light nips of his teeth that had Cara's hips bucking against him in search of relief.

He needed some of that himself.

When she tugged on his hair, indicating she wanted him to move things along, he had no problem complying. He stepped back long enough to help her open the button on her jeans and shimmy out of them while he pulled off his pants and tossed them aside.

He braced his hands on either side of her head and looked her over, top to bottom. "God, you're beautiful."

She blushed but didn't move to cover herself. Instead she reached out and touched his cheek. "Thank you."

He replied by kissing her and within seconds, they were skin to skin, her soft body melting against his. Her breasts pressed against his chest, she smelled like wildflowers and Mike couldn't wait another second.

"I want you in my bed," he said with a possessive growl.

"So what are you waiting for?" She grinned, and he scooped her up. In his tiny apartment he didn't have far to go in order to get her where he wanted her: on his bed, ready and waiting.

Cara thought her heart was going to explode inside her chest. Mike might be silent some of the time, but when he spoke, every word counted, and tonight everything that came out of his mouth affected her in a profound way.

She scooted backward, positioning herself in the middle of the bed, watching his handsome face while he followed her movements with his heated gaze.

His features were hard and determined as he once again braced his hands on either side of her head. "I need you." The words sounded pulled from a place he rarely visited, rarely shared.

"I'm yours."

And she was, no matter how much she knew it would hurt her in the end. She didn't look, didn't meet his gaze, not wanting to see panic or questions there. Instead she reached between them, grasping his hard, hot length in her hand, and guided him to where she needed him most.

Then she let herself look. His eyes were dilated with need, his face taut, but when he plunged deep, his expression softened and every wall she'd erected around her heart crumbled.

She felt him inside her as he moved—every long glide out and every deliberate thrust back in felt like it had a direct line to her heart. She didn't want to think so much. She wanted to feel what he did to her body, not how he affected her emotions.

Wrapping her legs around his, she yanked hard, knocking him off balance. "Switch," she said, taking control. Maybe then she could chase away the pesky feelings getting in her way.

Surprisingly, Mike agreed, and soon she was on top and in charge like she'd wanted. She stayed that way until he laced his hands through hers, the simple gesture causing a lump in her throat.

As always, no matter the position, she didn't remain in control. He met her rhythm with ease, taking her up and close to peaking faster than she'd thought possible. Her body clasped him tight, making him almost a part of her. So instead of feeling less, Cara felt far more, more of his incredible power and the way he mastered not just her body but her mind—and her heart.

Thankfully that was her last coherent thought before he released one hand and slipped his fingertips to her *there*, pressing the exact spot and sending her flying into the hardest, longest climax of her life. Mike thrust up one last time, and she heard her name on his lips as he came right along with her.

She didn't know how long she rode out the glorious wave, but she milked every last ounce of pleasure he gave before she collapsed on top of him, breathing hard, feeling him do the same beneath her.

His fingers tangled in her hair as he rolled her to the side and pulled her against him.

They lay in silence, and Cara tried to gather her emotions together and rebuild the walls she'd constructed. To do that she had to think rationally. She felt something for Mike, she accepted that. What else did she expect for not having casual sex all that often? When she did sleep with a man, it began to mean something. Okay, that was wrong too. It was Mike. He affected her like no man ever had, so of course she felt something for him.

But she didn't know him well enough or long enough to be in love with him, and she wouldn't let herself reach that point. How she'd stop it, she didn't know. But she'd damn well try.

In the meantime, she knew if she tried to untangle herself and leave, she'd wake him up, so she resigned herself to falling asleep now and worrying about everything else tomorrow.

* * *

Cara and Mike shared breakfast at his place. They each ate a bowl of cold cereal, toast, and coffee before he drove her home. She waited for the awkwardness between them that never came. They had chemistry and were comfortable together, two things that she knew from past experience was extremely rare.

She finished her coffee, and he dropped her off. He didn't treat her like a one-night stand, walking her to the door and kissing her good-bye before heading into the station early. Cara called Havensbridge and left a message for Daniella, a promise that she'd be there around nine A.M.

Then she showered, quickly dried her hair and pulled it into a messy ponytail, and grabbed her keys, ready to go, when her cell rang.

A glance at her phone told her Mike was calling. She couldn't deny the pleasure she received from seeing his name on the screen. "Hey," she said as she answered.

"Hey yourself. Listen, I know it's your day off, but I called Judge Baine, the guy who presided over the drug and money case. His wife said I could talk to him this morning. I was wondering if you wanted to come along."

"You bet!" she said, excited to get details on the case and also happy he'd thought to include her.

"I should warn you, though, it might be another dead end," Mike said, sounding none too pleased.

"Why?"

"His wife explained that he has Alzheimer's, and though he sometimes has lucid days, they're rare, and so far today isn't one of them. But she still said we're welcome to try. Said she never knows what's going to trip his mind back into the present."

"Oh, Mike. I'm sorry." Cara felt his disappointment as if it were her own.

"Me too, but what can you do? If this doesn't pan out, we'll just have to keep finding other leads."

There it was, that *we* again. True, she was partnered with him on this—in fact, it was her case first—but the fact remained that he was the chief and the people potentially involved were close to him. He could have excluded her and there'd be nothing she could do about it. Instead, as personal as this was for him, he made her feel like she was as much a part of things as he was. And she liked it. Liked it a lot.

"Cara? I said I'd be by in thirty minutes to pick you up. Okay?"

She blinked, realizing she'd been lost in her own thoughts. "Sure. But I promised Daniella I'd go to Havensbridge this morning."

"I don't have any afternoon meetings. I can come with you." He paused. "If you think that's okay."

"I don't see why not," Cara said, touched he'd offer.

"Great. See you soon." He disconnected the call.

Thirty minutes later, Mike arrived and five minutes after that, they pulled up to a beautiful Colonial-style home that had been meticulously cared for and maintained. Cara wasn't overly familiar with this side of town, but she knew the houses here cost a pretty penny.

She let out a long whistle. "Nice."

"Very." Mike raised his glasses and studied the house before dropping them back over his eyes. "Let's go."

The judge's wife met them at the door. She was an older woman with gray hair and a friendly expression on her face. "Mike Marsden, welcome," she said, gesturing for them to step inside.

"Thank you for letting us come," Mike said. "This is Officer Cara Hartley."

"Nice to meet you," Cara said, shaking the woman's hand.

"Pleasure," the other woman said. "Marshall's in the den.

It's where he spends most of his days." She started walking toward the room.

Mike glanced at Cara and shrugged, and they followed her into a room filled with sunshine. Obviously Mrs. Baine loved and cared for her husband. She'd opened the shades and put real flowers around to make for a cheery atmosphere and space.

"Marshall, you have company."

The judge turned his gaze from the television, which had *Wheel of Fortune* on the screen. At seventy-three, the judge was still a young-looking man with salt-and-pepper hair, who had retired because of his condition and not because he'd been ready to leave the bench.

He glanced at Cara and Mike with clear eyes. "Well, who do we have here?"

"I told you the new police chief, Michael Marsden, was coming to visit, remember? And he's brought Officer Cara Hartley with him. They want to ask you a few questions," his wife explained, as she walked over and smoothed non-existent wrinkles from the blanket on her husband's lap.

He squeezed her hand, and she stepped away. "I'll go get some refreshments," she said.

"No, please don't go to any trouble," Cara said.

"We won't bother you long," Mike said to Judge Baine.

She nodded. "If you change your mind, let me know." With a wave, she walked away.

Mike and Cara settled into chairs across from the judge. "So how can I help you two young people today?" he asked.

"We need you to go back about thirty years," Mike said. "To a case about a guy stopped for a traffic violation who had drugs and thousands of dollars of marked bills in his trunk."

Mike had been smart in laying out the facts for the judge. Even if he'd seen hundreds of drug cases over the years, he surely hadn't had many that involved marked bills.

Judge Baine raised his gaze to the ceiling, and Cara figured he was thinking back. She glanced at Mike, who studied the older man but waited patiently.

"That'd be 1983, right?"

"That's right," Cara said softly.

"Oh, my years on the bench, the stories I could tell you." And for the next twenty minutes, with the television and Pat Sajak blaring in the background, that was what he did, allowing Cara to understand why people said those with Alzheimer's had no problem with long-term memory.

It was short-term memory that caused more of an issue, and that became clear when the judge wound down his storytelling and focused on Cara. "I'm sorry, do I know you?"

She blinked in surprise. "I—uh—"

"She's with me, Your Honor," Mike said, speaking deferentially to the older man.

"Oh, Rex. Didn't I tell you not to come see me here at home?"

Cara's eyes widened in surprise, and Mike flinched as if Judge Blaine had slapped him—instead of calling him by his biological father's name.

Mike leaned forward in his seat. "It's Mike. Mike Marsden, Simon's son."

"Remember to keep this from your partner. He's as straight as they come, and we can't risk him finding out," the judge said in a warning tone.

Cara's gaze shot to Mike, but he was focused on the older man.

"What can't we risk Simon knowing about?" Mike asked him.

Suddenly, the older man looked around frantically. "Did you hear that? Someone else is here. They're talking and listening to us. I told you we can't talk here," he said, sounding panicked.

"It's just the television." She spoke in what she hoped was a soothing voice, but the judge didn't calm down.

"Mary, Mary?" the judge called out loudly, tossing the blanket off his lap. "Who else is here?"

Mike and Cara rose from their seats at the same time his wife came running in.

"I was worried he'd get like this. Was he able to help you with information before he got upset?" she asked, wrapping an arm around her husband.

"He did his best," Cara assured the woman.

As if by silent agreement, she and Mike edged toward the door, knowing their visit had come to an end.

"Would you mind letting yourselves out? I don't want to leave him alone," his wife asked.

"Of course. We'll be fine," Cara said.

She followed Mike through to the entryway, out the front door, and back to his truck. He didn't say a word as he started the engine, nor did she ask him to. She knew he needed to process what he'd heard and come to his own conclusions.

"Can you take me home to get my car? I need to head over to Havensbridge." She knew Mike wouldn't be coming with her now.

He turned to face her. "You don't want to talk about what we just heard?"

"Not until you're ready." Clearly the judge had known Rex Bransom thirty years ago, and they obviously shared a secret they hadn't wanted Simon to know. Whatever Mike's next step, he deserved space to figure it out on his own time.

He blinked in surprise but remained silent.

"Take me to my car?" she asked again.

Mike shook his head and laughed at the irony. Unlike most women, Cara seemed to know he needed time to wrap his head around this mess, and instead of talking nonstop or pressing him for his feelings, she was letting him be.

Yeah, she was unique all right. No wonder she'd gotten to him. And there was the irony. She made him want to open up. "I've always done my best not to think about him," Mike heard himself say.

"Rex," she whispered.

"Yeah." He rubbed his burning eyes with the back of one hand and thought about the judge's words. "I can't say I'm shocked that the guy who abandoned my mother and me was into something shady. At least he's stayed out of our lives, and I've been grateful for that."

Though sometimes, when he was younger, Mike had wished his real dad would come back and say he'd made a mistake, he'd never meant to leave, and Mike would have both Simon and Rex in his life. But then he'd grown up and realized that only a coward ran off on his commitments— like he'd run from Tiffany. He'd hurt her, but she hadn't been pregnant, and he'd made his escape before things got any more out of hand.

By getting Ella pregnant, Rex had an obligation he'd ignored. Mike had vowed never to be like him, and after coming too damned close, he'd kept his promise by keeping women at arm's length. He was better off without Rex Bransom anywhere in his life.

"But he's got the answers you need," Cara said, getting to the crux of the issue.

"Yeah." And the thought of tracking Rex down after all these years turned Mike's stomach.

"You could try talking to Simon again."

He nodded. "I thought of that. But he already clammed up on Sam, and that means he must know something about the money in the evidence locker, or Rex, that he wants to keep to himself. And I don't want him overstressed during his treatment."

"You love him," Cara said softly.

Mike couldn't help the smile tugging at his lips. "Yeah. He put up with me." To Mike, that meant everything. "So what are my choices? Track down my wayward real father or harass a sick man for answers." He blew out a breath in disgust.

Cara reached out and placed a hand on his shoulder. "You aren't in this alone."

"I appreciate that, but yeah, I am." He'd always been alone or felt that way.

"No, that's in here." She tapped his head. "You've got a family that loves you. They don't consider you adopted or not one of them. Do you understand how lucky you are to have siblings? A mother you can go to? A father you love who *will* get through this?" Her voice cracked.

And he realized it was because she had none of those things. As shitty as his life felt at the moment, she was right. He had a support system, even if he didn't always feel like he deserved them.

He lifted one long curl of her hair and twisted it around his hand. "You're a pretty wise woman."

She shrugged. "I don't know about that. I just think I'm an honest one."

He grinned. "Well, what you said about family? That's given me an idea. Before I have to face looking for my old man, maybe I'll ask my mother what she remembers about that time."

Cara blinked, startled. "Your mother? Why?"

Mike narrowed his gaze. "Because she was around, she knew Rex and Simon, and maybe she can shed some light on things. I know she can handle talking about the past. She's tough." But Cara's wide-eyed stare made him uneasy. "Any reason I shouldn't ask?"

Cara looked out the window at the empty residential street ahead of them. "No. Of course not. You should talk to your mom. You're right. She may remember things."

"Good." Talking to his mother would buy him time to come to terms with the fact that sooner or later he'd have to track down his father and face his past.

"Before I visit my mother, I'll bring you home so you can get over to Havensbridge."

"You're going so soon?" she asked.

"Why put it off? Unless Dad's awake and we aren't alone.

Then I'll hang with him for a while and talk to her next time he goes to chemo on Monday."

"Okay."

He pulled the truck onto the street and headed back to Cara's. The townhouse community where she lived was new, the units not too large or too small, the yards in the back private enough to keep all residents comfortable. He liked that she had a place of her own, away from the turmoil with her parents.

He parked in front of her condo. "I'll pick you up at seven tomorrow night for dinner with Ethan and Faith."

"Oh! Right."

He tugged on her ponytail. "Did you forget?"

She faced him with a sheepish grin. "Of course not! I just wasn't thinking about it at the moment. And now that you reminded me . . ."

"What?"

"I need to go into town and buy something to wear." She bit down on her lower lip, and he wanted to pull it into his mouth and nibble for himself.

"Don't make yourself crazy. They're old friends and they're just like us. Ask Dare."

"Okay, fine." Her cheeks flushed with embarrassment. "I'll see you tomorrow night." She turned and reached for the door.

"Cara, aren't you forgetting something?"

She swiveled back to him. "What?"

He leaned over and cupped his hand behind her head, pulling her close. "This," he said, sealing his lips over hers.

She moaned and responded immediately, opening her mouth and sliding her tongue against his. God, she was so damned responsive, easing the ache that had been present in his chest since Judge Baine's outburst about Mike's real father.

"I've got to go," she murmured against his mouth. But she didn't back away.

"You sure?" He licked at her already moist lips.

"No. Yes. Yes." She sat up, blue eyes glazed, cheeks pink, ponytail messed from his hand.

He couldn't tear his gaze from her pretty face.

"Stop looking at me like that," she said, reaching for the door once more.

"Cara, when I bring you home tomorrow night, I'm staying over."

"Is that a promise?" she asked, her eyes gleaming with desire.

He nodded. "Now *go.*"

She laughed before hopping out of the truck and running to her front door. He waited until she was safely inside before driving away.

Nine

Mike strode into his parents' house with dread. A real case of need to know, don't want to know. His mom had asked him to come on Saturday instead of Friday, so he'd put off any confrontation or discussion until today. Kojak greeted him in the foyer with yapping barks, and Mike scooped the little dog into his arms.

"Michael!" His mom met him in the den, ready with a hug and a kiss on his cheek.

"Hi, Mom." He hugged her back.

"I'm so glad you're here."

He smiled. "I'm glad I'm here too. It's nice to see you more than every couple of months."

"Really?" she asked, her eyes filled with uncertainty.

He leaned back against the comfortable sofa cushion and paused to think. Not because he wasn't happy to be here but because he knew what she meant. Was he happy to be in Serendipity, living here and not in the city?

"I'm enjoying it more than I thought I would," he admitted.

"The job? Or being here?" His mother was dressed in a chocolate-brown sweat suit, looking as sharp as ever, despite the tiredness drawing deeper lines in her beautiful face.

"Both," he said easily. So far he had no signs of antsiness or wanting to leave the small town where he'd grown up.

"That's good!" His mom sounded as surprised as he felt. "Does Cara have something to do with that?" she asked, leaning forward and pressing personal issues as only a mother could.

He grinned indulgently. "Have I ever discussed my private life with you?"

She laughed. "As long as she makes you happy," Ella said, putting her own interpretation on his words.

The correct interpretation, but Mike wasn't about to tell her that. She'd be pushing him for more than he was ready to think about or admit. For all he knew, he'd wake up tomorrow needing the freedom of getting lost in Manhattan.

"Mom," he said in a warning tone.

"Fine. Just so you know, your father and I approve. In case you were wondering."

He wasn't. He never had before. But a funny warmth spread through him now. Mike cleared his throat, reminding himself that he was here for a reason. "Where's Dad?" he asked.

"Taking a nap. But he's doing well with his treatments, and the doctor is really pleased."

Mike let out a long breath. "I'm glad."

"Me too. They say this exhaustion and weakness will go away after he finishes chemotherapy. I hope they're right."

"I've heard it takes a while for people to come back to themselves," he cautioned her. "Some people are never quite the same." He spoke gently, but wanted to prepare her.

She nodded, swallowing hard. "I know, honey. But I need to think positively to get through this and your father, and his will to live and get better . . . it'll be fine."

"I agree." He sat forward, elbows on his knees. "Mom, I need to talk to you."

"Of course. What is it?"

Mike broke into a sweat. He couldn't remember the last time he'd broached the subject of Rex. Though he meant it when he'd told Cara his mother was strong, neither one of them would enjoy this talk.

Better to get it over with, he thought. "I have questions about Rex Bransom."

The color leeched from her face.

Mike rose and was beside her in an instant. "Are you okay?"

She nodded. "I'm sorry. I wasn't expecting . . ."

"I know. But something's come up from years ago, and there are things I need to ask you."

She nodded slowly, color returning to her cheeks. "You can ask me anything, you know that."

Assured she'd recovered from the shock, he returned to his seat on the couch. "Here's the situation." Mike explained everything: the mayor's request to clean up corruption, how it had led to the evidence room and the money, and how he and Cara had ended up at Judge Baine's house and the man's Alzheimer's-induced ranting. "But there's truth to some of what he said. There has to be. At the very least, he linked himself to Rex and admitted holding out on Simon. And Dad—well, Sam tried to talk to him about that time right before he got sick and he shut down completely. Wouldn't say a word."

Ella rose and paced the room.

Mike let her absorb his information before asking, "Mom, was Rex involved in anything back then?"

She turned, but didn't meet his gaze.

"Mom?"

"Look, back then I was so absorbed in being pregnant and Rex's reaction and then his leaving . . . I'm telling you the truth." She clenched and unclenched her hands. "But I can tell you this," she said softly. "Rex liked a challenge; he skated on the edge."

"Like me," Mike muttered, more to himself than to her.

"You don't skate on illegalities, Michael. There were good parts of Rex, and those are the things you inherited from him. Don't do this to yourself."

He shook his head, agreeing with her on some things, not on others. "So I'm back to where I started. Either I push Dad, which I can't do while he's so weak, or I find Rex and get the answers myself."

His mother swayed on her feet.

Mike muttered a curse, rose, and wrapped his arms around her, leading her to the sofa. "Sit."

She did as he instructed.

"I'm getting you something to drink. Hang on." Mike went to the kitchen and returned with a glass of orange juice. "Here. Drink this."

He sat next to his mother while she drained the glass.

"Thank you."

"You're welcome. I'm sorry to do this to you now."

She shook her head. "Work or not, you have every right to ask about your father."

They sat in silence for a few minutes, until she looked up at him. Reaching out, she touched his hair, running her fingers through the too-long strands in a motherly gesture he remembered from childhood. "You look so much like him, you know."

He glanced away. He didn't know. Wasn't sure he wanted to.

"I'm sorry I didn't keep any pictures. It was thoughtless of me, but I was young and I didn't want Simon to think I still held a torch, you know?"

He nodded, not wanting to know the answer to that question either.

"So you want to find him?" his mother asked.

"Want to?" Mike let out a harsh laugh. "No. But I need to."

"I've been in touch with him."

The words came out so whisper soft he thought he heard wrong.

He whipped his head around and looked at his mother. "Say that again."

"I've been in touch with Rex."

Disbelief and a sense of betrayal ripped through him. When? How? "I thought he was MIA."

His mother hung her head. "He was. And then a little while ago, he friended me on Facebook."

"That's why you got so upset at that family dinner. All that talk about Facebook and old flames." He shook his head in disbelief. "What did he want?" Mike asked through clenched teeth.

"He was curious about you," she whispered.

Pain lodged in his chest. "Too little, too late," Mike muttered. "Why didn't you tell me?"

"I couldn't! Imagine how Simon would feel if he knew Rex was asking about his family. Especially while he's in treatment."

"What about me? What's your excuse for keeping me in the dark?" he asked through the red haze of anger, hurt, and frustration that clouded his thoughts and his vision.

"This. Your anger at him. Your ambivalence about yourself. You're so afraid you're like him—I know you personalized that mess with Tiffany, though heaven knows that girl was a clinging vine. But now you're home and you're here . . . I didn't want to jeopardize your peace of mind." She closed her eyes, weariness and strain evident in her face and how she'd hunched her shoulders.

He reached out and pulled her close. "You should have told me," he said, unable to stay furious at his mother.

"I know. Even Cara said so, but I didn't listen."

Mike froze. "Cara knows?"

His mother moaned. "Oh God. I'm sorry. That same night, we were talking about her parents, and I said I understood what it was like to doubt your choices. I didn't plan on telling her, but I guess I needed someone to talk to because before I knew it, I had. And she said you should know, and I made her swear not to tell you."

"Okay," he said, to appease his mother.

Cara knew. He thought she understood him. Thought he could trust her in a way he'd trusted no other woman. Yet she'd sat with him at the judge's house, listened to him say he needed to find the father he hated, and she'd known his mother was in touch with the man. And still she'd said nothing.

"Michael Marsden, don't you dare be mad at Cara," his mother said, shaking his shoulders. "I put her in an awful position."

"Maybe." But he was sleeping with the woman, revealing himself to her on all sorts of levels. *She should have told him.*

"Don't worry about it," he told his mother.

"You aren't upset with her?"

"I'm seeing her for dinner tonight," he said, evading the question.

"That's not an answer." His mother's voice was stronger now. She'd composed herself and was back to her forceful self.

"It's all I have at the moment." He rose to his feet. "Where can I find him?" he asked of Rex.

She swallowed. "He's in Nevada."

"Vegas?" Mike asked.

His mother nodded.

"Figures," Mike muttered.

"What are you going to do?" she asked, wringing her hands as she spoke.

He met his mother's gaze and answered honestly. "I have no fucking idea."

She blanched at his language, but she didn't correct him, obviously knowing he deserved the outburst.

"I have to go." He leaned over and kissed her cheek. "Tell Dad I said hi."

"Mike, please. Calm down and let's talk again before you do anything."

He wasn't making any promises. "I love you," he said, before walking out the door and into the cold sunshine and bright light of day.

He was numb. Angry. Hurt. Pissed. And he had to work it all out before he picked up Cara tonight and took her out with old friends. Or the night he'd been looking forward to was going to end up being a nightmare instead.

Cara was more excited about dinner than she let herself admit. But before she could focus, she needed to do some grocery shopping because her fridge was empty. She pushed a cart up and down the aisle in the Food Mart, following the list she'd made. She often cooked on Sunday, freezing some meals for the week, so she stocked up on both basics and snack foods.

As she turned into the last aisle, she paused the cart by the milk, looked up, and saw her mother standing with a small basket in her hand, studying the orange juice.

"Mom!" Cara said, before she could think through that she'd been avoiding her.

Natalie Hartley glanced up. "Cara!" She strode over and hugged Cara, her pleasure in seeing her daughter obvious.

Despite Cara's frustrations with how her mother chose to live her life, Cara adored her and missed her like crazy. She tried hard not to let herself think too hard about how much—or she ended up sad and melancholy. The holidays were especially hard. Cara often ended up at the Marsdens' or with Alexa and her dad, instead of being with her own parents.

"How are you?" Cara asked, inhaling the floral, fragrant scent she associated with the better parts of her childhood.

"Fine." Her mother's gaze darted to the left and right before focusing on Cara. "What about you? Are you well? Happy?"

Cara swallowed the painful lump in her throat. "He's here, isn't he?"

Her mother couldn't even go to the grocery store by herself. She was surprised he'd left her alone in an aisle. "He went to pick up soda we forgot. Talk to me quick, before he comes back. Are you well, honey?"

Cara nodded. "I'm good."

"My baby, a police officer. I'm so proud," her mother said, tucking Cara's hair behind one ear.

She blushed. "Mom." Cara shook her head. "I—"

"Nat, let's go now!" Cara's father's voice interrupted her midsentence.

She'd been about to tell her mother she missed her.

"I have to go." Natalie's shoulders had slumped, and she didn't look Cara in the eye. "I love you."

"Tell him one minute. We're just talking." Cara heard the plea in her voice.

"Baby, move it. It's time to make lunch," her father ordered.

Cara looked over at Greg Hartley. Still handsome; his salt-and-pepper hair slicked back off his face, his eyes burned with anger as he looked between Cara and her mother, who'd already taken a step away from her daughter.

It wasn't difficult not to say hello to her father.

And he deliberately ignored her. He hated that she'd become a cop. He hated it even more that she refused to acknowledge him as her parent, denying him the respect and control over her he craved.

"Nat, now." Her mother jumped at the low bellow.

She turned her back on Cara and walked away, head down, as she curled into herself.

Cara hated him. She hated how her mother gave in to whatever he wanted without care to her own needs. If cutting herself off from her parents was the only way to avoid seeing this painful sight, she'd continue to do it. No matter how big a hole her mother's absence left in her chest or how much the fear for her safety ate away at her. Her mother had made it clear she didn't want Cara's help. There was nothing else she could do.

Except help those who wanted it, Cara thought. Stuffing the pain down where it belonged, Cara finished up her shopping, took the groceries home, and did cleaning around the house.

On Friday, she'd spent more time at the shelter than she'd planned because Daniella was obviously depressed after discovering that she'd need continuing education courses to update her paralegal license. The timing would take a while for her to get up to speed and capable of being rehired. That meant more time at Havensbridge, and the young woman was lonely, talking about alternatives like going home. As in back to her ex. Cara was nervous and spoke at length to Belinda about keeping Daniella busy and talking, to prevent her from leaving.

Though Cara could relate to many of the women who came and went from the shelter, Daniella and her sad blue eyes reminded Cara of her mother's. The run-in was still fresh, causing her to miss her mom even more.

By the time Saturday afternoon came, she'd managed to shake off the depression and allow her excitement about her date with Mike to come through. She spent the morning at Consign and Design in town and bought a new April Mancini original skirt at a very reasonable price. The leopard print was gorgeous and the short length showed off her legs, which were normally hidden under a uniform or blue jeans; she added her favorite black patent boots, along with a silk black camisole and a cream-colored blazer.

One last look in the mirror and she was ready to go. Ready to see Mike.

The doorbell rang and, with a last bout of nerves in her stomach, she headed for the door and let him in.

"Hi." She greeted him with warmth, stepping back to admire the view.

Wearing dark denim jeans and a black button-down shirt and not a speck of razor stubble, he was the sexiest thing she'd ever seen. He smelled delicious too.

"Hey." He didn't crack a smile as he stepped inside. His expression looked dark and forbidding, and a sudden chill skittered over her skin. One that had nothing to do with the brief blast of cold air from outside.

"Ready?" he asked.

"I just have to get my purse and jacket."

He shoved his hands into his front pockets and waited without making small talk and without looking at her at all.

She swallowed hard. His greeting was nothing like she'd expected. Okay, so he wasn't admiring the view as she'd done with him. She told herself that was fine, even as disappointment welled inside her.

But his closed expression put her off and unnerved her even more. He looked nothing like the man who'd dropped her off yesterday afternoon with a blistering kiss and a promise to stay the night.

"Umm . . . is everything okay?" she asked as she picked up her small bag from the couch.

"Any reason it wouldn't be?" he asked in an ice-cold voice.

Her discomfort turned to alarm. "You tell me."

He glanced at his watch. "We're going to be late," he said, without answering her question.

"And I don't give a damn." Cara wasn't going anywhere with Mike in this mood. She tossed her bag back onto the sofa. "Talk."

He turned to face her, his eyes and expression glacial. "I went to see my mother today."

Uh-oh. "What did she say?"

Disappointment flashed across his handsome face. "Are you really going to play this game? You know exactly what she said. That she's been in touch with my father on Facebook and *you knew.*" He spat the words like an accusation.

Cara's stomach twisted in tight knots, but she straightened her shoulders, standing by what she had—or hadn't—done. "It wasn't my place to tell you." She'd felt angst about it, felt guilty, but in the end, there was only one choice she could make, and she remained silent.

He shook his head back and forth slowly. "I talked to you about my father. I don't talk to anyone about him, including my family." His eyes blazed with anger and betrayal, causing her heart to pound harder in her chest.

"I know." And Cara had valued every ounce of information he'd given her, no matter how small. "And I appreciate that you let me in." She stepped closer, placing a hand on his shoulder, but he stepped out of reach.

She did her best not to shiver at the rejection. "I begged your mother to tell you, but she didn't want to upset you. She insisted, and I gave my word."

"That's it?" He glared at her, not giving an inch. "You saw me after the judge's house. You knew how conflicted I was. And all you can say is you gave your word?"

She nodded, pulling her walls back up because she wasn't getting through to him. "My *word* is everything. It's what defines me."

He raised an eyebrow. "That cut-and-dried?" he asked.

"You're damned right. Want to know why? Because I know what it means not to keep it."

He narrowed his gaze.

Cara went on. "Every time my father swore he wouldn't touch my mother again, he gave his word. He promised over and over he wouldn't hit her again. He wouldn't belittle her. Demean her." Cara's thoughts went back to the scene at the grocery store the other day. "Order her around, demand she walk away from her own daughter at his command." Cara's voice caught, but she forced herself to go on. "He makes her feel like she's nothing. And every time he promised not to do it again, he did. He broke his word. And each time was worse than the last."

She felt rather than saw his shock. The atmosphere changed between them, chill turning to warmth, but Cara didn't want Mike softening toward her because of pity. He needed to understand why she'd keep a promise no matter what.

"I learned early on, the only thing that matters is whether a person can keep their word. That's what defines who I am as a human being. That's what makes me different from him." Her voice cracked, but she wasn't going to fall apart on him. "So no, I didn't tell you what I knew because I promised your mother I wouldn't."

This time he came to her, his body heat bracketing her where she stood. "Cara."

She shook her head, unable to believe that the night she'd looked forward to had gone so far off course. Yet she didn't blame him for being hurt or angry with her.

"Look at me," he said, his voice gruff and a lot warmer than when he'd walked in.

She wasn't ready, but he turned her to face him. "I, of all people, know what it's like to not want to be like my father. I was pissed at everything, and I overreacted. Took it out on you because I couldn't have it out with Rex." His half-grin disarmed her own anger and hurt.

She sighed. "I wanted to tell you, but I couldn't."

"I get that now."

And Mike did. Talk about blindsided. All his righteous

anger dissolved in the face of her admission. This woman had the ability to twist him in knots, making him feel things completely foreign to him. They had more in common than he realized, wanting not just distance from a parent they despised but proof they were nothing like them.

He ran a hand through his hair. "Should we go?" he asked, eager to put the discussion behind them. No good could come of talking about it anymore.

She eyed him warily. "That's it?"

"Do I look like the type to hold a grudge?"

She burst out laughing. "Yeah, as a matter of fact, you do."

He rolled his eyes, knowing the tension had broken. "Let's go, okay?"

She inclined her head. "Okay." She seemed happy to let it go too and reached for her bag.

With his anger gone, he exhaled long and hard, finally getting a real look at the enticing female he'd picked up for a date. Her long, dark hair, normally pulled back in a ponytail, fell over her shoulders; bangs skimmed her forehead; and she'd put on more makeup than he was used to seeing on her. The effect, combined with the sexy outfit she'd chosen, blew his mind.

This wasn't Cara the cop. It wasn't Cara who filled out a pair of jeans and looked damned good in a worn T-shirt. This was a sexy siren who'd dressed with him in mind, and he'd shown up here blasting her for hiding things from him instead of admiring her.

"I'm an ass."

"You said it, not me." Her lips twitched in amusement.

"I'm sure you thought it," he muttered. "You look beautiful."

She blinked, obviously startled, before smiling widely. "Thank you."

"It's what I should have said from the beginning. Can we start over?" he asked, extending his arm for her to take.

He knew they'd have to discuss the case sooner or later, just as he'd have to decide what to do about looking up his old man. But those weren't things he needed to dwell on now.

She nodded slowly and licked her glossed lips. "I'd like that."

That easily, they were back to normal, leaving Mike to marvel yet again how different Cara was from other women he'd been with who chose arguments for the sake of arguing. Tiffany especially had liked tantrums in order to get something she wanted out of him. No woman he'd known had just simply stated her feelings instead of keeping them inside until they boiled over. Cara made it a habit. There was no guessing where he stood with her, and he liked it.

Twenty minutes later, they'd pulled into the driveway at the house on the hill. Cara, eyes wide, marveled at the twinkling lights coming from on high and the large mansion rising in front of them.

"It's a town landmark, but I never get used to seeing it," she said in awe.

He knew what she meant. He and Cara came from working-class families, and though Mike grew up in a nice house in a decent neighborhood, their four-bedroom home could probably fit in the pool behind the mansion.

"It is something," he agreed.

They parked and walked to the door, and Mike rang the bell. A few seconds later, the door swung wide and a teenage girl stood before them.

"Hey, Tess," Cara said to the girl.

"Ooh, you got yourself a hot one," the teenager said, glancing at Mike.

"I most certainly do." Cara winked at her, shocking Mike completely.

He opened his mouth to speak, but no sound came out.

"Mike, this is Ethan, Dare and Nash's smart-mouthed sister, Tess. Tess, Mike Marsden. The *police chief*," Cara said, emphasizing his job description.

"Oh. Shit." This time Tess grew silent, and Cara burst out laughing.

"Are you going to invite us in or let us freeze to death out here?" Cara asked.

"Come on in," the teenager said grudgingly.

"Gee, thanks." Cara's light laughter washed over him.

Tess stepped back, and Mike noticed she was wearing a fitted top over jeans, her clothes too tight to be comfortable, but a typical teenager outfit from what he'd seen around town.

"Tess, did you get the door?" Ethan asked, the sound of his footsteps coming closer.

"Duh," she muttered.

Ethan met them in the foyer with a smile, but he glanced at his sister and asked, "What's with the attitude?"

"You said company, not the chief of police," Tess hissed at him, her cheeks pink.

"I'm not here on official business," Mike said, hoping to put her at ease.

Ethan laughed. "I should hope not. She's been off probation for a while now."

"What?" Mike asked, sure his friend was kidding.

"A long story for another time," Ethan said.

Tess looked at him, narrowing her eyes. "I can't believe you!" With a solid foot stamp, she took off, heading back upstairs.

"Bye, Tess," Cara called out.

"Bye," the teen yelled back.

"What was that all about?" Mike asked.

Ethan shook his head and laughed. "That was Tornado Tess. Come on into the den and I'll tell you all about it." He gestured for them to follow him into a large room with a bar in one corner and a big-screen television in another. "Faith is upstairs with the baby. She'll be down soon."

"Ooh, can I go on up and take a peek?" Cara asked.

Ethan grinned like a proud father. "Sure. Just follow the

smells," he said, making Mike wonder how the hard guy he'd known in high school had gone from rebel to parent with seeming ease.

Mike shuddered.

Cara laughed and headed out the door. He watched her walk out, her tight behind swaying in that little skirt and short jacket.

"Damn, you have it bad," Ethan said.

Mike raised an eyebrow. What could he say? He'd been caught.

"So what's it like being a father?" He changed the subject.

Ethan grinned. "I wasn't ready for it either."

"Hell, you're old enough to know if you're potentially getting your wife pregnant."

Mike shook his head at his friend, and Ethan burst out laughing. "I was talking about love, not kids."

"Who the hell said anything about love? We're just having fun."

Ethan walked to the bar. "At least you didn't say it was just sex. Scotch?" he asked.

Mike nodded. "Thanks." He already knew it wasn't just anything. Not that he'd get into that with Ethan.

"It's amazing being a father." Ethan poured two glasses of alcohol and handed one to Mike.

The man switched subjects like a pro. "Are you talking about Tess or baby diapers?" Mike asked, joking.

"Both." Ethan met his gaze, his expression as serious as Mike had ever seen it. "I thought I'd grown up when I moved back here, and I had, but Tess, she turned me into the man I wanted to be. Faith did the rest. Then she gave me our daughter." Ethan raised his glass. "To women," he said, the foolish grin of a man in love on his face.

Mike wasn't that far gone, but he had to admit Cara had him in an unfamiliar place that had him reeling. Mike raised his glass and took a large gulp, needing it to feel more centered.

"Want to see my princess?" Ethan asked with pride.

"What's her name?" Mike asked.

"Allie. After my mother, Alicia."

Mike nodded, understanding the sentiment. He followed Ethan out of the den and up the long circular stairs.

Soft female voices sounded from a room at the end of the hall, where a light glow illuminated the darkened hallway. Music played from another room, the heavy rock telling him where Tess, the teenager, had gone.

Mike paused outside the baby's room and, with Ethan, looked inside. To his shock, Cara, not Faith, held the tiny bundle in her arms. Before he could process the warmth spreading through him, Cara leaned in and pressed her nose to the baby's head. "I love the smell of baby," she whispered.

"It's the Johnson's Baby Shampoo. Makes you want to eat them up," Faith agreed.

"She's so precious," Cara said in awe. "I was afraid I'd break her."

Faith waved a hand dismissively. "From the way you changed that diaper, you're a natural. All ready for when you have one of your own."

Ethan stood beside him, the silence charged. Mike felt as uncomfortable listening to the women's dialogue as he did having his old friend undoubtedly put his own spin on what he thought Mike was feeling. Hell, he barely knew himself.

"I don't know if that'll ever happen," Cara said, surprising him. "I'd need to believe that relationships can last and that there's someone out there who I'd trust with my whole heart not to hurt me."

The way her mother had been hurt. Mike heard the unspoken end to her sentence, her quiet words and painful thoughts a sucker punch to his gut.

She didn't think she believed, but she so obviously yearned for what Faith had—and Cara deserved that kind of love and devotion. He wasn't the guy to give it to her, and for the first time in his life, Mike was disappointed that he couldn't be what a woman needed.

Not *a* woman.

This one.

No hearts involved, wasn't that what he'd told her? If that were true, then why did his chest ache so badly now?

Ethan cleared his throat, and the women glanced up. "Hi!" Faith said. "Come on in."

The quiet spell that enveloped Mike broken, he followed Ethan into the room, but Mike knew this night would stay with him for a long, long while.

After they put the baby to bed, Faith and Ethan said good night to Tess and checked in with the housekeeper, Rosalita, who would be babysitting for the evening. They had dinner in a neighboring town at a steak restaurant, where they were seated in a small booth.

With Cara next to him, she invaded his personal space. Cara's scent, a new warm, musky fragrance, cocooned him in a sexual haze. It was a miracle he'd been able to focus on conversation with the hard-on he had beneath the table. Faith and Ethan seemed happy to be out for grown-up time, so they ordered a bottle of wine and lingered over drinks, dinner, and dessert.

By the time they headed back to Cara's, Mike realized he'd had a genuinely good time. He couldn't remember the last time he'd gone on a regular date with another couple and was even more shocked to discover that not only had he liked it, he wasn't itching to get back to New York or his solitary life.

All he could focus on was getting Cara into bed and keeping her there.

Ten

For a night that had been a roller coaster of emotions, Cara ended up having a really good time. She'd adored Faith's baby, the sweet, innocent smell providing her with unfamiliar warm fuzzy feelings floating in her brain. Then she'd looked up to see Mike staring at her with a hot but unreadable expression on his face, and if she hadn't handed the baby back to her mother, Cara might have ended up letting a deeply buried yearning creep inside. She couldn't afford to think about things like babies, family, or even long-term relationships. The very thoughts were anathema to her on a normal day, but with Mike in her life, they were downright dangerous.

She'd been grateful when Ethan said it was time to go, and they'd said their good nights to Tess and Rosalita and headed off for dinner, just the adults. Cara had relaxed and let go, drinking more wine than she was used to, and even now, on their way home, she still felt a happy buzz.

Mike pulled into the driveway of her condo and cut the engine of his truck. Before she could focus, he'd come around to her side and opened her door. She fumbled for the seat belt, the fuzziness from the wine making her fingers less than nimble, and she couldn't suppress a very un-Cara-like giggle.

"Let me." Mike immediately leaned over her and unbuck-led the seat belt with one easy click, releasing her.

She turned to hop out of the high truck seat and came into direct contact with his hard body, and his large hands came to her waist. It was all she could do not to lean farther into his warmth and the intoxicating scent she'd come to associate with Mike.

Instead of stepping back and giving her room to climb out, he lifted her out of the seat and deliberately allowed her body to feel the hard length of his as he lowered her to the ground.

She teetered a bit on her heels and wrapped her arms around his neck, telling herself it was so she wouldn't fall.

"Cara," he groaned, burying his face between her neck and shoulder. "Sitting so close to you at the restaurant, your bare thigh touching mine, your sexy scent distracting me, I've been hard all night."

Her body clenched tight at his blunt words, and she let out a moan, arching her hips into him and tangling her fingers in his hair.

"Inside," he said, grabbing her hand and heading for the door. "Keys?" He held out a hand.

She fumbled opening her purse but found the set and handed them to him so he could unlock the door faster than she ever could, and they stepped inside.

Between the rush of cold air and the desire flooding her veins, she'd more than shaken off the effects of the wine, but she was more than happy to let him take the lead. For one thing, he was hot doing it, and for another, as long as he wasn't telling her what to do in every other part of her life, she'd cede control in the bedroom. When she'd decided that, she had no idea. But this was Mike. He liked to be in charge there, and she liked to give him what he wanted. Who cared as long as it worked?

And when it came to *this*, they definitely clicked.

She shucked off her jacket, letting it fall to the foyer floor. Next she bent over to remove her boots, only to feel Mike's hand slip beneath her skirt and find the lacy Victoria's Secret panties she'd chosen, knowing he was staying over.

His hand caressed her ass, and heat flooded her everywhere.

"Cara, baby," he murmured, his voice rough.

But his words stopped her cold and she whirled around to face him. "Baby?"

Realization dawned, and he narrowed his already dark gaze. "Okay, that's it." He grabbed her hand and pulled her over to the couch, settling her on his lap. "The word obviously slipped out of my mouth. Again. I need to know why you react the way you do."

"I don't want to talk about it."

"Tough." He lifted her hand and pressed a hot kiss against the rapidly beating pulse point in her wrist. "Now tell me so I can understand and we can get past it," he said, his tone implacable.

He wouldn't give her an out, and she blew out a frustrated breath. "Look, I know I'm being ridiculous." Because Mike used the word as an endearment.

And other people used it too, as a joke or a friendly comment, and Cara snapped at them every time. Sam and Dare thought she was a feminist, and she didn't bother correcting them. Nobody had ever pushed her about it before.

"I didn't say you were ridiculous. I just want to know why it bothers you." He kept his hand intertwined with hers.

"Fine," she snapped, feeling cornered. "It's what my father says to my mother. Baby, bring me a drink. Baby, get me the newspaper. Baby, stop being such a goddamned drama queen. Baby, shut the fuck up and cook dinner." And *Baby, you need to listen when I tell you to do something* before he let loose with his fists.

Beneath her, Mike stiffened at her words, then finally forced himself to relax. "Thank you for telling me," he said at last.

She heard the heartfelt sentiment behind the words. "Guess I'm more screwed up than you thought, huh?" She managed a laugh she didn't really feel.

"No more than me, *baby.*" Before she could react to the word, he'd lifted her hand and run his tongue over her sensitive skin.

She shivered, feeling the cool trail of moisture all the way to her core, and she unconsciously wriggled deeper into his lap, seeking pressure where she ached the most.

"Notice that?" he asked.

All Cara felt was a pure shot of desire. "Notice what?"

He chuckled. "Desensitization to the word. I'm going to work at it until every time you hear *baby*, you think of me doing something wicked to your body and the bad memories no longer resurface."

"You think you can accomplish that?" she asked in a husky voice, unbelievably touched by his response.

He shrugged. "I hope so. I know it'll be fun to try."

He blew on the damp skin of her wrist and with an answering sigh, she shifted positions until her thighs bracketed his and her sex came into direct contact with his erection.

"See?"

She laughed.

He leaned in and pressed his lips against hers, the pressure light at first, teasing her with soft kisses and leisurely licks of his tongue. He didn't let up. She wasn't sure how long they remained that way, kissing, nibbling each other's mouths, fondling one another over their clothes. All she knew was that this kind of foreplay wasn't something the guys she'd been with usually indulged in, not when sex was the end goal. But Mike didn't seem in any hurry to get to the finish line, since he was clearly enjoying this and so was she.

He cupped her breasts in his hands, teasing and plucking at her nipples through the bra and the silk, until they were hard peaks. Only then did he lean down and suck one rigid tip into his mouth. A wave of sensation struck and she felt the pull as if he were suckling on her bare skin. She arched her back and he bit lightly. More excitement whizzed through her, moisture seeped into her panties, and actual tremors shook her body.

He slid a hand beneath her shirt and into her bra, tweaking her other nipple with his thumb and forefinger. All the while, he continued to torture the first breast with long delicious pulls and mini love bites, reading her body and what she needed with perfection. Soon she was writhing against his erection and feeling an ever-increasing arousal beating at her harder and faster.

Mike lifted his head and looked into her eyes. "Let go, baby," he urged before returning to his task. He pinched with his hand, bit with his teeth, and white-hot bursts of light shimmered around her as her orgasm exploded. She was lost, rocking against him, when suddenly he grabbed her hips and held her tight, keeping his hard, hot length against her as she came and came.

Afterward, Cara discovered she hadn't been the only one to climax, and Mike mumbled something about feeling like he was seventeen again. Laughing, they'd moved from the couch to the shower where she'd washed him thoroughly, learning his body in a way she'd never done with another man. He'd reciprocated the favor and they fell into her bed, damp and clean, but she was nowhere near exhausted.

"Mike?" she asked at the same time he pulled her against his gloriously naked body.

"Yeah?"

"You tired?"

In response, he flipped her onto her back and pinned her arms over her head against the mattress. "Are you?" he asked, staring into her eyes.

She shook her head, and a sexy grin edged his lips.

"Okay then." Mike let other parts of his body talk for him, sliding his erection back and forth across the lips of her sex.

"Mmm," she said, moaning at the intimate friction that felt so good.

"Like that?" he asked, doing it some more, his penis coming into direct contact with her sex.

"Oh, yes." She threw her head back and moaned.

He shifted until he held her wrists with one hand and slid his free one between their bodies, positioning himself at her opening. "You ready for me, baby?"

Cara thought she purred.

In the back of her mind, she knew what he'd called her, but now that she'd told him the truth, the word had lost its former power. This wasn't a man demeaning her and making demands. This was a man looking to thoroughly ravish her.

She bent her legs in welcome. Mike's eyes darkened and he thrust deep, wholly possessing her.

"Holy shit." His entire body shuddered.

She understood. She felt him everywhere, filling her up inside while his hot body blanketed her outside. And then he began to move in a sensual glide as he picked up rhythm and tempo. Holding on to her wrists, he still managed to drive into her harder and faster each time. It didn't matter that she'd just come a little while ago; he played her body that well and soon she was on her way once more, waves rushing at her from all sides as the pleasure grew.

She met each thrust with wild abandon, relishing the feelings he inspired. The way he covered her with his body caused a building friction to grow with each slam of his erection thick and full inside her. Her orgasm started as a slow tingle deep but when he came, shouting her name, he threw her up and over.

Wave after wave overwhelmed her. "Oh, oh, oh, God, Michael, harder!" She barely recognized her hoarse shout.

Somehow he heard. He obeyed, pistoning into her over and over until the dizzying waves subsided and he fell over her, crushing her into the mattress.

She didn't think she could move. Didn't want to. When Mike rolled off her, easing himself out of her, she felt the loss. Then he shifted positions and suddenly pulled her against him tight.

"Night, baby," he murmured. And fell asleep.

Mike awoke feeling . . . different. Something had changed last night; he knew that even before opening his eyes. He lay on his back, his usual sleep position, Cara sprawled over him, her head on his chest, one leg wrapped around his. No feeling of suffocation in sight despite the fact that they'd connected last night. Really connected.

Like most guys, Mike considered himself an expert on sex. What went on between him and Cara went beyond. Each time they were together, something profound shifted inside him. He didn't know what it was, and he wasn't about to go looking into it either. That might send him running.

And he wasn't ready.

He lifted a long strand of her jet-black hair and ran his fingers back and forth over the long strands, thinking. She was more wounded than he realized, more self-contained. She didn't ask much of him and seemed surprised when he did something that affected her emotionally. At first he attributed it to her feelings about him—she didn't expect much of him and wouldn't ask for much either. Only now he was beginning to wonder if she didn't expect it of anyone.

Which spoke more about her issues than it did of his. Interesting. The more she withheld, the more he wanted to know. And the more he knew, the more he wanted. Definitely not his usual M.O.

She stirred in his arms, and he suddenly found himself looking into her big blue eyes. Not a bad way to wake up. "Morning."

She smiled. "Morning."

His phone rang, muted from being in his pants pocket, but he heard it just the same. "I should check that," he said with regret.

"And I should look at mine. You kept me so busy last night I didn't think about it." Her cheeks turned pink at the admission.

He grinned, feeling an absurd amount of pride at the notion that he'd been that distracting. "Okay, check your phone and meet me back here for a morning quickie before you have to go to work."

She groaned at him, but the flicker of excitement in her eyes told him she'd be completely willing.

He rose and pulled his phone from his pocket. "Erin," he said. "I'll call her later."

"Oh, no," Cara said. Obviously she'd missed more important calls than he had.

"What's wrong?"

"Three missed calls from Havensbridge." She hit a button and put the phone to her ear.

Mike tried not to focus on her naked body while she was obviously upset, but he couldn't turn away. She had the most gorgeous curves along with toned muscles from working. Womanly despite the hard demands of her job.

"What do you mean, Daniella left?" Cara asked, her voice rising.

Mike tossed his phone onto the nightstand and came up beside her. She listened and finally spoke. "Yeah. I understand. Call me the minute you hear something. Thanks." She disconnected the call and threw the phone onto the mattress in frustration.

"The woman you've been worried about?" Mike asked.

She nodded, the pain in her eyes unmistakable. "She left the shelter late last night. Just walked out and didn't tell anyone where she was going. Dammit!"

He eased her onto the bed, but she remained stiff and unyielding. "Cara, calm down and talk to me," he said in a firm voice, in order to get through to her.

"One of the other girls said she tried to call me and I wasn't there for her. I let her down. Now she probably went back to her ex. There's nowhere else she'd go. Her family doesn't live near here." Tears streamed down her cheeks.

Mike had never been good with female waterworks or theatrics, except this wasn't any of those. Cara, like Erin, didn't cry easily. These tears were heartfelt and real; he felt like a hand was squeezing his chest as he brushed the moisture with his thumb.

"For all you know, she wanted to tell you but nothing you said could have made a difference."

She swallowed hard. "You don't know that." She pulled in a shuddering breath. "But thanks for trying to make me feel better." She forced a smile he knew damned well she didn't feel.

"Don't."

She blinked at his rough voice. "What?"

"Don't hide your feelings from me," he said, surprising her and himself. "You're hurting. I get it, but I won't let you pretend that you're fine. Not with me."

She hiccupped and her body shook, but she didn't reply. Instead she pulled herself together before his eyes and for some reason he didn't understand, it bothered him that she wouldn't lean on him.

"What's your plan?" he asked, instead of pushing her.

"Work. What else can I do? She's not a missing person; I can't force her to come back to the shelter. If I follow her home, I might provoke her ex. I have to trust she'll come to me if she needs me. Assuming she lets herself trust me again." Cara shook her head in frustration. "I have to shower and get to work." She pulled out of his arms.

He let her go, sensing nothing he said would help her now. She started for the bathroom, leaving him feeling useless and uneasy at her withdrawal. The door shut behind her and he left her alone, knowing she needed time. He kicked back on her bed, bracing his hands behind his head, determined to ignore the sound of running water. The thought of the water sluicing down her back and over her skin. Naked skin.

She finally opened the door, steam coming out of the bathroom along with the enticing warm scent that only served to arouse him more. She stepped into the room with a fluffy white towel wrapped around her, her damp hair falling over her shoulders.

"Hey," she said softly.

"Hey."

"Sorry I took it out on you." Her somber expression offered all the apology he needed.

He held out his hand. "Come here."

She eased into his arms and curled up against him. "I'm scared," she whispered. "I'm afraid that when Daniella's ex sees her again, he won't welcome her with open arms but closed fists."

He brushed her hair off her face and tucked her beneath his chin. "You can't take on the world's problems. No matter how much you want to."

She let out a heartfelt sigh. They sat that way together in silence that was . . . easy and right.

"Thank you," she said, quietly but with real meaning.

"You're welcome."

She blew out a long exhale and curled more tightly into him, her guilt and fear painfully obvious. He wished he could take it away, but he couldn't. Instead he'd be here for her now, and if Daniella surfaced.

His biggest fear wasn't that she'd come to rely on him.

No, his worry was that when he finally faced the fallout from Simon and Rex Bransom's past, he'd be the one needing and relying on her.

After the call from the shelter, Cara arrived at work in a bad mood, one that remained for the rest of the week. Though she still volunteered at the shelter, Daniella's absence gave her a stomachache, and she couldn't help but worry about her. Mike began instituting changes in their schedules, so she was on her own for daytime shifts. Not having a partner made her more aware of everything going on around her, and though the downtime was harder, the job became more challenging, the decisions her own.

When they were at the station, neither Mike nor Cara behaved any differently. He didn't pay extra attention to her, and she didn't go seeking any. And even if people had seen or heard about what went on between them at Joe's, nobody commented. There was no fallout from their relationship from anyone.

Except Sam, who decided it was his job to warn her daily about his brother's bachelor tendencies and lack of staying power. As much as Cara appreciated his concern, she was tired of hearing something she already knew, accepted, and didn't want to think about until she had to.

A couple of times during the week, Cara took periodic drives past Daniella's last known address, hoping for a glimpse but not finding one. She had to suppress the urge to ring the doorbell to the apartment, even during the day, afraid if Daniella's ex-boyfriend saw her, in uniform or not, she might inadvertently set the man off. She knew how her father's temper spiked when her mother spoke about enjoying other people's company, and how he'd then crack down to prevent her from expanding her social circle or having interests outside him.

Finally, what felt like an endless workweek ended and

Cara came home, changed into sweat clothes, poured herself a large glass of cranberry juice, plopped down in her favorite chair, and breathed in deep. Nothing to do for two whole days, and the timing couldn't be better since she needed a break from everything.

She hadn't seen Mike alone, and she pondered calling him. Would it seem like a booty call? Or would it seem like she was too clingy if she didn't wait to hear from him? Hmm. Why did she care what it seemed like when she wanted to be with him? The worst he could do was say no, and based on some of the covert looks he'd given her when he thought no one was looking, she didn't think that would be the case.

She was just about to go looking for her cell phone when the doorbell rang. Putting her glass down on a coaster, she rose and headed to see who had stopped by. Sometimes her neighbor went away for the weekend and asked Cara to watch her cat while she was gone. Cara loved animals, but her work hours didn't make it fair to have a pet, and she wouldn't mind a little time with a fur baby.

She peeked out the window beside the door and blinked in surprise. Mike stood waiting, dressed in faded denim and his leather jacket, one arm braced on the molding outside.

She opened the door for him with a grin. "Mike!" She couldn't hide her happiness at the surprise visit.

"Guess that assures me of my welcome." He slipped one arm around her waist and hauled her against him for a long, hard kiss that she returned with an equal amount of enthusiasm.

"Mmm," she moaned against his lips. "I missed this."

"I missed you," he said, stepping around her and walking farther inside.

"What's up? Have you eaten dinner? I haven't but I was about to make myself something." She gestured toward the kitchen.

"I can't. I'm on my way out of town." His words took her

off guard, and she actually felt as though a knife stabbed her in the heart.

"Where are you going?" she asked, forcing air into her lungs, pretending she wasn't panicked at the thought of him leaving.

He could be headed anywhere for any reason. Just because Sam had been warning her for days about his inability to stick didn't mean he was going anywhere for good. Not yet.

"Vegas. To find my father."

"Oh. Wow." Thank God. It wasn't back to New York. It wasn't permanent.

But her reaction to his announcement that he was leaving town told her in no uncertain terms she was getting too close, letting herself get too used to him here, in Serendipity.

She exhaled hard. "I didn't know you'd decided on a plan." She focused on the case and his past, not on her own silly emotions, which needed to be tucked back into the box she normally kept them in. The box that had stayed easily sealed off before Mike came back to town.

"It was a last-minute decision. I could have contacted him on Facebook, but that would give him control to decide whether he wanted to see me. I decided the element of surprise would work to my advantage. Maybe if I catch him off guard, he'll reveal more about his time here." He laid out his thought process with ease, but Cara caught the tight set of his jaw and knew that nothing about this decision was simple.

"How did you find him?"

"I had someone I trust do some digging, then hired a P.I. Turns out Rex hangs out most nights at a place called Shots. Some dive not known for its high-end liquor or clientele. So I know where I'll be going when I hit town." Mike frowned in obvious disgust.

Cara didn't think first, she just said what came to mind.

"Want company?" As soon as the words escaped, she could have kicked herself.

No doubt he didn't want anyone around to witness his reunion with the father he'd never met. A man he'd always hated . . . and, Cara suspected, wanted to know anyway. Which was the exact reason he shouldn't take this trip alone.

Eleven

Mike hadn't considered asking Cara to go along. He handled his shit alone, especially the personal stuff. Yet for some reason, he hadn't hesitated to say yes when she'd asked. He refused to let her pay for her ticket, and he was lucky enough to snag her a seat next to him. She was unusually silent throughout the flight, but he didn't think much about it. He had plenty to keep his mind occupied, the idea of meeting his real father for the first time churning his stomach. She must have understood because she bought magazines and a Patricia Cornwell novel, and delved into those in place of conversation.

An hour in, the pilot reminded them to put their seat belts on because of expected turbulence. Mike glanced at his buckle and Cara did the same, checking and double-checking before returning to her book—until the plane took what felt like a quick dip and consecutive bumps continued to shake the aircraft.

Cara sucked in a breath and grabbed Mike's arm as the big jet continued to bounce around in the sky. "Oh my God, oh my God." She repeated the phrase, her nails digging into his skin, leaving deep grooves in his flesh.

The plane jerked again and he covered her hand with his, prying her fingernails up and threading his hand into hers.

"Sorry."

"It's fine." He glanced at her pale face. "Have you ever flown before?"

"A couple of times, but I've never gotten used to it." She shook her head and glanced down, her cheeks pink.

"Why didn't you tell me flying bothered you?" he asked her, touched that she'd offered to join him anyway.

She shrugged.

He grinned. "I know why. You want me to think you're tough."

"I *am* tough," she said, glaring at him.

He chuckled and reached out, tucking her hair behind her ear. "That you are."

She lifted her eyes to his, warmth shimmering there at his honest assessment. Then she smiled, her gratitude and emotions there for him to see, socking him unexpectedly in the gut.

"So, where are we staying? I didn't think to ask." She changed the subject and he was grateful.

"The Bellagio." When she'd said she was coming on this trip, he'd changed his reservation from the unassuming MGM to a place she wouldn't soon forget.

"Really?" she asked, her eyes opening wider. "The hotel from *Ocean's Eleven*? The one with the huge waterfalls?"

He'd obviously chosen well. The normally sedate Cara squealed in delight, making him extra glad he'd switched.

"Wait until you see the room," he said, squeezing her hand and noticing how she'd forgotten all about the turbulence. "And I made a dinner reservation tomorrow night at Delmonico's in the Venetian." He wanted to show her what

Vegas had to offer, including a gondola ride, something he'd never imagined wanting to go on.

"Are you sure about all this?" A tiny crease formed between her brows as she crinkled her nose in concern. "I know this has to be expensive and—"

He cut her off with a finger over her lips, and her pretty blue eyes dilated to a deeper hue. He was about to remove his hand when she nipped the pad of his finger with her teeth.

"Damn," he muttered as his cock jumped in his pants, swelling against the rough denim of his jeans. "Unless you want me to make you a member of the mile-high club, I suggest you cut that out." He pulled his hand back before he jumped her right there in her seat.

She grinned, mighty pleased with herself, making him laugh.

"Behave," he muttered.

"If you insist." She eased back into her seat, facing forward, an impish and irresistible smile still on her face.

Mike shifted in his seat, knowing he'd be uncomfortable for the rest of the flight.

"Oh! It's calm now. Thank you for distracting me," she murmured, now completely relaxed.

Unlike him, he thought wryly. He hoped he could wait to get to Vegas and check in because he needed stress relief before facing his father.

He needed Cara.

From the moment the plane took off until now, when she stepped into the large *suite*—not a room, a *suite*—Cara had been in awe. She didn't know what it was costing Mike, and to her surprise, she didn't plan to ask. Instead, she'd decided to let herself enjoy.

And enjoy she did. Mike clearly wanted her, pinning her

to the California king in the center of the room as soon as the bellman left them alone. From there, they christened the bed—more than once, at which point it was after midnight, Nevada time.

They spent the next day doing fun things, like taking a tour of Madame Tussauds museum, playing roulette, making love, showering, and heading to dinner. At Delmonico's, Cara ate the best steak of her life. She and Mike talked about everything and nothing, with the exception of the night ahead and his hoped-for meeting with Rex Bransom.

With Mike, she was at once comfortable and always aroused, enjoying her time with him whether they agreed on the topic at hand or not. He was easy to be with. Too easy, and she had to keep reminding herself she couldn't get complacent or convince herself Mike was someone who'd be around for long.

After dinner, they returned to the room to change clothes before heading over to Shots. On the ride up in the elevator and then back in the suite, Mike grew increasingly silent, and Cara gave him his space. She'd packed quickly, but she'd deliberately chosen the outfit she'd worn the first time she and Mike were together, a short skirt and her favorite cowboy boots that allowed her to strap on her ankle holster and small Glock. Airline rules allowed them to bring their weapons but not ammo, and they'd bought bullets earlier in the day. Just in case. They both felt more comfortable knowing they were armed.

The television blared the sound from a movie as they dressed without speaking. Cara wriggled into her cropped top with a deep V, pleased when Mike stopped to watch, his eyes drawn to her cleavage before he shook his head and pulled his gaze away. At least she provided a distraction for him.

They headed for the lobby; Mike kept her hand tight inside his. Although most people around them were more dressed up for the evening, the women in high heels and sequined short dresses, once they arrived at Shots, a dive bar on a side street far off the main strip, Cara and Mike's casual attire worked just fine.

Unlike the light, welcoming atmosphere at Joe's, the mood at Shots was heavy and dark. What lighting existed was minimal, and the place catered to a skeevy clientele that made even Cara, a seasoned cop, uncomfortable. As if sensing her emotions, Mike reached back and grasped her hand, pulling her close beside him as they made their way through the crowd.

She didn't know his plan for tonight, and she hadn't wanted to ask. She'd take her cues from him.

Mike glanced around the dimly lit bar, wondering if he'd recognize his old man on sight. His mother hadn't kept photographs around, and though Mike could have looked through old yearbooks at the high school or Googled, something always held him back. Maybe on some level, he'd always known this day of reckoning would come, that he'd have to face his father, and he'd wanted to do it on his terms.

He took in the smoky bar, the class of people here, and his stomach churned. He was about to push his way through the crush and buy a drink when a loud, masculine burst of laughter caught his attention and somehow he *knew*.

"What's wrong?" Cara asked.

"What makes you think anything's wrong?"

"You're squeezing my hand so tight I think you broke something." She pulled her hand from his and shook it out.

He frowned. "Over there." He tipped his head toward the back corner from where he'd heard the sound.

Cara sucked in a sharp breath. "He looks just like you," she said in awe.

Mike nodded, sensing he'd been given a glimpse into what he might look like in twenty or so years, but from the other man's obvious outgoing personality, that was where the similarities ended. Rex sat in the corner, holding court. There was no other word to describe how people around him gravitated to the booming laugh and deep voice. He was telling a story, and the people surrounding him seemed to hang on his every word. And by his side was a woman who couldn't be more than twenty-two if she was that, wearing a tube top with no support for her ample breasts, makeup that had been caked on and bleached blond hair teased high, obviously trying to look older than her very young age.

Mike moved on autopilot. Retaking Cara's hand because he wasn't willing to leave her here to be picked up by some douchebag, he moved forward and pushed through the throng of people.

With each step, Rex Bransom's voice grew louder. "And then I told her, sit back and watch a pro because Rex here's gonna buy you anything your heart desires. Isn't that right, baby girl?"

Nausea swept through Mike. "Is that before you knock her up and leave her high and dry for the next twenty-nine years?" He, who never spoke without deliberation, spewed his deepest thoughts.

Rex paused midgulp and choked on his beer. Dark eyes rose to meet Mike's, then opened wide in recognition. "Everybody scram." He waved his hand, and his crowd grumbled but dispersed. All except the woman wrapped around him like a snake.

"You too, baby girl."

"But Rexie," she complained, rubbing up against him in an attempt to get him to change his mind and let her stay.

Mike held the other man's gaze, hoping the hatred he felt was evident because he sure as hell wasn't holding back.

"Go." Rex unhooked her arms from around his neck and stood.

With a whine, the woman headed for the bar. "I'll be waiting right here," she called back over her shoulder.

Rex didn't tear his eyes from Mike's. "Son."

Mike glanced over his shoulder before looking back at

Rex. "You can't possibly mean me, because the only man with the right to call me that is Simon Marsden."

Only the slight tic in one eye betrayed any feeling. "So that's the way of things."

"What other way would there be?"

Rex nodded and appeared to eye Mike with newfound respect. "Sit." He pointed to the chair one of his minions had vacated.

Mike folded his arms across his chest and remained standing.

"Who's the pretty lady?" Rex's gaze landed on Cara and stayed too long for Mike's liking.

"Cara Hartley," she said, stepping forward.

"She's not your concern," Mike said, holding out his arm so she wouldn't step forward for a handshake or any other contact.

"So you're not here to make nice, and you're not here to introduce me to your woman. Why don't you tell me what's brought you to my neck of the woods?"

It was time to dive into the reason he'd come, to find out what the hell Rex Bransom had been up to in Serendipity. "Now I think I will sit." Mike pulled out a chair for Cara before easing himself into a seat beside her.

Rex did the same, settling back into his chair.

"Why the hell are you bothering Ella?" Mike hadn't planned on saying that either.

Rex blinked, appearing stunned and even a little hurt. "Is that what she said? I'm bothering her?"

A steady throb began in Mike's left temple. "That's my interpretation."

Rex leaned forward.

Mike angled back.

"Did it ever occur to you that I might want to know how my family's doing?" Rex asked.

Damned if he didn't sound sincere, and that more than anything made Mike sick to his stomach.

Beside him, Cara let out a small sound of disbelief. Mike ground his back teeth together, as surprised as she was.

"Family doesn't disappear for decades." And Mike didn't want to prolong this agony any more than necessary.

If tortured, he might admit to having been curious about his old man, but as he'd suspected, he didn't like what he'd found. "I'm here for one reason only. To ask you what you know about money still lying around the evidence room in Serendipity from a case you worked back in 1983. Marked bills ring a bell?" He watched the other man closely, wanting to catch both the shock—which was obvious—and any other emotion that crossed there.

"Is crime down so much in that podunk town that you cops have nothing better to do than chase down old cases?" Rex asked with disdain.

Podunk town? There was no better description to indicate that Rex was happy to have left Serendipity and the people in it behind. And hadn't Mike felt the same way? And hadn't he ended up in Atlantic City, a place not too dissimilar to Vegas? Mike had a job. According to his P.I., Rex did occasional work with the local PD. In other words, he was a snitch who got paid for his observations. Mike's stomach clenched some more.

You traveled all the way here for that?" Before Mike could answer, Rex turned toward the bar. "Sal, get me another scotch. Neat."

Mike narrowed his gaze. Talking about the family he'd abandoned hadn't driven Rex to need another drink, but the old case had.

Rex refocused his gaze on Mike. "You got so many questions, why didn't you just ask the man you call Dad?"

Mike straightened his shoulders. "You mean the one who did your job for you? Who stepped up when you couldn't be bothered? There's no way I'm going to upset him now, not with what he's going through."

Rex jerked as if Mike had gutted him. "What's wrong with Simon?" he asked, suddenly sounding as if he cared.

Cara shifted in her seat, and Mike answered before she could offer up anything. "Nothing you need to concern yourself with."

He hadn't meant to slip and give Rex any information about his family. "Tell me what you remember, and I'll get out of here and you'll never have to see me again. I'm sure that's what you want anyway."

Rex scowled, his expression turning dark. "You have no idea what I want. Not now and not back then." He paused, and the silence between them grew heavy. "Sometimes we do things because we have to. Want has nothing to do with it."

Mike rolled his eyes. He'd flown cross-country only to have him speak in riddles. If he'd wanted to waste his time, he could have stayed at the casino and dropped money at the tables.

But he'd try one more time. "Money?" he reminded Rex. "Marked bills found in the trunk of a car you stopped for speeding? Does any of this sound familiar?"

Rex slammed a large hand against the table, causing it to shake under the force. "Leave it alone, *son*."

"And I told you not to call me that." Just being in Rex Bransom's presence made Mike feel like a small, unwanted boy. There were too many times he hadn't appreciated what Simon had done, focusing instead on what this man hadn't. At the moment, Mike resented the hell out of having had to track him down.

He'd had enough and rose from his seat. "This was a waste of time. Come on," he said to Cara.

She dutifully rose from her chair, and Mike knew she was doing what he asked in order to make this as easy as possible on him. He appreciated it more than he could express.

To Mike's surprise, Rex stood as well. "You might not believe this, but it was good to meet you."

"The feeling isn't mutual," Mike muttered.

A flash of pain flickered in eyes similar to Mike's own before Rex masked it. "Glad you brought your lady. She's a fine-looking woman. Don't make the same mistakes I did."

"Don't worry. I'll never turn my back on the people who mean the most to me."

He grasped Cara's hand and walked away without looking back.

Cara felt Mike's tension and anger vibrating through him and didn't know how to ease it. She wasn't even sure he'd want her to. They returned to the hotel in silence, and she waited until they were alone in the suite.

He stalked over to the bar and poured himself a drink, downing it in one gulp.

"Mike?"

He shook his head. "Not now."

He was shutting her out. She couldn't say it didn't hurt, but she understood. She'd wanted to make the overture and she had, but whether he wanted to talk was up to him. And he clearly did not.

She opened a drawer, pulled out the nightgown she'd brought with her, and walked into the bathroom. After being in the smoky bar, she needed to feel clean before getting into bed.

She stripped out of her clothes and stepped into the luxurious shower. It took her more than a few tries to understand which knobs turned on the overhead spray, but once she managed, the water cascaded down her back, warming her up—at least from the outside. Inside she was cold from Mike's rejection. No matter how much she got it, she'd made this trip to help him. Once he'd accepted her offer, she hadn't expected him to turn her away.

As she lathered up with the soap provided by the hotel, which smelled fruity and delicious, she thought about the short meeting with Rex Bransom. The man was more self-contained than Mike. Other than his initial startled surprise at seeing Mike, he hadn't slipped, hadn't given anything away. And when he didn't want to answer, he used Mike's weak spot—the word *son*—poking at the open wound. No question, the man was a bastard. Her heart broke for Mike, who she was sure was as hurt as he was confused.

She tilted her head up toward the hot water, rinsing the shampoo out of her hair, the spray washing over her like rain. It felt so good, she wondered if she could install this kind of shower in her condo. She laughed at the silly thought.

She heard the creak, and then Mike's hands gripped her forearms as he pressed his body against hers, his erection solid at her back.

"Forgive me?" he asked, nuzzling his face into her neck.

She sighed, her body softening along with her heart. "There's nothing to forgive. You needed space."

"And you always give me what I need. Even if I don't know what that is myself." His gruff voice rumbled in her ear.

He hadn't wanted to talk, but he was obviously happy to forget his troubles inside her body. And she didn't mind. Sex was what they did best together, was what she could count on from him.

He slid his finger through her slick heat, moisture easing the way for an easy glide. Desire rippled through her and she arched into his hand.

"You're so wet for me, baby."

She moaned only to have him stiffen behind her. "Fuck. I can't believe I call you that. I've been calling you that. Hell, I tried to convince you it was okay. Then *he* said it and it sounded so damned demeaning." His arms were still wrapped tight around her.

Cara sighed and leaned her head against his shoulder.

"From Rex to her? It *was* demeaning. God, Mike, she was all of twenty-one—and that's if she was even legal! He didn't care about her. He liked the attention, the idea of a young woman who idolized him and hung on his every word. We both know that's not how I see you."

That got a laugh. "No, you don't automatically do anything I say."

She grinned. "Independent. That's me," she said, before her thoughts sobered.

Mike didn't know another woman who could make him laugh—during sex or about this whole screwed-up situation.

"Besides, didn't we already undergo desensitization therapy?" she asked, wriggling her backside against his erection.

She turned to press a kiss against his solid chest. Her soft lips teased his skin, arousing him even more as she continued to explore. She ran her tongue over the flat peaks of his nipples until he let out a harsh groan, and then she nipped harder and he thought he'd come right then.

"Uh-uh." Her pleasure mattered, not his. He dropped to his knees. He breathed out, teasing her with a rush of air. Her thighs trembled. He placed his lips on her sex, drawing the tight bud into his mouth and suckling hard.

She cried out and thrust her hips forward. Grasping her waist to steady her, he kept up the pressure, knowing exactly what she liked and needed most. He brought her up quickly but didn't let her climax; instead he released her as soon as she was near, causing her to moan in frustration, to buck her hips and beg for more.

Mike merely chuckled and ran his tongue along her outer lips, teasing her some until she wrapped her fingers in his hair and pulled. "Please," she begged.

He soothed her with a lick along her slit. Her knees buckled and he lifted her in his arms and carried her to the bed, where he laid her down on the thick bedding and eased his body down on top of her.

"Did you really think I'd let you come without me inside you?" He brushed his lips over hers.

She met his gaze, her eyes dilated with pleasure, hazy with desire. "I wasn't thinking at all."

He laughed and kissed her hard, thrusting his tongue inside her mouth while savoring the feel of her soft, satiny skin beneath him.

But she was restless and shifted beneath him. "Move, dammit." She punctuated her order with a squeeze of his butt cheeks.

"Good to know you want me . . . baby." He forced the word out of his mouth. No way would he allow his father to control any part of his life, especially this.

Her answering kiss indicated she knew how hard it had been for him and melted more of his heart. Oh hell, she already owned it, he thought, raising his hips and sliding his erection along her damp heat. She shuddered beneath him, as if mini climaxes were racking her body already, and he took advantage, thrusting into her hard and deep.

"Michael," she said, on a groan, the way he'd come to expect.

"I love it when you say my name like that, when I'm deep inside you."

A sultry smile lifted her lips.

He pulled out slowly, feeling her clutch around him, then drove back in once more. She raised her knees, pulling him farther into her heat, and he picked up the rhythm, in and out, his sole focus on the intensity of the feelings she inspired. Harder, faster, she met him thrust for thrust, her sexy moans increasing every time their bodies joined.

He loved the sound of sex, the grinding of bodies, but this was so much more. He'd never walk away unscathed. Bracing his hands beside her, he lowered his head, taking her lips in a hard, much-needed kiss. Her sex clenched him, milking him tighter. A tingling in his gut signaled the onset of climax. He stiffened and shuddered, imploding inside and out. He came, the release physical as much as it was emotional, the sensations pulling him under as he came harder than ever before.

From a distance, he heard her cries, gasps, the "Oh Gods," that signaled she'd joined him for the ride. Spent, he sprawled on top of her, certain he'd never breathe well again.

A little while later, he lay with Cara curled in his arms. The longer they rested in silence, the more time he had to dwell on his meeting with Rex.

Leave it alone, son. Those words told Mike that Rex knew more than he'd admitted, but he'd been smart enough to hit Mike where it hurt to get himself off the hook. And Mike had allowed it. Still, even if he'd pushed, Mike was under no illusions he'd have been able to break Rex.

His answers didn't lie in Vegas any more than they did in Serendipity. They were bottled up, unlikely to be revealed. He ought to call the mayor, tell her they'd hit a dead end and call it a day. But Mike didn't like unfinished business. He hated it even more when it pertained to his life.

In the midst of the chaos with Rex, a surprising need for home surfaced. Mike wanted to talk to Sam and Erin, to feel a part of the family he'd tried so hard to distance himself from. That need surprised him.

Cara stirred, shifting and rolling to face him. "You okay?" she asked.

"I'm with you, so never better." He leaned over and kissed her.

She smiled and curled back into his side. "Except I wasn't talking about us. I can practically hear you thinking."

He chuckled, not surprised how well she read him. "I've got a lot on my mind."

"Want to talk about it?" she asked, extreme caution in her voice.

No doubt because he'd been such an ass the last time she'd approached him. "I would, if there were something to discuss. Rex is a no-good son of a bitch who'd rather hurt his own son than reveal information. That about sums it up, and there's nothing I can do to change it."

Cara exhaled hard. "All true. But you shouldn't dismiss how he made you feel."

"I *feel* like I don't want to have anything to do with the man, but since his blood is running through my veins, I really can't control that either." He wished he could take back the sarcastic bite in his voice, but it was too late.

"Mike—"

"Look, I know you're here for me and . . . I appreciate it." He cut her off before she could poke at the wound his father opened in him. No matter how well meaning, he wasn't up to it. "I just need to work through it myself."

"Mmm," she said, and the sound vibrated through him. "Been there and thought that many times myself. I get it."

For the first time, he sensed that she really did. Funny thing was, he hated the thought of her going through any of her personal garbage alone. Still, that was exactly what he needed right now.

"I can't wait to get home," he muttered.

"Having that bad a time?" she asked lightly.

"Not when I'm with you." He squeezed her tighter. "I just need to get away from here."

"I get that too." With her head snuggled in the crook of his arm, he couldn't see her face or read her expression. "Besides, you already showed me the best of Vegas, so I really can't complain that you're ready to leave."

He twirled his finger in her hair, guilt riding him that when he should still be enjoying the next twenty-four hours, he wanted to get out of the state his father lived in as soon as possible.

"Come," he said, nudging her shoulder.

"Where?"

There was one more sight they'd yet to enjoy together. "Get dressed. I want to go outside and see the light show." Personally, he could live without it, but he remembered her delighted expression when she talked about seeing the lights.

"Are you sure? We could call the airlines now and get on the next flight home," she offered.

"Not until after you've seen the light show." He rolled her onto her back and pinned her to the mattress. "And definitely not until after I've seen your face when you do."

Twelve

Mike came home from Vegas, caught up on sleep, and insisted Cara do the same. He gave her a few days off and took some for himself. As soon as he felt more human and got a handle on his emotions, he called and met his brother and sister for lunch at The Family Restaurant.

He arrived last, as usual. His siblings were waiting, their meals and his ordered and on the table. They looked at him with concern.

"You texted us to say you were going to Vegas to meet Rex Bransom. Then we heard nothing for three days," Erin said, chiding him in an exact replica of their mother's voice.

Mike settled in a chair across from her. "I didn't mean to worry you."

"I heard you dragged Cara along with you." Sam made it sound like an accusation.

"She offered to go," Mike said tightly.

"Sam, leave him alone," Erin urged.

"No, let's finish this conversation once and for all." He and Sam hadn't gotten past Mike's seeing his brother's best friend, and Mike was tired of pretending everything was fine between them when it wasn't. "Do you want Cara for yourself? Is that it?" Mike asked his brother.

Sam clenched his jaw. "No. I just want to know that when you pick up and leave—and you will because you always do—you won't leave her heart stomped beneath your feet."

Mike groaned. "All I can tell you is that I've been honest with her from day one." He opened and closed his hands, fisting them beneath the table. "I don't want her hurt any more than you do."

Sam expelled a harsh breath. "I believe you. I just . . . her father's a bastard. Her mother takes it. Cara's never stayed in a relationship long. She won't put herself out there for fear of being hurt, but she's different with you." He shook his head. "And I can see disaster coming from a mile away. But I love you both, so . . ." He raised his hands in front of him. "I'll stay out of it."

Mike knew what it took for Sam to step back. There was no better man, no one more loyal than his brother. "Thanks, man."

"Okay, now that you two have settled things, what happened in Vegas?" Erin asked.

Mike drew a deep breath. "I met him."

"And?" Erin asked in a whisper.

Mike closed his eyes, and the memory of Rex Bransom flashed before him. "We look alike," Mike admitted. "We . . . spoke alike. He's more outgoing. He enjoys being the center of attention. I don't. But I'm afraid that in here"— he tapped his chest, over his heart—"we're more alike than I want to believe."

He felt his brother's hand slap him on the shoulder. "That's bullshit," Sam said, defending Mike so strongly that he almost believed it himself.

Almost.

"He left. So did I. He abandoned a woman—"

"Don't go there," Sam warned him. "Tiffany was nothing like Mom."

That, at least, was true.

"Mike, you're one of the best men I know." Erin, her eyes wide and damp, met his gaze. "And that's because you're like Simon, not Rex."

He didn't reply.

His sister covered his hand with hers. "Hey. You have to believe me."

Mike didn't know how to feel or what to believe. It was Rex's blood running through his veins. Rex, who couldn't stay in one place, who never gave a piece of himself to anyone he came into contact with. Mike's search for Rex had revealed that the man jumped from state to state, never forming ties or relationships. Mike was much the same.

"Forget him," Sam said. "Call the case cold for good and put it behind you."

Mike didn't know if he could. "He called me *son*. And afterward, I never felt more dirty in my life."

His siblings looked at him with pity, which had him squirming in his seat.

"What about Mom and Dad? You going to tell them what happened?" Sam asked.

"I've spoken to Mom. And as soon as Dad finishes his last treatment, we agreed to sit him down and explain everything, including that Rex contacted her through Facebook." He'd already told his brother and sister the background before he went to Vegas.

"Oh, to be a fly on the wall for that conversation," Erin said, with a shake of her head. "Good thing their bond is tight enough to withstand anything."

"Amen," Mike said.

"So. Does anyone have any good news to talk about?" Erin grinned.

"Same old," Sam muttered.

They finished eating in relative peace, for which Mike was grateful. His cell rang as he was finishing, and he took the call from work.

He listened without much interest. "Just leave it on my desk," he said to the desk sergeant on call. "I'll get to it when I come in tomorrow." He disconnected the line.

"Anything important?" Erin asked.

Mike shook his head. "Someone left an envelope for me." And he hoped that was the most interesting thing that happened to him for the rest of the week. He could do without drama and excitement for a little while.

Cara had been back in Serendipity for almost a week when Alexa finally had time to meet her at Cuppa Café Saturday morning. Cara needed a female friend fix desperately, and she'd had to wait until her friend's day off.

"Sit. I have your drink ready and waiting," Cara said when Alexa arrived. "I have so much to tell you!"

Alexa shrugged off her winter coat. "I wish you'd told me you needed to talk! I'd have made time sooner," she chided.

Cara waved a hand. "As if I'd ever ask you to drop a patient or turn down an emergency. You're a workaholic, but don't worry. I know that if I needed you, you'd be there for me. I guess I wasn't ready to share just yet."

Alexa listened, her eyes glazing with a bit of envy at the description of Las Vegas—at least before meeting Rex. From the suite in the Bellagio, to the most intimate dinner she'd ever experienced, to the light show, where Mike had encircled her in his arms and held her while they watched, Cara was falling hard.

"Your man sounds yummy. Are you sure we're talking about Mike Marsden?" Alexa asked on a laugh, as she drew a sip of her black coffee.

Cara winced at the way her friend drank to keep herself

awake and downed her own heavily sugared latte. "I'm sure. When he's hot, there's nobody sweeter."

"But?" Alexa prodded, waiting for Cara to pull her thoughts together and answer.

Which wasn't easy. The *but* was the whole reason she was here with her friend. Cara was falling hard, and it had to stop. Her runaway feelings were getting out of hand, and she needed a reminder that anything more than a hot affair with Mike would burn out fast. And she needed to hear it from another woman, not from Sam.

Cara swallowed hard. "But when he's cold . . . Brrr."

Alexa narrowed her gaze. "So he's not Mr. Perfect."

Cara shook her head.

"Good. Who is?" Alexa grinned. "Glad to know he's as human as the rest of us."

Cara sighed. "Listen, we talked about this a few weeks ago at Joe's. I know who and what Mike is."

Alexa tipped her head and eyed Cara with those appraising, smart eyes. "And you love him for it."

Cara blinked, stunned at her friend's words. "No. No, of course not." She couldn't be in love. "I told you I'd only love a man who I can trust with my whole heart. I need security and predictability. Not someone who blows hot and cold, or who's reminded me more than once he's not interested in anything permanent." Her heart squeezed at the reminder, but that was what she wanted out of this talk. The brutal truth said out loud. "I need to know what to expect from a man, and when."

Alexis shook her head and put her empty cup down. "Not every man is your father."

Cara's stomach cramped. So maybe she wasn't looking for anything quite that brutal. Still, Alexa had a valid point. "True. And I'm not saying Mike's anything like my dad. He wouldn't hurt me—or anyone—that way, but I don't have to wonder if Mike's the guy I can entrust my heart to because he doesn't want it." She rose and tossed her cup in the trash. "I'm so glad we had this talk!"

"Cara Hartley, sit yourself down!"

Cara stared at her normally quiet, sedate doctor friend. So did everyone else in the small café. In order to avoid making a scene, she lowered herself back into the chair. "Who are you and what have you done with my friend Alexa?"

"I *am* your friend, and as such, I'm here to tell you to get your head out of your ass," she said, much more quietly this time. "Mike took you with him to Vegas to meet the man who abandoned him for the first time. And you don't think he's someone you can trust your heart to?" Alexa held up a hand. "And I don't want to hear about some relationship he had when he was pretty much still a kid himself."

"I don't need his past as proof. He told me so himself! His exact words were, *no hearts involved*!"

Alexa frowned. "In the beginning, maybe. But now you're the one keeping yours sealed shut."

"That's right, and it's called self-preservation, thank you very much. And now I have to go to Havensbridge. I'm hoping someone heard from Daniella."

"Still nothing?" Alexa asked, concerned

"No." Cara drew a deep breath. "Listen, I appreciate that you're looking out for me, but I knew what I was getting into with Mike. And I asked you to meet me today because . . . maybe I am falling for him a little bit and I needed the reminder of why that's a bad idea."

"I'm sorry I couldn't give that to you." Alexa shook her head. "I guess I need to believe someone can find the right guy."

Personally, Cara thought Alexa could find that man if she stopped working so hard and let herself look around. But she knew better than to have the old argument.

"That's okay," Cara said instead. "I gave it to myself."

Alexa rose, walked to Cara, and gave her a hug. "I just want you to be happy, and honestly? Being with Mike makes you happier than I've ever seen you."

Too bad it couldn't last. But Cara didn't say that.

"Are you free for dinner tonight?" Alexa asked. "I have a rare free evening. I was thinking maybe dinner and a movie?"

Cara nodded. "That sounds wonderful." It had been too long since Alexa had given herself permission to relax, and Cara definitely wouldn't mind continuing their time together. They made plans for the evening, and Cara headed out the door.

At Havensbridge, no one had heard from Daniella. Cara spent the afternoon talking to a new woman who'd come in while Cara was in Vegas and encouraging her to look into self-defense classes in which she'd expressed an interest. All the while, Daniella's absence, which was now going on two long weeks, weighed heavily.

That night, a snowstorm hit, forcing Alexa and Cara to change their plans. They ordered dinner in and watched the movie *Friends with Benefits*, which left Cara shaking her head at the romanticized ending.

"When was the last time a woman ended up with Prince Charming? One who organizes an entire flash mob to impress her?" Cara rolled her eyes, though she'd secretly loved the movie.

Alexa laughed. "It's a *movie*; can't you just enjoy it without analyzing it to death?"

Cara laughed, but she knew that when a guy said he didn't do permanent, she'd better listen.

Alexa left before the snow got any worse, and Cara holed up in her condo, watching the beautiful snow fall outside her living room window.

She must have dozed off because she woke to the distant ringing of her cell phone, the sound coming from her bedroom.

She ran, hoping to catch the caller before they hung up. "Hello?"

"Cara?" Her name sounded like a whisper, but she recognized the voice.

"Daniella?" Cara gripped the small phone in her hand.

"I don't know what to do," the other woman said in a small voice.

"Are you hurt?"

Silence.

"Daniella? I'm not going to judge you. I just want to know if you're okay." Cara realized she was trembling and lowered herself onto the bed.

"I'm fine. But I need to talk to you."

An opening, Cara thought. A small one, but it was there. Cara squeezed her eyes shut tight and prayed. "Where can I find you?"

"Umm . . ."

"No pressure. We'll just talk, and afterward you can walk away if that's what you want."

The silence was deafening while the time that she waited for an answer stretched on. "The McDonald's off Route 80," Daniella said, and then Cara heard a click.

Heart pounding, Cara glanced down. She was wearing a pair of pink sweats and a T-shirt. Good enough. She wasn't taking the time to change and risk Daniella leaving. She strapped on her holster and gun, pulled on her jacket, and was in the car within five minutes of the phone call.

The drive there normally took fifteen minutes, but thanks to the heavy snow and roads, which hadn't yet been plowed, it ended up being a thirty-minute drive. Thirty long minutes in which Cara inched along in her car, with too much time to think. Her first impulse was to call Mike and tell him she'd heard from Daniella, but Cara slammed the brakes on that idea immediately.

After Vegas . . . no, that wasn't right—before Vegas, when Mike had shown up on her doorstep and told her he was headed out of town, her panic at the notion of his leaving told her in no uncertain terms that she was coming to rely on him too much. To put things back in perspective, Cara had to remember that this was her life. She'd been

self-reliant before Mike arrived, and she'd have to go back
to going it solo once he was gone. No reason not to exercise
the same behavior now.

Finally the Golden Arches came into view, and Cara
pulled into the parking lot, which was already covered with
an ever-thickening layer of snow. A small McDonald's off
a highway, it wasn't a full-service family restaurant but one
where truckers and travelers stopped for a quick meal or cup
of coffee. Tonight, the dimly lit parking lot was fairly empty.

Cara entered through the front door and was surprised
to see Daniella behind the counter. No one waited in line to
order, and Cara stepped up to greet her. "Hi," she said softly.

"Hi." Daniella smiled. It didn't reach her eyes.

Cara wondered if she'd ever see her truly happy and
prayed with everything in her that she would. "You got
a job!"

"As soon as I went back, Bob said since I ran away
once, I have to earn my keep. But he keeps a close eye
on me," Daniella admitted, her cheeks flushing with
embarrassment.

Cara winced, but she'd promised not to judge. "At least
it gets you out of the house."

Daniella nodded. Her eyes filled with tears, and she bit
down on her lower lip, obviously to keep from crying.

All Cara wanted to do was bundle the woman up and
bring her home, but she knew that acting emotionally wasn't
an answer. She couldn't bring home everyone she helped at
Havensbridge, no matter how badly she wanted to.

"Can I get a cup of coffee?" Cara asked, hoping to give
Daniella something else to concentrate on.

"Sure. My manager is in the back. She's really a sweet
woman, and she said I could take my break when you got
here. I'll just tell her to come out and cover for me."

Cara nodded.

A few minutes later, Cara and Daniella were seated
across from each other in a small booth.

A middle-aged woman walked over, carrying two cups of coffee. "On the house. Take all the time you need," she said.

"Thanks, Bev."

"Thank you," Cara said.

"No problem." She nodded at Cara before walking away, taking her place behind the counter.

"She seems nice," Cara said.

"She's been very good to me." Daniella sounded surprised, as if she'd seen too little kindness in her life.

"How long have you been working here?"

"A little over a week." She glanced into her coffee cup.

Cara studied Daniella carefully, taking in the fading bruise on the girl's jaw. Without meaning to, Cara reached out and brushed a gentle finger over the discoloration.

"I tripped—"

"Not with me, okay?" Cara whispered.

Daniella's eyes once again filled with tears that she was unable to keep from spilling over her cheeks.

"Daniella, I know I promised no pressure, but you have to leave. You can stay at Havensbridge and—"

The young woman clenched and unclenched her fists. "I want to leave him. I do. That's why I called you. But I like working here. I like having somewhere to come every day. It's not like being a paralegal, but I feel good about myself. And I can do this part time and make money while I take online refresher classes."

Cara nodded, pleased that Daniella not only had made the decision but had more of a plan than when she'd been at Havensbridge the first time. "That's good. I'm sure Belinda will have a way to make things work. It's just transportation you'd need, right?"

"Right—except Bob knows I work here." She shook her head in frustration. "He shows up at odd hours, to check up on me."

Cara wasn't surprised.

"Damn right I know where you are every minute of the day." A shadow loomed over their table. Cara looked up and into the eyes of one very pissed-off—and if she wasn't mistaken, drunk—man. "I drive you here and pick you up because you've proven you can't be trusted."

Daniella shrank lower into her seat.

Cara felt the pressure of her holster and breathed out hard. She straightened her shoulders and met the man's gaze, refusing to let him intimidate her as he obviously wanted to do.

"I'm sorry, do I know you?" She deliberately dismissed him with her tone.

"Bob Francone. Who the hell are you?" He braced his hands on the table, leaning over them, distinctly threatening.

Cara wasn't impressed. She smiled broadly and reached into her pocket. "I'm Daniella's friend. Officer Cara Hartley." She flashed her badge.

"You stupid bitch!" Bob raged at Daniella.

A whimper escaped the younger woman's lips.

Time to take control of this situation, Cara thought. She slid to the edge of the seat, intending to stand, but Bob remained blocking her way. "Excuse me."

Bob ignored her. "You're friends with a *cop*?" Bob asked Daniella instead.

"Please don't make a scene," Daniella said, the words coming out more like a plea.

"*I* shouldn't make a scene." He barked out a laugh. "You called a goddamned cop and I shouldn't make a scene?"

"That's correct. Now I believe I said excuse me, you're blocking my way." Cara nudged his thigh with her knee. "I'd like to stand up."

"And I'd like you to get the fuck out of Daniella's life," he said, too loudly.

"That's not your call to make," Daniella said, surprising Cara and making her want to applaud at the same time.

"Shut up!" He slapped her, sending Daniella sprawling back on the seat.

Cara pulled her gun. "Step back now." She leveled her weapon.

Daniella scrambled up once more, her terrified gaze on Cara's gun. "Bob—"

"I've got this, Daniella." Cara's gaze never wavered from the man.

He eyed the gun, then Cara, warily.

"Look, Bob, I've already got you on assault. I've asked you to step out of my way twice now. I'm sure you don't want to add false imprisonment of a police officer to tonight's charges."

Sirens broke the charged atmosphere, the sound growing increasingly louder. Bev, Cara realized, must have called the police.

Panic flickered in Bob's eyes, and before Cara could register his intent, he grabbed Daniella by the hair and yanked her out of the booth. Cara jumped up and trained her gun on Bob, who'd wrapped one beefy arm around Daniella's neck. Her face turned red and she grabbed at Bob's arm, attempting to pry his grip away from her airway.

"Let her go," Cara said calmly.

"Go to hell. She's mine," he said, his eyes wild.

"She's her own person, Bob. Release her now, okay?"

From the corner of her eye, Cara realized Sam had quietly come in from the back entrance, with his partner, a rookie named Ted, alongside him. Thankfully Bob hadn't seen them enter. No doubt he'd freak out even more once he did. But he hadn't drawn a weapon and Cara didn't know if he had one on him. All she could do was hope that Sam could easily take him from behind.

"Bob, if you love Daniella, you don't want to hurt her. That puts us on the same side. Let's end this now." Cara imperceptibly nodded at Sam.

He stepped up behind the man, jamming his gun into

Bob's side. "It's over," Sam said, nudging Bob with his weapon.

That quickly it was over. Without warning, the big man released Daniella and dropped to his knees, blubbering like a baby.

Cara pulled the girl away from Bob, whom Sam easily subdued.

"I'd never hurt you, Dani, you gotta know that," Bob said as Sam cuffed his hands behind his back and proceeded to read him his Miranda rights.

Bev wrapped an arm around Daniella, comforting her as a mother would a child. Cara exhaled long and hard, pleased that this had ended so quickly and easily.

"Thanks for calling the police," Cara said to Bev. "That was a smart move."

Bev, a gray-haired, stout woman, merely shrugged. "Seemed like common sense. He shows up here every day at different times, watching Daniella, making threats. I've seen his type before." She frowned and patted Daniella's back.

"I'm sorry," Daniella murmured.

Cara shook her head and smiled. "No apologizing for someone else's behavior, remember?"

Daniella nodded.

"I'm going to need you both to come down to the station and give your statement. Will you press charges? And file for a restraining order?" Cara asked Daniella. "I'll be right there with you."

Daniella nodded.

Cara was under no illusion that this arrest or an order of protection would end Bob's abuse, but it would document it and maybe act as some sort of deterrent.

"I'm proud of you," Cara told Daniella, squeezing her hand.

"I need to call my son—he's the owner. He'll come in so I can come down to the station," Bev said.

Cara inclined her head. "Good. I can drive Daniella now and you can meet us. Let me go see what's going on. I'll be right back."

Cara walked over to Sam, who was about to escort Bob out to the squad car. He handed the now-calm man over to Ted. "I'll meet you at the car."

With a nod, Ted prodded Bob and they headed out the door. "Dani, I'm sorry," he called out.

She turned away without answering.

Cara shook her head in disgust. "Daniella said she'd press charges."

"That's good," Sam said.

"I can drive her over now. The manager needs to lock up and she'll meet us at the station so we can all make a formal statement," Cara concluded, since she was off duty when the incident occurred.

"She okay?" Sam tipped his head in Daniella's direction.

Cara nodded. "She is. I just hope she stays that way." She'd seen too many women, her own mother included, back down and change their minds once faced with the reality of testifying and pressing charges.

"And you? Okay?" Sam eyed her critically, as he always did after any kind of incident.

"Just another day at the office," she said with a grin.

Sam shook his head. "Smart-ass," he muttered. "See you at the station."

Cara spent the rest of the night filling out forms and making sure Daniella was settled. Bev insisted that Daniella go home with her, and Daniella agreed. As long as she was somewhere she felt safe, there was no risk of her returning to the apartment she shared with Bob. For now, the bastard was in jail, but after his arraignment in the morning, he might get out on bail. And Daniella would have to make some smart and hopefully permanent decisions.

*   *   *

Sunday dawned cold and sunny after the snowstorm the night before. Mike had spent all day yesterday at the station catching up on endless paperwork, which was still piled high on his desk, and he'd met with the tech guy to go over the potential computerization of files. Last night he'd spent at Ethan's playing poker with guys they'd gone to school with, where Mike had won a decent amount of cash and caught up with old friends. Not a bad way to spend a Saturday night, short of seeing Cara and spending the night in her bed.

He hadn't seen her much since their return from Vegas, their schedules keeping them apart. He'd been busy, but he thought about her often. Although he was getting used to it, stranger still was that he missed having her around—in his bathroom, sharing drawers, and in his space. There was never a time when being apart from a woman bothered him. He'd even invited her to the family dinner tonight, but she'd begged off, claiming she was exhausted. Considering he'd woken her when he called this morning at eleven, he didn't doubt it.

At his parents', Mike handled chores his father used to do himself, like shoveling the walk clear of snow and de-icing the driveway. Sam and Erin pitched in to do their parts as well. Between the three of them, Mike hoped they kept Ella and Simon's lives running as smoothly as possible until this nightmare ended.

No wonder people whispered the word *cancer*. The damned disease took a toll on everyone within loving distance of the person afflicted. But Simon appeared stronger today and hadn't been napping when Mike arrived.

Mike kicked the snow off his boots and left them along with his coat and gloves in the laundry room to dry. Dinner was their normal affair, joking with each other, and for the first time in ages, even Simon participated, leaving Mike with a feeling of warmth about his family he hadn't experienced in too long—if ever. Maybe meeting Rex had given him a newfound appreciation for all he had here in Serendipity.

"Where's Cara tonight?" Mike's mother asked over dessert.

Mike paused, his spoon full of his mother's delicious bread pudding midway to his mouth. "Home. She said she's exhausted and asked me to send her apologies."

"Which of course you forgot to do," Erin teased him. "I don't blame her for being tired after last night's excitement."

"Excitement?" Suddenly uneasy, Mike laid his spoon down on his plate.

"Someone hasn't checked the blotter today," his father said, laughing as he glanced at Mike. "I can relate. There were Sundays I didn't want to know what was happening in town. I figured if the world was falling apart, someone would let me know. That's what deputy chiefs are for."

"I was the assistant D.A. on call last night," Erin said.

Mike's mouth grew dry. "What happened?" he asked his brother, who he knew had been on duty.

"Cara didn't tell you?" Sam asked.

Mike shook his head.

"Shit," Sam muttered. "I thought you knew or I would've said something sooner."

"Tell me now," Mike said.

Sam cleared his throat. "We got a call about a disturbance at the McDonald's off Route 80. Manager said a drunk guy was threatening one of her workers. Ted Shaeffer was with me. We arrived to find the perp with his arm around his girlfriend's throat and Cara holding a gun on him."

Mike's stomach churned, his gut firing on all cylinders. Cara wasn't on duty last night, but if she was involved in something, there was only one other person who could've been there too.

"Was the woman's name Daniella?" Mike asked.

Sam nodded. "Cara was off duty when she got a call. She met Daniella at McDonald's and her boyfriend showed up. Abusive asshole," Sam added, and Ella didn't reprimand him for his choice of words. "We defused the situation without bloodshed."

Mike nodded, not surprised. He hadn't been worried about Cara handling herself or being in a difficult situation. Hell, he'd trust her to have his back any time. What did shock him was the fact that she'd heard from Daniella and yet she hadn't called him last night and she hadn't mentioned it this morning.

"Who is this Daniella?" Simon asked.

"A young woman who Cara took under her wing at Havensbridge. She left a couple of weeks ago and nobody's heard from her since. I knew how worried Cara was, so I spent some time calling a couple of neighboring area hospitals. Just in case," Mike said. Yet Cara hadn't let him know that Daniella had surfaced.

"Daniella agreed to press charges and testify. She even took out a restraining order, which took guts."

"That poor girl," his mother said softly. Ella shook her head, her eyes filled with sadness. "Nobody should have to go through something like that."

"What about Cara?" he asked. "She was okay afterward?"

Sam nodded. "I'm sorry, man. I really thought you knew."

"It's okay." Mike appreciated that his brother cared, and he knew that Sam had finally accepted Mike's relationship with Cara.

"She was fine. She gave her statement, made sure Daniella was taken care of, and went home."

Alone, Mike thought. She'd gone through her own form of emotional hell, one that probably brought back all sorts of painful memories and fear for her mother, and she still hadn't called him at any time afterward. Damn stubborn, independent woman, he thought, rising from his seat.

"Mike? What's wrong?" his mother asked.

Simon put a hand over Ella's to calm her. "It's fine. Let him go. He has a lady to talk to."

Leave it to his father to understand. Mike smiled at the old man. "Thanks for dinner, it was delicious."

"Don't worry, I'll do all the cleanup," Erin said, dismissing him with a wave of her hand and a grin that let him know he owed her.

"Hey, take it easy on her," his brother warned him about Cara.

He supposed some things would never change, and he stopped short of telling Sam that how Mike treated his woman was none of his damned business. That would only cause more trouble than he had the time or patience to deal with.

The only person he wanted to shake sense into was Cara.

Thirteen

Cara had a massive headache. By the time she'd gotten home last night, she'd fallen into bed exhausted but had trouble sleeping. Normally the adrenaline of a situation at work would lead to a crash and a good night's sleep, but this wasn't work. Everything about Daniella felt personal to her.

She had flashbacks of Daniella cringing when Bob yelled, slinking down in her seat as if trying to become invisible, taking the slap as if it were normal. It all reminded Cara of her mother's body language and behavior, hence the nearly debilitating headache.

She took a couple of Advil and was about to lie back down on the couch, a place she'd been most of the day, when her doorbell rang.

She padded across the room in her bare feet and peeked out. Catching a glimpse of Mike, her heart fluttered faster.

She swung the door open wide. "Hi!" she said, surprised but not unhappy to see him.

He stood in his leather jacket, a serious expression on his

handsome face. "Hi." He stepped inside and immediately turned to face her, stepping into her personal space.

His brows furrowed tight, and she curled her fingers to prevent herself from smoothing out the wrinkles. She needed to know what was going on in that head of his first.

"What's wrong?" she asked.

"I thought we had a relationship." He pinned her with his dark, steady gaze, and her pulse rate tripled.

He was angry and she had no idea why. "Umm, we do?"

"Not sure?" he clipped out.

"Of course I am! What I'm not sure about is your mood and what's causing it."

"I'm getting there. So we're in a relationship."

She nodded, suddenly too warm in her own skin.

"Yet you not only heard from Daniella, you went to meet her, ended up pulling a gun on her boyfriend, and I had to hear about it from my brother and sister?" he asked, his voice rising.

Despite his anger, she wasn't the least bit put off. She knew no matter how upset he became, he'd never hurt her. She was more intrigued by this sudden wave of emotion he was turning her way.

"You weren't on duty last night or today, so you heard it from them?" she asked, trying to understand.

"At dinner with my parents, yeah. So why didn't you tell me when I called this morning?"

"Because you woke me and I wasn't exactly thinking clearly!"

"I can understand that, but after you woke up? All day when you weren't feeling well, when you were upset, it never dawned on you to give me a call? Let me comfort you?"

"Wait. You're hurt that I didn't tell you I'd finally heard from Daniella?" This seemed so out of character for him, she didn't know what to say.

He looked at her, stupefied. "Hello? Of course I'm hurt! If I heard from my father and didn't call you, wouldn't you be?" he asked, the storm passing from his eyes, replaced by a calming, more wounded look that touched her deeply.

She swallowed hard. "I thought about calling you. On the way there."

He narrowed his gaze. "Then why didn't you?"

Oh, this was going to be hard. Honesty always was, but he deserved the truth. "Want to sit?" she asked.

He tipped his head to the side, his cocky stance answering for him.

"Guess not. I wanted to call and that's why I didn't."

"Which makes no sense."

"Maybe not to you. But when we started this"—she gestured between them—"I said you were going to break my heart, remember?"

He nodded, wariness in his dark eyes.

"Do you remember what you said?"

Awareness dawned in his expression, and she noted the exact moment when he recalled his statement.

"I said *no hearts involved.*" His voice sounded scratchy and rough.

Good, since those words were like sandpaper on her already bruised heart. "I knew if I was going to let myself get involved with you, I'd have to keep up my walls. But you're an intense guy, and what's between us is too."

He let out a harsh laugh. "Tell me about it," he muttered.

She smiled. "Yeah. Those walls crumble pretty quickly when you're around. The thing is, if I'm going to survive you leaving—whenever that is—I have to keep living my life without relying on you."

"And letting me know what's going on with you is relying on me too much?" He spread his hands wide, not getting it.

"That's right. It is." Already the condo that had always felt like home seemed emptier when he wasn't here. "I can't let myself get used to calling you and sharing the little things when soon enough you'll be gone and I'll be on my own again." Just the thought had her shivering.

"Jesus. Is it really that easy for you?" he asked, as if he were the wounded party.

"Are you kidding? Nothing about being with you is easy!" She'd give him her heart on a platter if he asked, but he hadn't. He wouldn't. And the pain that would slice through would be sharp enough without adding to it by knowingly letting him in.

He pulled her close, wrapping his arms around her tight. "Join the club, baby."

She managed a laugh at his use of their word and laid her head against his chest with a sigh. He smelled good, his musky warm scent sending her senses reeling.

"I still wish you'd called me," he said, his lips against her hair.

"And I wish I didn't care about you so much, but we don't always get what we want." She turned and started to walk away, to give herself much-needed space and distance.

Not because she was angry or upset but because she wanted to jump into his arms and lose herself in everything that was Mike. And losing herself wasn't something she could afford to do. She thought of her mother, giving up her sense of self for a man who couldn't give her what she needed. Mike wasn't abusive like Cara's father, but he couldn't give her what she deserved either.

"Cara." He grabbed her arm and spun her back to face him, the pain on his face indicating he wasn't happy about their situation. "I feel more too." He stroked a hand across her cheek.

"But it doesn't change anything, does it?"

He winced, and she had her answer. Just because she'd expected it didn't mean it didn't hurt. "I'm starving," she said, focusing on something she could control. "I'm going to heat up some lasagna. Want some?"

He shook his head. "I ate at my parents'."

Without waiting for his reply, Cara headed toward the kitchen. Her bare feet stuck out of her navy, overly large

Serendipity PD sweat pants, her bare waist peeking beneath her cropped top, her ponytail swishing against her back. She'd never looked more appealing. Mike groaned and followed her.

She had so many valid points, he didn't know where to begin. Did his feelings for her change anything about his future intentions? The truth was, he didn't know. Everything about his return to Serendipity was unexpected, from the overwhelming depth of feelings he had for this woman to the lack of desperation to leave. But Simon was feeling stronger and he would come back as chief, which would put Mike out of a job.

Could he stay in Serendipity as a detective or cop? Did he even want to? He didn't know, and until he did, he wouldn't give her false hope.

He waited until she'd put her dinner in the microwave before capturing her between his body and the kitchen counter. She studied him in silence with too-wise blue eyes.

"Know what I like most about you?" she asked.

The question surprised him. "My good looks?" he quipped.

She slipped her hands around his waist. "Other than that."

"My charm?"

She managed a laugh. "Besides that—you've always been up front with me. Knowing where I stand makes whatever happens more bearable."

He smiled at the compliment. One that somehow, deep inside, didn't make him feel very good about himself at all.

Mike stayed while she ate dinner. He asked if she wanted to talk about Daniella or her situation, but she said no, she'd done enough of that all day. So they discussed things like the state of the computer system at the station and Annie and Joe's upcoming wedding. Mike watched an episode of *Law & Order*, which she loved and he found ridiculous, so he focused on her devouring half a pint of Ben and Jerry's instead. Her lips wrapped around the spoon and she slowly savored the ice cream, licking the treat with her tongue and moaning with each chunk of cookie dough she found in the tub.

He couldn't take another minute and not pick her up and carry her to bed. He had no doubt she'd let him, too. She wasn't one to hold on to hurt or disappointment. Discussion finished, she hadn't brought it up again, nor did she punish him with moodiness or any inkling of disappointment.

As they chatted about everyday things, as she seemed content, his mood worsened, which only pissed him off. He had a woman who accepted his life and wasn't making demands. He should be relieved. Hell, he *should* be sinking into her willing body and taking everything she was willing to give. But she'd had a rough weekend and though he knew sex would be a good temporary distraction, he couldn't shake the feeling that sleeping with her tonight, when their feelings were so raw, wouldn't be fair to her.

She met his gaze over her spoonful of ice cream and grinned.

Okay, maybe her feelings weren't raw after all, but his were. He was feeling unsettled after their intense talk, almost . . . unhappy that he was getting everything he wanted and thought he needed out of a relationship.

So instead of staying, he kissed her good night and headed home.

Monday morning, Mike stared at the mound of paperwork on his desk that seemed to have grown over the weekend. He had a part-time administrative assistant, a fifty-five-year-old woman named Rachel who liked to mother him and the rest of the officers who worked under him. Thankfully she was on this morning, and when she walked in with two cups of coffee, he gratefully accepted his and they got to work.

While she sifted through the various papers, Rachel made notes, updated his calendar, and sorted everything into piles for filing later on.

An hour later, they were nearly at the bottom of his inbox. True, his schedule was full for the week, but he was up and running efficiently once more.

"I'm not sure what I'd do without you," he said to Rachel.

"Your father used to say the same thing. If I'm making myself indispensable, I'm doing my job right." She smiled, and she looked younger than her light silver hair usually made her look.

"My father's a smart man." Mike smiled at the thought of Simon in this same seat.

"And you've got a lot of him in you. The respect you command from your officers, the way you don't take the mayor's BS—pardon my French—and of course, your way with the ladies." She laughed. "Not that you'd do anything about all that attention they give you. You're like your daddy in that way too."

"Attention?" Mike asked. Since he'd been back in Serendipity, he hadn't noticed any women paying him special notice.

"Another way you're like Simon, God bless him. Once he laid eyes on your mama, there wasn't another woman who could distract him."

Mike didn't know which comment to tackle first, so he went with the easiest. "You don't say? Dad was a goner from the beginning?" He wanted to hear more about Simon and Ella in the early days, after Rex left and they'd gotten together.

He often wondered if Simon had done the right thing and fallen in love later, or if he'd always had a thing for Ella but the coast wasn't clear until Rex left town. He'd also been curious about his mom, whether she'd married Simon out of desperation or true caring. He didn't doubt she loved him now, but in the beginning? Mike shivered, knowing he was more afraid to know that part of the story, whether being pregnant with Mike had compelled his mother to make a choice she wouldn't have otherwise.

He forced himself to refocus on Rachel, who was looking at him with a funny expression on her face. "Did you hear me?" she asked.

"Sorry. I got distracted."

"I said, Simon always loved your mama, even when she was with that scoundrel, Rex . . . Oh!" Rachel slapped a hand over her mouth. "I'm sorry. That was thoughtless of me."

Mike shook his head. "You spoke the truth. No need to apologize." Everyone, it seemed, knew Rex Bransom hadn't been a man worth knowing.

Cheeks still pink, Rachel looked to Mike's desk, pulling a manila envelope from the bottom of his inbox. "This is the last thing. It has your name on it." She handed the package to Mike without meeting his gaze.

"It's okay, Rachel. Really."

She nodded. "Thank you. I'm going to take these stacks and head over to the filing room." She gathered the papers and quickly made her escape.

With a groan, Mike lowered himself back to his seat, package in hand. He didn't recognize the writing but realized this had to be the envelope he'd gotten a phone call about over a week ago. He'd forgotten all about it and obviously it'd been buried beneath piles of paperwork.

He opened the envelope and a clichéd black book fell out, along with a note. A quick read told him it was from Judge Baine's wife:

In a lucid moment, my husband asked me to give you this. Old mistakes that he paid for by living with his guilty conscience that eats away at what few good moments he has now. As many suspected, the old Winkler place was, in fact, a brothel. Many otherwise good, prominent men kept it going—until the time you were asking about. Now you have the list in your hands. Do with it what you must. My husband has more than made up for his sins, at least to me, and he's barely aware of what's going on around him most of the time, anyway. But he did want to clear his conscience, and I followed his wishes.

Mike glanced up at the ceiling in his office. "A lead as well as some answers. Thank you, God."

He jumped up and headed for the squad room, intent on finding Cara. He found her at her desk, typing in reports on the barebones system they had. Soon, though, his new system would be in place and even when he was gone from here, he'd have made a lasting impression.

That mattered to him, he realized. This place, a small police station with dingy walls, an air conditioner that needed to be replaced, and the people in it, *mattered*.

"Hi!" Cara glanced up from her desk.

Beautiful blue eyes focused on him and immediately brightened his day. "Hi. You have some time?"

"Umm, sure. Let me just save this . . ." She hit a button and pushed her chair back. "Ready. What's up?"

He looked her over, loving how she appeared so in control and sexy in her uniform. "I have a lead on the money in the evidence room. Or at the very least, I have a list of names and information I can't discuss here."

"Then let's go."

She was dropping everything? "Don't you have work to do?"

"I'm on top of things."

"Good. I want to look at this in private. Can we go to your place?"

"Sure, but yours is closer."

Mike paused. "But yours is warmer." And he didn't mean temperature. He liked the homey feel of her condo, and for the news he assumed he'd be getting, he didn't want to be in his sterile room over Joe's Bar.

*   *   *

Back at her condo, Cara made them grilled cheese sandwiches while Mike sat down at the kitchen table, pad and pen in front of him, Judge Baine's black book open wide.

"It looks like a ledger," she said, glancing over from where she stood at the stove, frying up lunch.

"It is, but it's not used like one. Not exclusively anyway. There's a list of names here. Prominent businessmen with initials underneath their names."

She slid the spatula beneath the sandwiches, flipped them one more time, placed them on plates, and carried them to the table. "What else is there?"

He flipped through the book, coming to empty pages.

"Flip further," she said, taking a bite of her sandwich. "And eat before it gets cold. I worked hard on these."

He grinned and took a bite. His eyes glazed over. "Delicious. This isn't just grilled cheese."

Pleasure filled her. "I'm not sharing my secret recipe. Besides, it's not like you'll ever cook it. If you want it, you'll have to come to me and get it."

"That would be my pleasure." He started to reach for her, but she slapped his hand.

"Work first," she said, tapping the book with her finger.

"Can we play later?" His eyes darkened at the suggestion, and her heart skipped a beat.

She'd been disappointed when he'd kissed her and gone home last night, but a part of her understood. They'd both admitted to deeper-than-planned feelings, and sleeping together last night would have been a very bad idea. She'd have ended up *feeling* way too much. This afternoon, though, they were back on familiar playful ground, where she at least had a shot at keeping her emotions in check.

"Maybe," she said, teasing him. "Now keep looking."

He turned the sheets of paper one by one, finally coming to another set of filled pages. "Bingo. Women's names."

"I bet you can match those to the initials underneath the men's names."

A quick scan back and forth proved her right. "Okay, so the initials are names of women," he said.

"One question answered. Let's focus on the men. Any names you recognize?"

"Other than the judge? Only almost every one," Mike muttered. "Judges, politicians, family men, men with money, working-class guys . . ." He shook his head in disgust.

"Is Simon in there?" she asked gently.

He skimmed the pages more than once before meeting her gaze. "No." His eyes shimmered with relief. "No, thank God."

So whatever Simon knew, he hadn't been cheating on his wife.

"What about—"

"Yeah. Rex is here," he said, reading her mind. "And not just as a patron but as a benefactor. Hell, it looks like Rex helped fund the place. There's cash notations next to names, including Rex and . . . oh shit."

"What?" She leaned in close.

"Martin Harrington, Faith's father, is in here." He slammed the book closed. "It's like a bird's-eye view of the sex lives of the men in Serendipity."

"Eww."

He nodded in agreement. "Let's break this down. What do we know?"

"We've confirmed that the Winkler place was a brothel and that the old boys' network kept it going." Having finished her sandwich, Cara pushed her plate away and took a long drink of her water.

Mike, too, took the last bite of his sandwich and added his plate to hers. "What about the money in the evidence locker?"

"We know marked bills were found in both the trunk and the evidence locker, so we know there are ties to the Winkler place. We know many prominent men in Serendipity were involved, and we know whatever it is has been over for years," Cara said.

"So we have more information now than we did before, but we're still at a dead end, and unless we want to question every man on this list and bring all this dirty laundry to light after thirty years, we're still at a dead end. And the only two people we have asked aren't talking."

Cara rose and placed her hands on his shoulders, massaging the tight knots, engaging all her senses as she worked her fingers through his shirt and into his skin. "All you can do now is wait until you feel Simon's strong enough to push for answers."

Which put this case back on hold.

"The mayor left a message this morning. Hell, she called last week."

"Just tell her you've reached a dead end. It's not a lie."

"It's not the truth, either."

She stilled her hands and leaned her cheek against his. "We haven't found anything that needs to be revealed."

He inclined his head. "And I bend the rules all the time when it suits me. And it suits me now. I just need to know."

"I get that." She kissed his cheek, savoring the masculine scent and the rough stubble against her lips.

His appreciative groan rumbled through her at the same time his cell phone rang. "Dammit." He grabbed his phone. "Yeah." He listened to the caller on the other end. "Thanks, Erin. I'll let her know." He disconnected the call and turned to face her.

"What?"

"Bob Francone made bail."

Cara sucked in a startled breath. "Because it wasn't the first time, I thought they'd keep him locked up. But I'm a cop. I know better." She kicked the leg of his chair, but he was still sitting in it and the pain seared through her toe. "Ouch. Shit. Damn!"

"Hey." Instead of letting her continue taking her frustration out on herself, he did what he should have done last night instead of leaving. He scooped her into his arms and carried her out of the room.

"Hey! Put me down. I have to call Daniella and let her know."

"Erin already did. That's her job, remember?"

"Then she needs protection."

"Which we can't give her. Her job is off a federal highway and she's staying with someone who lives outside Serendipity. But she has a restraining order—"

"Which means nothing, and you know that!" She wriggled in his arms, but he held on tight. Damn, he liked the weight and feel of her. "Stop moving," he said, pressing his lips against her neck and licking her there.

She sighed and let out a soft moan. "If I do, can I call Daniella?"

Mike closed his eyes, realizing so much about her in one short second. "Cara, you can't take care of everyone. You can't control what's going to happen. Sometimes, you just have to let things *be*."

She cuddled into him, her actions speaking more of trust than lust, and his heart melted. "Mike?"

"Yeah, baby?"

"Can I call Daniella now?"

Mike said the only thing that came to mind. "If I agree, can we end up in bed?"

Fourteen

Cara spent the rest of the week working and remembering the amazing sex she'd had with Mike on Monday afternoon. He'd kept her in his arms, picked up her cell off the counter, and waited as she'd called Daniella, got voice mail, and left a message. Next thing she knew, he couldn't keep his hands off her—and vice versa. He lay over her, skin to skin, and breathed her in. She felt him inhale and groan, his entire body shaking. Then he made love to her.

She knew the difference. He took control as usual, but the reverence in his touch was different; the way he caressed her with his lips, his hands, his mouth—was different. When he entered her, his gaze drinking her in as he thrust deep, he owned her. She knew it even if he never would.

Now, on Friday, her day off, she could barely concentrate, but she'd promised Alexa they'd go dress shopping for Joe and Annie's upcoming wedding. Cara wasn't a girly-girl who loved shopping, unlike Alexa, who enjoyed the whole process even if she didn't get off work much to indulge. They drove to the nearest mall, twenty minutes away, and Cara let Alexa do her thing. She pulled a variety of dresses for each of them, choosing an assortment of colors, lengths, and shapes. Cara wasn't big on bright colors, so in between her friends' choices, she tossed in some basic black too.

After what felt like an endless morning, Cara slid into a black, silky, one-shouldered dress that draped in the right places and that she felt very comfortable in.

"Come out and let me see!" Alexa called from the fitting room next door.

Cara walked into the hall in her bare feet and faced Alexa, who glowed in a short dress covered in gold sequins. "That dress looks fabulous on you!" she told her friend.

"I love it too. I think this is the one. As long as we find shoes and a bag today, I'll be all set."

Cara groaned. "I thought we were finished after this." She looked over her shoulder into the mirror for a full-length glance at her image. Yep, she was happy with this one.

"No. Next we accessorize." Alexa planted her hands on her hips. "What are you wearing?"

"A dress." She rolled her eyes at the stupid question.

"Going to a funeral?"

"Hey, that's not nice. This is a cocktail dress and you know it."

"It's a basic black dress, and it does nothing special for you." After that disheartening pronouncement, Alexa walked around Cara in a circle, and nodded once. "Right. Nothing special. Did you try the red one?"

No, Cara had not tried the red one because she'd stand out at the wedding like a sore thumb. "I could have worn that to Vegas. It's not appropriate for the wedding. It's at Joe's Bar!"

"Yet you love me in this?" Alexa waved her hand up and down the glittering number.

"You're more outgoing."

"You're such a chicken. You want to blend into the wood-work? Why? You've got a hot body and a hot guy who'll want to see it. Go change. I want to see the red dress."

Cara sighed and headed back into the fitting room. There was no arguing with Alexa when she was in this kind of determined mood. "I'll never find shoes to match," Cara called out through the slatted door as she struggled to adjust the tightly fitted dress.

"That's what silver is for. Now get out here and let me see."

"Did anyone ever tell you that you're bossy?" Cara muttered, tugging on the hem.

"Only my interns, my staff, my patients, and my friends."

Cara opened the door and stepped back into the hall.

"Oh my God. Stunning. Turn." Alexa made a spinning motion with her hands, and Cara dutifully followed directions. "Perfect!"

"Look at my cleavage!"

Alexa grinned. "Exactly! Stunning. Classy yet bold. Let's go. We have to find shoes."

Cara sighed and shut the dressing room door. Before changing, she glanced at her reflection in the small mirror. She did love how the dress hugged her curves. She'd just never picked out such a statement color before.

"You only live once," Alexa called out from her room next door. "Stop overthinking it and change."

Cara laughed and decided her friend was right. She'd buy the dress and make a statement. They paid for their dresses and took them downstairs to pick out shoes.

"Do you have a date for the wedding?" Cara asked.

Alexa shook her head. "With who? The same people who come through my office doors? Or the ER?"

"And whose fault is that? You work too hard! There are plenty of single, good-looking guys in Serendipity, and you know it."

"I really don't want to talk about it, okay?" Alexa asked, sounding like she meant it.

Cara narrowed her gaze. "One of these days I'm going to figure out why you won't let me in when it comes to talking about romance. You sure don't mind digging into mine."

"You deserve to be happy in a relationship, Cara."

"So do you," she reminded her friend.

"We don't always get what we want," Alexa said softly.

And Cara merely nodded, knowing truer words had never been spoken.

Cara and Mike were on the way to the movies in a multiplex about twenty minutes away from Serendipity. They'd just started out when his cell rang and his mother asked if he'd come over.

"I'm with Cara," he said into the speakerphone.

"Bring her along!" Ella immediately said, no hesitation.

Cara's chest tightened. She appreciated how the Marsdens always made her feel welcome and not like an outsider. Sometimes she felt more a part of their family than her own.

"Do you mind?" Mike mouthed to her so his mother wouldn't hear.

"Of course not." She smiled to reassure him.

About half an hour later, they were gathered in the family room of his parents' house with Erin and Sam, waiting for Ella and Simon, who were upstairs.

"Any idea why we're here?" Mike asked his siblings, who sat around his parents' family room with them on a Friday night.

Erin shook her head. "They just said they wanted to talk, but not to panic, it wasn't bad news." Her brows crinkled in confusion.

"Okay, so we're all in the dark."

"At least it smells like we're getting dessert," Sam said with a grin.

Erin rolled her eyes. "Can you think about something other than your always empty stomach?"

Personally, Cara agreed with him. The delicious aroma of coffee brewing scented through the house, making her hope there was some kind of cake to go along with it. But she didn't say anything, merely glanced at Sam, and they both laughed knowingly.

Mike, whose arm was around her shoulder, tightened his hold. Cara tried not to be too pleased by the unnecessary proprietary display. Instead, she focused on Kojak. The little dog had made himself at home in her lap, and she petted the fluffy white head, wishing she were able to get a dog of her own.

"What's with that look?" Mike asked.

Cara couldn't help but smile at how well he read her. "Kojak's cute. I wouldn't mind a pet, but my shifts are too long. It wouldn't be fair for an animal to be alone all the time."

He eyed her with a funny expression on his face, but before she could question him, Ella and Simon walked into the room, their arms linked together. Their show of unity wasn't just an act. Anyone who'd grown up in Serendipity, who'd been to town events Simon had presided over as chief, who'd attended gatherings with this family, knew that Simon and Ella's love was steady and real. Illness had only strengthened the bond, and Cara envied them the life they shared—sickness and all, she'd give anything for a love that enduring and real.

"What's up?" Sam asked, leaning forward in his seat.

Erin stared at her parents, her eyes wide and her expression curious.

Mike feigned relaxation, but Cara felt the stiffness in his arms and knew whatever their pronouncement, it was as important to him as to his siblings.

Whether they were being deliberately dramatic or not, the next few moments of silence dragged on endlessly.

Simon and Ella smiled at one another with love, then turned that gaze on each of their children, causing Cara a moment of discomfort. "I should go and let you all talk," she said, suddenly feeling like an outsider who didn't belong.

She started to rise, but Mike held on tight while Simon stepped forward. "Nonsense. If anyone has a right to hear this news along with the family, it's you." He smiled warmly at Cara and she drank in his words, relaxing back beside Mike on the sofa.

"Thank you," she said softly.

"My pleasure." He grinned, and Cara realized Simon looked happier than she'd seen him in a while; though he was still frail as a result of his treatments, there was a definite glint in his eye that she hadn't noticed the last time she'd been here for dinner.

"Well, stop keeping us in suspense," Sam said.

"He's in remission!" Ella said, obviously unable to keep the news in any longer.

The next few minutes were a blur of happy hugs, kisses, and tears of joy as they celebrated the news. Cara gladly participated, knowing the family's relief as well as her own. Simon was a wonderful man, dedicated not just to the family who adored him but to the town he loved. He'd been police chief of Serendipity for as long as Cara could remember, and before his illness, he'd been a great boss . . .

Her thoughts trailed off as the reality of the good news set in. Simon's remission meant he'd be ready to resume the reins at the station again soon. Simon would come back to work, and Mike would step down. He'd be out of a job in Serendipity. Nothing compelling would keep him here, and he'd return to his solitary apartment in Manhattan, his undercover work, and his women. Like Lauren.

The ache in her chest hurt so badly she couldn't breathe, making her wonder if this was what a heart attack felt like.

While the family talked, Cara picked up Kojak again, finding comfort in the dog's soft fur, and she buried her face in
his fluffy body. If she were going to survive Mike's leaving,
maybe she'd have to get a dog after all.

What kind of person was she that she'd turn a wonderful
celebration of life into a memorial? She ought to be ashamed,
Cara thought. She swallowed the pain in her throat and
promised that she'd pull herself together. As long as she was
in this house, she'd smile and be happy. She'd save the wal-
lowing for when she was alone.

A status that was coming soon enough.

"Hey," Mike said, sitting back down beside her, concerned by the pained, fragile look on her face. "You okay?"
First Cara had tried to bolt before his parents' news, and
now she'd all but withdrawn into herself.

She nodded, her eyes watery. "It's such great news. Overwhelming, actually."

"Unexpected, too. I had no idea he was going for a scan
or anything."

"I'm sure they didn't want to either worry you unneces-
sarily or get your hopes up just in case things were status quo."

He nodded, grasping her free hand that wasn't holding
the dog. "I'm glad you're here to share the celebration." He
grinned at her, beyond thrilled that his father had beaten the
damned disease.

She smiled back. Oddly, it didn't reach her eyes.

He wanted to pull her out and find out exactly what was
wrong, but Ella announced coffee and cake, Sam whooped
in happiness, and he knew they couldn't escape yet.

"I can always count on my youngest boy and his stomach," his mother said, laughing.

"Even I'm hungry for some of your mom's chocolate
cake," Simon announced.

Mike slid his hand into Cara's. She scooted the dog off
her lap and they headed for the kitchen, but he had the

distinct sense something was off. He just had no time to ask what was going on in her head. Over dessert, the celebration continued with family jokes and fun toasts to Simon, despite that fact that the only drinks on the table were coffee cups.

Sam cleared his throat and looked at Simon. "Here's to your shoving my big brother out of your office and reclaiming your rightful place as chief."

No sooner had Sam raised his glass than Mike realized *exactly* what was bothering Cara. He was startled that he hadn't thought of it sooner, but his father's good health news had overshadowed everything else. Suddenly his own stomach cramped as he understood the source of her worry.

He reached beneath the table and squeezed her hand. She didn't squeeze back. And considering that he didn't know what the hell to say—or do—he didn't blame her.

When the doorbell rang, Mike was relieved because it took the pressure off. Pressure he was starting to feel in his chest, and he wasn't certain whether it was because he could finally think about leaving Serendipity or because he suddenly didn't want to go.

"I've got it," Simon said, and since this was probably the first time in ages he'd been excited to have company, everyone let him do the honors of answering the door.

"So, Erin, how was—"

"What the hell are you doing here?" Simon's voice carried into the dining room, interrupting whatever his mother was about to say and scaring even Mike.

"I haven't heard that tone since I borrowed the car when I was fifteen," Mike muttered, rising from his seat.

Everyone scrambled to see what had Simon so upset, Mike heading out first.

"You aren't welcome here," Simon said, and Mike's gut twisted into a painful knot as his gut told him exactly who the unexpected visitor was.

Sure enough, Rex stood in the doorway, his gaze running over Simon. "Is that any way to greet an old friend?"

"Rex!" Ella said, her dismay at seeing him as obvious as Simon's.

"Hey, beautiful! You look even younger in person than you did online."

Cara sidled up beside Mike and slipped her hand into his, silently offering her support, but Mike had a feeling it was Ella who was going to need it.

"You've seen her online?" Simon asked, his suddenly wary gaze shooting between his wife and his former best friend.

Mike drew a steadying breath. "How about we do this inside?" He didn't need the neighbors witnessing this spectacle.

"You've got five minutes," Simon muttered, and stepped aside so Rex could enter.

Mike felt his brother's and sister's gazes darting from Rex to Mike, as if looking for the similarities, and Mike's skin crawled in fear that they'd find some.

"Could we get some privacy for this meeting?" Rex had the balls to ask of Simon.

"No. This is my home," Simon said, his voice clear and strong. "My wife and my children. My son," he said, his gaze falling pointedly to Mike. "You're interrupting a family dinner, so we'd appreciate it if you had your say and then were gone."

Rex's face flushed. "I heard you had cancer. I wanted to come see that you were okay." He shifted on his feet, obviously surprised he hadn't been welcomed with open arms.

There was a narcissistic bent to Rex that Mike hadn't been aware of before now. He'd honestly thought Simon and Ella would be happy to see him after all these years.

"You heard about me how?" Simon asked.

Mike's heart pounded in his chest. Both he and his mother had avoided telling Simon anything about being in contact with Rex. They'd agreed to wait until Simon didn't have so much to worry about, until the cancer was gone. But Rex's timing took that choice away from them.

Ella placed a hand on Simon's arm. "He reached out on Facebook a few weeks ago," she said.

"Then I went to Vegas to run down a lead on that cold case I'd been asking you about," Mike added, refusing to let his mother take sole responsibility. "I mentioned not wanting to burden you because you had too much going on."

"So when Rex asked me what was up with you, Simon, I told him," Ella said. "Mike and I decided we'd tell you everything once we knew you were healthy. I had no idea Rex would just show up here after all these years." She scowled at the man who, though he was Mike's father, had intruded on them all.

"But apparently we ran out of time," Mike said, shooting Rex a disgusted glare.

"You've been in touch with him," Simon's gaze dulled as he looked at his wife. "And you went to meet him." He turned that disappointment on Mike.

And he didn't like the sick feeling in his gut caused by hurting the man he considered his father.

"Simon—"

"Don't worry, Ella. We'll talk later." To Mike's relief, he didn't sound angry at his wife. "And son, so will we." He turned an understanding gaze on Mike.

That was Simon. Angry for an instant, calm and understanding for a lifetime. More than anything, Mike wanted to be like him.

"As for *you*." Simon jerked toward Rex. "What makes you think we want you here after all this time? My wife says she didn't expect you. Mike, did you invite him?" he asked, his tone completely neutral.

If Mike said he had, Simon would have accepted it. God, Mike admired the man even more—and he hadn't thought such a thing was possible.

"No." Mike folded his arms across his chest. "I didn't. I

asked him a few questions, then made it clear I wanted nothing to do with him."

"Guess those are the only people in the room who get a vote where you're concerned, and they stated their choice. I appreciate that you made the long trip, but there's nothing here for you anymore. That was *your* choice almost thirty years ago."

Rex shook his head in denial. The complete shock on his face told Mike he'd really expected to be welcomed. "I came because you have cancer. Because we go way back. And because we have history."

"Well, the cancer's gone, and now so are you." Simon headed for the door.

"I wouldn't be so quick to throw me out," Rex spat suddenly, his voice low and not nearly as nice or accommodating. "Your so-called son is looking into the money in the evidence locker. What are you going to do when he finds out what you did?" His words sounded like the threat they were meant to be.

All eyes looked to Simon.

"I'll talk to my family. I'll take my punishment. But they won't hear anything from *you*." This time Simon did head for the door and opened it. "Your welcome here ended the day you left town."

Rex stiffened, his big body reverberating with anger. "As I recall, you sent me packing."

Mike whipped his head around. "What?" He glanced at his mother.

Tears shimmered in her eyes, but she didn't have the shell-shocked look Mike had expected. Clearly more was going on here, and only the second generation was in the dark.

"Dad?" Sam stepped forward, but Simon held out a hand. "I'll explain everything." He gestured with a broad sweep. "After he leaves."

"You'll be sorry. You had thirty years of peace. Do you really want to stir the pot now?"

Mike had had enough. "Sounds to me like you're the one stirring the pot." He stormed over to Rex, grabbed his arm, and escorted him outside.

"I'm your father," Rex said.

"Simon's my father."

"But my blood is running through your veins."

Mike tried like hell not to let his panic at that thought show. Instead he held on to the support of the four people back inside who cared about him.

Five if he counted Cara.

Mike spun and reentered the house, slamming the door shut behind him. In the family room, his brother and sister were peppering Simon with questions, shouting over each other in their need to be heard.

"Hold up and wait for Mike. I don't want to have to repeat myself."

Mike eyed Simon with pride, admiration, and love, seeing him in a new light.

The man had staked his claim as Mike's *father*—in front of a man who claimed biological rights, no less—and he'd done it at his own personal expense.

Simon had raised him. He'd gone to every sporting event, academic function, and graduation Mike ever had. And he'd never once acted as if Mike meant any less to him than his own children. Despite this, Mike had always felt less important, less worthy than the others—thanks to insecurities instilled by the mere knowledge that his real father had abandoned him. In Mike's mind, he'd figured deep down Simon felt the same way.

He'd been dead wrong. And he was ashamed for giving Simon so little credit. Whatever had gone down all those years ago, Mike didn't give a damn. He'd protect Simon with everything he had.

He stepped up to his father and pulled him into a quick hug before joining Cara, who sat quietly in an oversized chair.

"Are you okay?" she asked softly.

He nodded. For the first time, he really was.

"I should go and let Simon talk to you all alone," she whispered.

He snaked his arm around her waist, anchoring her in place. "It's your case too, and these are the answers we've been looking for." Besides, he wanted her here for the rest of the reveal.

"Tell them, Simon," Ella said, her voice strong.

Mike suddenly realized that his mother knew everything. All along, she'd had the answers they were looking for. Of course she did. Ella and Simon were a tight unit, and they hadn't gotten that way by keeping secrets. Damn, but he'd underestimated her too.

Simon stood at the head of the room, facing his kids. "The rumors you all heard were true. The Winkler place rented out rooms by the hour. They had girls that were imported from Manhattan for the use of whatever locals were willing to pay. And the Winkler boys, as they were known, only took cash. That cash came from both prostitution and drugs, since the boys worked for a syndicate that operated out of Manhattan."

Mike glanced at Sam. They sat in silence, waiting for the rest.

"Plenty of people wanted the brothel shut down, myself included, but there were too many men in high positions involved."

"Like Judge Baine," Mike said, understanding how high and deep this small-town scandal went.

Simon nodded. "Like Marshall. And old Mayor Ferber. Of course, periodically, people would make a ruckus and mothers would petition and the place would go dark for a while, only to open up again when things quieted down."

"How was Rex involved?" Mike asked.

Simon gave Mike an understanding nod. "As I found out later, he was on the take. With the old police chief involved, Rex became the rookie who was sent out on call every time a complaint came in. He made sure evidence got buried, things stayed quiet, and he was paid well for his trouble. Same as Judge Baine."

"What happened to mess it all up?" Sam leaned forward in his seat.

"What always happens. Stupid shit trips people up. The feds were on to the syndicate in New York. They had marked money in play to find out what businesses they were using to launder drug money. The feds had a highly placed guy in the cartel by that point, and he made sure the marked bills made it into circulation in each business. Including the Winklers. Then one day, there were picketers at the motel. Things got ugly and the cops were called in—except Rex was out on a routine call and he couldn't get over there first to hide or ignore evidence. I found more cash than a motel should have and it was all marked."

Mike listened as all the pieces fell into place.

"Everyone must've known it was only a matter of time before the cops tied the Winkler place to the drug guys in the city." Simon shoved his hands into the front pockets of his sweats. "Before that could happen, Judge Baine let the guy out on bail."

"Then?" Erin asked, as interested as the rest of them.

"A few weeks later, one of the drug couriers from Manhattan was pulled over for speeding in Serendipity. The cops found a load of drugs in the car and money he was transporting back to the city. The bills were marked just like the ones found at the Winkler bust," Simon went on. "The feds were notified about the drugs and the additional marked money. But around the same time, they'd taken key syndicate members around Manhattan. Nobody needed the little fish who'd been arrested in Serendipity, and the case went cold."

"Which helped make it all go away quietly, letting everyone here in town off the hook." Sam let out a low whistle.

Simon nodded. "With the cartel finished in Manhattan, the source of the girls and drugs dried up here in Serendipity—and wherever else they were running illegal brothels. The Winkler place became town lore, and that was that."

Mike cleared his throat. "What about the cash in the evidence room? The money replaced with older bills?" He tensed, sensing this was where Rex and Simon's involvement came in.

Cara placed a hand on his back, and he was never more grateful for the support than at this moment. Hell, whatever came, he felt stronger facing it with her by his side.

"Rex had a gambling habit too." Simon ran a hand through his thinning hair. "He stole the money from the evidence room. I didn't catch him in the act, but I figured it out and he didn't deny it when I confronted him." He paced the length of the small room. "Of course, he expected me to keep it quiet."

Mike and his siblings remained silent, waiting for him to tell the story his way.

"By then, your mother was pregnant with you and Rex was panicked in every way you can imagine. He couldn't deal, he wasn't making your mother any promises, and I saw only one solution for everyone involved."

Ella, who had been sitting on the couch, rose and stood by Simon's side. "We were all good friends. I was dating Rex and I thought I loved him, but what I loved was the illusion of the man. By the time I found out I was pregnant, the bloom was off that rose already," she said, letting out a painful laugh.

Mike's throat swelled, and he couldn't bring himself to speak.

"I was pregnant and scared, but make no mistake, Michael, I wanted you." Moisture glistened in her eyes, and with the way her gaze held on to his, he couldn't not believe her.

His chest pounded and his heart hurt, but he knew with everything in him that his mother told the truth.

"And I'd always loved Ella," Simon said to his rapt audience. "If Rex had done right by her, I'd have kept silent. But he didn't, and she deserved so much more than that son of a bitch was giving her, which was nothing but grief."

Ella patted his back, urging him to continue.

"I had an old pocket watch that belonged to my grandfather and some other jewelry my mother had given me to put away for any woman I ended up marrying, and—"

"He pawned it all." Ella picked up the story. "To help me and fix things, he sold family heirlooms." Her voice caught on her words.

"I took the cash and went to Rex with a deal. Either he left town, in which case I would replace the money he stole, or he could stay, and I'd turn him in for evidence tampering, stealing, and whatever else the D.A. wanted to come up with."

"What did Rex say?" Erin asked.

"He ran like the coward he was," Ella said. "Then Simon asked me to marry him. He said he'd always loved me and he promised he wanted to raise the baby like his own. That's when I learned that real love was more than something you said in the heat of the moment. Love is real and enduring." She squeezed Simon's hand before lifting herself onto her toes so she could kiss his cheek. "And he's proven that love to me every day since."

Simon kissed his wife before turning to face his children. "Questions?" he barked at them, so like the Simon Mike remembered rather than the frail man of late.

"Not at the moment," Erin said, obviously stunned.

"Statements?" Simon asked.

Sam shook his head.

"Concerns?" Simon's gaze locked on Mike.

He swallowed hard. "If I've got them, I need time to think them through. I'm a little numb," he muttered.

Simon nodded. "Understood. Come to me if you want to talk."

"Or to me," his mother added, and Mike knew she meant if he wanted to discuss her relationship with Rex Bransom.

"Right now, I'm taking your mother upstairs and I'm going to find out why she thought she couldn't tell me she'd heard from Rex," Simon said in a tone that brooked no argument. "And I'm not taking *because you had cancer* for an answer."

Sam snickered, and even Mike had to laugh. Somehow, things had gone from deadly serious to back to normal in the blink of an eye.

And Mike hadn't been kidding. He needed time to process the entire evening before he could begin to make sense—of anything that had happened tonight.

Fifteen

After the scene at the Marsdens', Cara wanted to go straight home and talk to Mike, but she'd promised a coworker she'd cover his shift. Since she sensed Mike needed time alone, she figured it was just as well. Besides, she had no desire to get into a discussion of when he'd leave Serendipity. It was enough that she knew the time was imminent and she could prepare herself emotionally. No long, drawn-out conversation would make the inevitable any easier.

Because it was nighttime, she was partnered with Dare, which she enjoyed. They joked around and talked about Tess and his brothers' babies. She didn't forget about her problems, but between work and Dare, she found a much-needed distraction.

When dispatch radioed about an unwanted intruder at 111 Elm Street, home of Judge Marshall Baine, every one of Cara's nerves prickled in alarm.

"Ten-four. Car number seven en route," Dare replied, hitting the siren and turning toward the judge's house.

Cara wanted to give him a full rundown, but unless they found Rex, she didn't want to spill Marsden family secrets.

She prayed she was wrong.

She wasn't. They arrived to find Mrs. Blaine wearing a bathrobe, arguing with Rex on the front lawn, while the judge paced behind her, muttering to himself.

Cara shook her head and climbed out of the car. "Something wrong?" she asked Mrs. Baine.

"This man is harassing my husband." Mrs. Baine waved a hand at Rex. "He's ill and he can't handle stress well, as you know." She shot a pleading glance Cara's way.

"Come on," Dare said, approaching Rex. "The occupants of the house asked you to leave."

"And I'm not leaving until I get what I came for. I need to know if he's got something of mine. Something nobody wants to see the light of day," Rex said, eyeing Cara warily.

She sighed. "I think you need to accept that you've worn out your welcome in Serendipity, Mr. Bransom. Whatever happened in the past, you're the one stirring it up now. If you persist in continuing this, you're going to implicate yourself in something that was buried a long time ago."

"You know this man?" Dare asked.

"This is Rex Bransom. He's Mike's biological father."

Dare blinked in surprise. "Does Mike know he's around?"

"Unfortunately, yes."

Dare turned to the judge's wife. "Mrs. Baine, would you like to press charges?"

She folded her arms across her chest. "My husband has given the police chief all the information he has on the past. What happens is up to him. In the meantime, if Mr. Bransom leaves now, I'll forget this incident ever happened."

"Nobody can find out about this!" Judge Baine suddenly yelled, turning on Rex at a full run.

"He's attacking me!" Rex held his hands up to protect himself, but Dare stepped between the men and as gently as possible subdued the judge.

"Relax," Cara muttered to Rex. "You've shown up and agitated everyone imaginable. Now are you going to leave quietly, or am I going to have to arrest you?"

He scowled. "I'm going. But you tell that son of mine that if he knows what's good for his *father*, he'll bury that journal where no one can find it."

Cara narrowed her gaze. Having not been welcomed, he'd decided to ruin Simon's reputation instead. "Haven't you realized? Mike's not like you. He'll do the right thing even if someone gets hurt."

"Even Saint Simon?" Rex spat with disdain, making his point before ambling toward his car like he hadn't a care in the world.

And he didn't. As a cop, Rex knew the same thing Cara knew. The statute of limitations on evidence tampering was ten years, and really, unless they were talking murder, the statute would have run out on any number of crimes with which Rex could be charged. Nobody in Serendipity wanted him here, so his reputation couldn't get any worse. But Simon's could, and clearly that was Rex's goal.

Cara's chest tightened at the thought of the man she respected as her boss and as Mike's father suffering for bailing Rex out and doing right by Ella. Rex Bransom was a loose cannon for the entire Marsden family and the life they enjoyed here in Serendipity.

Cara watched until he'd climbed into his rental and driven away before refocusing on the scene behind her.

"Can I call an ambulance?" Dare asked Mrs. Baine. "Perhaps they can give him a sedative?"

She shook her head. "I'll call Dr. Al," she said of Dr. Alan Collins, Alexa's father. "He'll come over and tell me what's needed."

Dare nodded. "Okay. Need help getting him back into the house?"

Mrs. Baine shook her head. "Once everyone's gone, he'll calm down and go back inside."

Cara swallowed hard. "If you have any trouble, let us know?" She felt sorry for Mrs. Baine and the difficult life she now shared with the man she loved.

"I will. Thank you." She wrapped an arm around her husband and whispered calming words.

Cara and Dare headed for the squad car.

"Care to share what's going on?" he asked her.

She bit the inside of her cheek. "Umm . . . not really? It's not my story to tell. It's up to Sam and Mike," she said.

"Understood. We Barron brothers have had so many secrets, I'm not going to judge others."

"Thanks," she said with a grim smile.

"Think he'll leave town?"

Cara knew Dare referred to Rex. She thought for a moment and sighed. "I don't know. He's not welcome here. I'd say it was sad if he hadn't caused the hard feelings all on his own—and how he's behaving now isn't exactly encouraging anyone to think differently, you know?"

Dare nodded. "When Ethan came back, he wanted to make amends. Nash and I didn't want anything to do with him, but he dug in his heels—and everything he did showed us he'd changed, even before we were ready to admit or accept it."

"Not Rex. He showed up at the Marsdens' claiming it was because he'd heard Simon was sick, but when he wasn't greeted with open arms, he began issuing subtle threats."

Dare swore under his breath. "How's the family taking it?"

Cara stared at the long stretch of dark road in front of them as Dare drove. "They banded together. It was really nice to see."

Even she'd felt the us-against-the-world vibe that Simon had put up against Rex. He'd enveloped Mike in complete acceptance, and everything inside Cara warmed at the sight. She knew how badly Mike had needed that sign of belonging, and Simon had given it to him.

He could take that knowledge with him when he left and know that he had his family waiting for him when he returned. He deserved that, she thought, knowing how elusive he'd found it to begin with.

When their shift finally ended, Cara headed home and slept for a solid six hours. She woke to her alarm and a message from Daniella, whom Cara immediately called back. She learned that the young woman had moved in with Bev, who'd been like a mom to her, something Daniella needed since her own mom lived out of state. Bev's only daughter had moved across the country with her husband, so they each fulfilled a mutual need for the other. With Bev's support and guidance, Daniella had enrolled in online classes and was continuing her work at McDonald's. And so far, no word from Bob, who it seemed was respecting the restraining order.

Though it was afternoon, Cara needed coffee and breakfast, since the night shift always put her off schedule with the rest of the world. She stopped at Cuppa Café, where she ran into Kelly Barron, Nash's wife, double stroller and twin boys with her, and Annie Kane, Joe's fiancée. Cara joined the women for a little while, listening to Annie's wedding talk with a surprising sense of envy.

Cara wasn't the jealous type, unless she counted thinking about Mike with other women. She was genuinely happy for Annie, and yet a part of her couldn't help but yearn for what the other women both had. A man they could count on in their lives. Cara swallowed hard, forcing down the sense of disappointment that Mike couldn't be that guy for her. Instead she continued to smile at all the appropriate places in the conversation until she could gracefully make an escape.

Then, knowing Mike would want details about the incident with his father, she headed over to the station. The squad room was fairly empty, a few people bent over desks typing up reports, so Cara walked directly back to Mike's office.

She knocked and waited until he gave her permission to enter. Given their relationship outside work, the formality here always made her smile. She'd really miss knowing he was the one filling up this office with his larger-than-life presence.

"Come on in," he called out.

She stepped inside, closing the door behind her.

He glanced up and his eyes widened. He was obviously surprised to see her. But not upset because his lips curved upward in a pleased grin.

"I didn't expect you to be up and around," he said.

"I slept, but I thought you might want to hear what happened with Rex last night." And she really believed he deserved to have her tell him things beyond the basics in the report she'd filled out.

His jaw clenched at the mention of his biological father's name. "I read the paperwork."

"But I thought you might be curious."

Mike remained behind his desk, the air around them having chilled with the topic. "I appreciate that you left out any details of what Rex really wanted at the judge's house."

She shrugged. "It wasn't pertinent to the report. He created a nuisance; the Baines declined to press charges. Dare and I agreed that was that." Cara watched Mike for signs that he was upset, but all she saw right now was his professional demeanor.

"What does Dare know?" Mike asked.

"That Rex brought up a whole host of personal family issues and that's it. He respects your privacy," Cara said softly. "Dare knows what it's like to have the past come back and bite him."

Mike nodded. "Okay. Did he say where he's staying?"

She knew Mike meant Rex. "No. Since we didn't arrest him and he left somewhat peacefully, we didn't ask." She drew a deep breath before continuing. "But he knows you have the book with the information. That's why he came to the Baines' house in the first place. I guess he thought he could see if the judge had kept any documentation of his involvement."

"Who told him I had it?"

"The judge's wife."

"Did Rex say why he wanted it?" Mike asked.

Cara bit the inside of her lip. "He said if you know what's good for your family, you'll bury the information. I told him that unlike him, you'd do the right thing even if someone gets hurt. And he said . . ." She trailed off.

"Go on." His eyes flashed fire.

"He said, 'Even Saint Simon?' Mike, he's looking to hurt him."

Mike expelled a long breath. "Yeah, I got that impression," he said through gritted teeth.

Cara's heart went out to him. "And? What's your plan?"

"I've done nothing but think about what to do. We both know the legalities. That's not what this is about. Rex came here wanting to pick up where he left off. When he wasn't accepted, he decided to do the most damage."

She nodded. "My thoughts exactly. But Simon's reputation is at stake."

"I know. If this gets out, people may not look at him the same way." He ran a shaky hand through his hair. "I hate this," he muttered.

"So . . . what will you tell the mayor?" Cara asked, which she knew was the crux of his problem.

"Some version of the truth. I just haven't decided how to phrase it to do the least amount of damage. And now I'm finished talking about this." He walked out from behind the desk and headed toward her. "Lock the door," he said, surprising her.

His voice, deep and full of longing, found an answering pull inside her. "But we're at work."

His eyes darkened. "I'm at work. You're off duty. And I don't want to be interrupted."

She locked the door to his windowless office and turned back to find him right beside her. He braced his hands on her shoulders and lowered his head until his mouth captured hers. Cara moaned and leaned into him, needing everything he had to offer because she knew he would soon be gone.

He swept his tongue over her lips and she parted them, letting him inside. Mike wasn't gentle. He plundered, devouring her with a kiss that stole her breath, buckled her knees, and had her arching her hips into his. He twisted his hand in her ponytail and tugged, shifting her head so he could deepen his possession.

She let him, wanting nothing more than to crawl into him and stay there forever, hating herself for needing him so badly and unable to do anything about it.

He broke the kiss and groaned. "I needed that," he said as he pulled her close, suddenly connecting them in a more emotional way.

Cara understood how confused he was, not knowing how much to make public about Rex and Simon. "Are you okay?"

His laugh wasn't all that dark or painful. "Yeah, I am. Yesterday I saw my place in the family for the first time, and I'm grateful," he admitted.

She smiled at the insight she'd had all along. "You're the only one who doubted it."

He separated them, keeping his hand at her waist as he gazed into her eyes. "Anyone ever tell you that you're brilliant?"

She smiled. "No but I'll take the compliment."

"You should." He walked back around to his desk, gathering papers as he spoke. "I need to leave for a little bit. I want to go talk to my parents."

"Something I said?" she asked, curious.

"Yeah. It was. But I can't explain it. Not until I verbalize it to them. I just know I have unfinished business to wrap up there. Not only discussing what has to happen next with Simon, but laying the past to rest once and for all."

"I get it," she murmured. "I really do."

"You do know that you've been instrumental in helping me get through this, and I'm grateful."

Gratitude wasn't the emotion she wanted from him, but it was all she'd get. "Well then, my work here is done. I'm going to head home and get some more sleep."

"You do that."

He eyed her with that hot, steady gaze, and she wished he could join her. "Say hi to your parents for me." *And ask when Simon plans to return*, she thought, but didn't give voice to the words.

"Will do." He winked and turned back to his desk, obviously needing to finish up a few things before he could leave.

"Oh! Before I forget, I heard from Daniella," she told him.

He glanced up. "How's she doing?"

"She sounded . . . at peace." Cara nodded, knowing that was the right description. "She has a plan and someone in her corner. She's good." She smiled at the thought.

"I know how much she means to you. I'm glad things are working out for her. Erin said her ex was assigned a stupid prick of a public defender as his lawyer. Maybe that won't work in his favor when he goes to trial."

"Or maybe he'll cut a deal and disappear for good," Cara said, wishing for just that.

"We can hope," Mike muttered. "I have late-afternoon appointments and a dinner meeting, so I'll call you later?"

Not see her.

Well, that was for the best, she knew. "Sure. I have dinner plans tomorrow night. Catch you at Joe's on Wednesday?" she asked casually.

He glanced up from the papers on his desk, hesitating as if he wanted to say something important. "Sure thing," he said instead.

Disappointed and not wanting to delve deeply into why, Cara smiled and walked out the door.

Mike had an hour to head over to his parents' and talk before his crazy afternoon began with regularly scheduled meetings. He also needed to hash out what he planned to say to the mayor. The sooner he made an appointment with her, the sooner he could wash his hands of the whole mess, Rex included.

Or should he say, Rex especially.

Since his almost-arrest, he'd gone into hiding, but Mike didn't kid himself that the man had left Serendipity. There was an egocentric part of Rex that was still looking for validation here. From Mike, Simon, or Ella—Mike couldn't be sure. If he didn't get what he came for, Mike wondered how far he'd go in retaliation.

Mike approached Simon, hoping maybe Simon, who'd once known the man best, had a clue. Simon sat behind his desk doing some paperwork in the family room. "Hey," Mike said, making his presence known.

"Hey, yourself." Simon looked up from his desk. "What brings you here midday? They not keeping you busy enough at the station?"

Mike shook his head. "For a small town, they keep me busy enough. Meetings and more meetings."

Simon laughed. "Which brings me to my point."

Mike raised an eyebrow. "You have a point?"

"I do. Sit." Simon gestured to the sofa.

Mike acted on instinct, listening to Simon and lowering himself into the seat. "Dad—"

"Me first."

Mike clenched his jaw. He wanted to have his say, but the old Simon was back and he intended to go first. "What?"

"Maybe I should have done more . . . I always realized you kept yourself apart from me, from the family. That you didn't feel like you belonged, but I didn't know what else to do—"

"Dad!" Mike jumped up from his seat. "You couldn't have done more. Hell, you probably should have done less." He paused, being more honest than he'd ever been. "But I'm glad you didn't. Even if I was a pain in the ass."

Simon grinned. "I wouldn't have wanted you any other way. You challenged me, son. Nothing wrong with that. I'm just sorry you held yourself down to that man's standards and not up to your own."

Mike dipped his head, thinking about what Simon said. "I thought everything I did wrong was about me. It was about him, wasn't it?"

Simon stared in silence. Mike knew the drill. Simon liked to let his kids figure things out for themselves. It might have taken Mike almost thirty years, but he'd finally figured out that Rex's problems had nothing to do with his own. That didn't mean Mike didn't have his own issues, however.

"Whoever you are, whatever you do, you make your choices, Michael. It's not because Rex is your biological father."

"I'm beginning to prefer the term *sperm donor,*" Mike muttered.

To his credit, Simon laughed.

"Can I ask you a question?"

The man who'd raised him and denied him nothing nodded. "Did you do the right thing with the money and marrying Mom—and fall in love later? Or—"

"No *or* about it. I loved your mom from the day I laid eyes on her. Everything I did was for her."

"At great risk to your own career and freedom," Ella said, surprising Mike by walking into the room.

"I didn't mean for you to hear that," Mike said, hoping his burning cheeks weren't bright red.

Ella sat down next to Simon. "I'm glad I did because I think this talk is long overdue. You need to know—I loved

Simon even back then. I may not have realized just how much or what kind of enduring love we'd share, but I did love him."

"And Rex?"

"Lust, Michael."

"Okay, that's enough." He turned his head, unable to look his mom in the eye.

But Ella wasn't deterred or finished. "As for Simon, maybe it started different, softer, but it was always much more real."

Watching them over the years and even now, as they held hands, united as they discussed the past, Mike couldn't help but believe.

"And yes, I was grateful Simon offered me a future. What pregnant single woman wouldn't be? But once I was with Simon, I never wished Rex had stepped up—except for your sake."

Mike nodded in understanding, as Ella smiled gently at him. "You're entitled to have questions about us. In fact, I wouldn't be surprised if your views on relationships weren't skewed by things you wondered about but didn't ask." She eyed him with those wise, brown eyes, making him squirm.

He didn't know what she meant and, given the fact that she wanted him to discuss his love life, he didn't plan to ask. But that wouldn't stop her from continuing.

"You say you don't want a serious relationship. In fact, you believe you aren't capable of one because that would mean staying in one place, correct?"

When he didn't answer right away, she rolled up a magazine and smacked his leg.

"Hey!"

"Answer me," she said, a twinkle lighting her gaze.

"Why bother? You already think you know the answer!"

Simon snickered. "Haven't you learned by now? Humor her, son."

"You're right. I've never stayed in one place or with one woman very long. I don't think I can."

"Bullshit," his very proper mother said.

Mike blinked in surprise.

"You've been in Manhattan for a long time, haven't you?" He nodded.

"That's commitment. You came here when your father needed you? Also commitment. As for women, did you ever think you just hadn't met the right woman?"

Simon patted his wife's hand. "She's got a point. I wouldn't have stepped up to marry and love just any pregnant woman."

Mike's head was spinning, not just with all the emotional shit they were throwing at him, but really, who wanted to hear about his parents' sex life? No matter how far in the past? They'd given him plenty to think about, but it was past time to change the subject.

"When your mother was with Rex, I sowed my share of wild oats. I never thought I'd settle down with one woman," Simon said.

"Okay, enough. I appreciate the truth and the talk. I do. But I need time to digest it all, okay?"

"Fair enough." Simon swept his hand through the air, cutting off any further discussion. "Any thoughts on what you're going to do with the cold case?"

The older man didn't pull any punches, with anything. It was as if being given a clean bill of health from his cancer scare had brought the old Simon back, and for that Mike was grateful.

"Yeah, I've done nothing but think about what to tell the mayor." He ran a hand through his hair and met his father's gaze. "Listen, legally you should be fine. The statute of limitations on any past crime has run out. Nobody's going to prosecute, so a full reveal wouldn't jeopardize your freedom."

Simon's reputation? That was another story and explained why Mike was sick to his stomach over his alternatives. Because telling the truth was the only out that Mike could see that would put this whole damn thing behind the family once and for all.

"Before you say anything else, I need you to know something," Simon said.

Mike swallowed hard. "Go on."

"I'd never ask you to bury the truth to protect me. From the time I made the choice to replace the money, I knew there was a chance of being found out. I've lived with the knowledge that I did something I wasn't proud of. More than losing my job, I dreaded you kids finding out."

Mike shook his head, not wanting his father to feel bad. "Want to know one more thing? Honestly?"

Simon nodded. "Always."

"It's good to know you're not perfect after all."

His father burst out laughing, as did Ella.

"Oh, son. If I ever made you feel like I was—"

"You didn't. That was all me, living in Rex's shadow and comparing myself to you, Erin, and Sam." It felt damn good admitting that out loud, and it helped shed some of the weight he'd carried around with him for most of his life.

"Michael . . ." Ella's voice trailed off.

"It's okay. I'm fine. We're fine," he said to his mother.

Simon cleared his throat. "One last thing. Don't you worry about telling the mayor what you need to. I can handle it."

Mike already knew that now. Not that he liked what he had to do worth a damn. "What about your job? She might ask you not to come back."

The thought of Simon, the town's beloved police chief, stepping down for good, in possible disgrace, turned Mike's stomach. "Maybe she'd let you walk away without stating why." Mike would lean hard on the woman to give Simon at least that much dignity.

"Funny you should mention his job," Ella said. "Your father and I have been talking, and with his illness and everything, we realize that life's short and fragile." Her eyes glistened with unshed tears.

"That it is," Mike said, having confronted his father's mortality this year.

"We want to spend more time together," Simon said. "Make the most of these years."

"I've always wanted to travel," his mother said.

Mike wasn't following. "Wait. What are you saying?"

"I'm thinking of retiring anyway," Simon said, the bombshell detonating in Mike's brain.

"I did not see this coming," he muttered, more to himself than to them.

"Be happy for us, though." His mother smiled, and Mike couldn't do anything less.

He inclined his head. "Whatever you decide, of course I support you."

"Good. Then you won't mind my recommending that you be given the job beyond the temporary position? You've already made changes that have improved the department. Everyone's pleased with you—"

Mike's breath caught in his throat. "How would you know?" he asked, unable to broach the *other* subject—of him permanently taking on the job.

"I have visitors. I get phone calls. I'm damned proud of the work you're doing, son. You're bringing Serendipity into this century and though I might've fought it in here"—he tapped his heart—"I applaud it here." His finger went to his head. "I like the old ways, but I'm smart enough to know things need to progress."

"And there are plenty of people who could handle the force and continue to modernize." Suddenly unable to breathe, Mike rose from his seat.

"But the men and women already respect you," Simon said. "Just think about it."

He was thinking.

Take the chief of police job permanently?

Settle in Serendipity?

For all his thoughts about enjoying things here, until now, Mike had always had his safety net. Simon would return and life would go back to normal. Okay, so things here had begun to feel almost normal, he silently admitted . . . but how long until the feeling of being strangled returned? Until he grew antsy? Bored? Resentful? Given the way he was itching inside himself, with just the mention of him taking over for good, Mike figured not long.

"And think of how happy Cara would be if you stayed," his mother added.

Cara. At the thought of her, Mike's chest constricted painfully. How long before he broke her heart? "I have meetings," he choked out.

Ella rose, concern in her gaze as she reached for him. "Michael, please relax and just think things through. You're reacting on instinct, not reality."

Oh, shit. Mike wasn't ready for this. His mother was right. He needed to think.

Hell, who was he kidding? He needed to *breathe*.

Sixteen

Since his father's announcement, Mike was off kilter and completely thrown. In another life, he'd have had one foot out of town, but he had enough sense of responsibility to know he had things to wrap up here. And he had a woman he cared deeply for—maybe even loved—who deserved more than for him to pack up and leave without telling her.

It was Wednesday and Joe's Bar hadn't yet started hopping when Mike and Sam met up for chicken wings. Off duty, Sam decided to call friends to join them later on, and Alexa, Erin, Dare, and Liza and whoever else in Sam's crowd decided to show. Mike already knew Cara would be there, since she'd mentioned it when he'd seen her on Monday. He hadn't spoken to her since.

He hadn't picked up the phone.

Instead he'd spent the last two days alone with his thoughts and the occasional shot of whiskey for good measure. Not that he'd gotten far in his thinking, hence this sit-down with Sam.

Mike and his brother talked about family stuff for a while

before Sam studied Mike through narrowed eyes. "What gives?" he asked at last. "You look like you're jumping out of your skin."

Mike rolled his shoulders, but it did little to alleviate the stress.

"Last week you were mellow. Less antsy. What changed?"

Mike leaned in closer. "Dad's thinking of retiring. He wants to recommend that I replace him permanently."

Sam's eyes opened wide. "No shit?"

Mike gestured to Joe for a shot of whiskey. He wasn't on duty and he didn't want to think. "Wish I were kidding, little brother."

"What's Cara say about this?"

Mike narrowed his gaze. "She doesn't know."

Joe placed his drink on the counter and strode away, giving them privacy once more.

"Don't you think she'd want to know?" Sam asked. He tipped his beer bottle to his lips.

"Do not open your mouth," Mike warned his sibling. "You're the one always saying that you don't want her hurt. So let me handle this in my own way."

"Explain."

Mike rubbed the cold glass between his palms. "Every time I think about staying for good, my insides twist into painful knots. It's not something I ever considered. She knows it. Once I tell her all this . . . things will blow up fast. I need to find the right time and place."

Sam's expression showed his disappointment. "And here I thought that you'd been looking pretty settled and happy these last weeks."

So had he. "As soon as Dad asked me to stay, it was like a noose wrapped around my neck."

"Don't you think maybe it's time to grow up?" Sam asked.

"Go to hell," Mike muttered, grinding his teeth at his

brother's inability to understand. "Look at my history. I move through life quickly, no time to think too hard or focus too much because any time I did, it felt like I was suffocating."

"Didn't look like it last week," Sam muttered. "Or the week before that."

His parents had said something similar, but neither of them could possibly comprehend the choking feeling he experienced at the very thought of a commitment like that.

Mike shifted in frustration and decided to dig into his past for examples. "When I was here before, starting out and then again in Atlantic City, walking the beat made me crazy. I couldn't do what you do every day without going insane. When my superior got me the shot to do undercover in Manhattan, he did it because he knew I needed the excitement. The adrenaline rush."

Sam expelled a long breath. "Okay, so you aren't getting that rush in meetings. But do you still need it? Really? Or do you get it from other things in your life? Other *people*?" Sam leaned in closer. "One woman in particular?"

"I. Don't. Know." And that was the crux of the problem. Mike expected to need the variety and the constant thrill. Expected it, but as he thought about his brother's question, Mike could admit that lately, no, he hadn't missed the adrenaline rush.

"What about women?" Sam asked. "Since Tiffany, you've kept them all at a distance, right?"

"Yeah. No promises, no desire to make any. It worked for me." He drew a deep breath. "Then Dad got sick and asked me to come home."

"And you came back to Cara," his brother said, looking at him with that all-knowing gaze he'd perfected as an interrogator.

Cara did it well too. Mike saw detective in their futures and felt a sudden pang of disappointment that he wouldn't be the one to promote them.

"Cara's . . . different," Mike admitted. "Every time I'm with her, she unsettles me."

"And it's a beautiful thing to see," Sam said with a shake of his head and loud laughter.

Unsettled was an understatement, Mike thought, remembering how Cara had shaken up his well-ordered life. She still did. Each time he made love to her—and he'd long since stopped trying to convince himself it was just sex—was a huge damned emotional reveal.

But Mike wasn't going there in detail with Sam. Bad enough he sat here unloading his feelings like some damned girl. Because it was like Cara had unraveled him, piece by piece, leaving him at his most vulnerable, raw and exposed.

A place he'd never been. A feeling he'd never expected to have in this lifetime. And one, combined with the pressure in his career, that had him wanting to run.

"Don't you get it?" Mike asked his brother. "If I say I'll stay and I can't back it up with action, it'll destroy her."

Sam let out a low whistle. "I'll be damned," he muttered, speaking low. "You love her."

Mike met his brother's gaze and didn't answer. He couldn't. It was one thing for Mike to think it, another for Sam to say it out loud, he thought, his brother adding to the panic his father had recently instilled.

"She know?" Sam asked, interrupting his thoughts.

"Hell, I barely know how I feel," he gritted out, wondering how much more he could have thrown at him in a short time.

Mike looked down and realized he was flexing and unflexing his hand into a tight fist. The one thing Mike did know was that he'd always been up front with her. If he left, at least he'd know he'd never led her on.

"You two look awfully tense," Erin said, suddenly beside them. She wrapped an arm around each brother's shoulder. "Need me to referee?"

Mike forced himself to exhale and release the tension he

was holding—or at least attempt to. It was hard enough to talk to Sam. He wasn't ready to get into it again with his sister.

"We're just catching up. Nothing serious. We're finished now."

"Sure, I miss all the good stuff," she said, sounding like she did when they were younger.

Mike managed a laugh. He reached into his pocket for cash, tossed money on the bar for his tab, and rose to his feet. "I have to go take care of a few things," he told his siblings.

He needed to leave here before Cara showed up. She was too in tune to him and would read things in his expression he wasn't ready for her to see.

Sam eyed him with concern. "Don't go off half-cocked and do something stupid."

Mike shook his head. "I'm just going to wrap up a few things," he assured him.

Sam muttered a curse but let him go.

Mike climbed into his truck and headed to a Holiday Inn just over the border in a neighboring town. He'd put out some feelers and discovered Rex was staying there.

For the life of him, Mike didn't know why the man was hanging around and decided he needed a nudge to point him in the direction he needed to go. Nervous but refusing to let it show, Mike walked up the stairs to the third floor, needing to cloak himself in his righteous anger before facing the man.

He knocked twice and waited.

Finally, the door swung open and Mike found himself facing Rex. "Got a minute?" Mike asked by way of hello.

"Come on in." Rex waved a hand.

Mike passed by and walked into the room. Rex, he noticed, was living out of a suitcase, his clothes strewn all over. The one thing that was in order was the makeshift bar the older man had set up on the counter.

"Whiskey?" Rex asked.

"Why not," Mike said.

Rex poured them both a glass and handed one to Mike. "To us. Father and son." Rex raised his drink.

Disgust rose in Mike's throat. "What world do you live in? There is no us. No father and son. And let's be honest, you don't want that anyway." Mike paced the small hotel room, feeling claustrophobic being enclosed with Rex. "You didn't want a son when you had the chance. You didn't want me in the almost thirty years that passed since."

Rex watched and listened in silence.

And when Rex remained quiet, Mike continued. "What I couldn't figure out, at least at first, was what you wanted. I mean, yeah, you contacted Ella on Facebook, but that was just a rush, right? To see if you could still get her to jump at your charm?"

Rex folded his arms across his chest. "Go on. I'm really enjoying your attempt at analyzing your old man," he said with a smirk on his face and a sneer in his tone.

"Then I showed up. That must've played into your hand, getting your son to come looking for you, at least until you realized I was digging into the past."

Rex shook his head. "What makes you think I had any kind of agenda?"

"Simple. You're a narcissist, Rex. It's all about you. Ella responded to you, I came to you, and you showed up back in Serendipity—not because Simon had cancer, but because you expected to be welcomed with open arms. And when you weren't? Instead of leaving like a man, you set out to cause as much trouble for Simon as you could."

"He deserved it. He drove me out of my own hometown—"

"Bailed you out, you stupid bastard," Mike reminded him. "And he took a risk doing it. Hell, he married your woman, he raised your son—he took on all of the burden and responsibility you couldn't face. And how do you repay him after all this time? You threaten to expose him and ruin his reputation in *his* hometown."

Rex's once-amiable expression changed to a nasty, evil frown. "He turned you against me."

As Mike had thought, it was all about Rex. "You did that all on your own. I'm here to make you a deal, just like Simon did all those years ago. Leave town and don't come back."

Rex took a step forward. "Or what?"

Mike had this covered. "Or you'll find that no place and nobody in town wants anything to do with you. There will be no business that'll welcome you, no old friends that will be happy to see you. You're a man who needs the world to love him, people to dance to his tune, a three-ring circus to surround him with attention. You won't find it here."

"You son of a bitch," Rex said, his eyes darkening with anger.

"It takes one to know one," Mike said, placing his still-full glass on the desk with a loud thunk.

As he walked out, he realized he felt nothing for the man glaring at him from across the room except pity and contempt.

Off duty and alone, Cara was surprised to find herself standing outside her mother's apartment. She'd sat across the way, watching the entrance, waiting for her father to leave. There was an off-track betting site located farther downtown, and Cara knew the old man liked to hang out there. Along with his other out-of-work friends, he could be counted on to spend a good couple of hours there. Cara banked on it as she sneaked into the side entrance of the apartment building and walked up the stairs to see her mother.

A long time had passed since Cara felt the need for her mother. She was surprised she felt it now. But Cara hadn't seen or heard from Mike since work on Monday. He hadn't called her. He hadn't stopped by. And he hadn't been in to the station, at least not when she'd been there. She felt his absence in the deepest places inside her, and it hurt.

Along with the emptiness came the desire to talk to her mom. To feel her arms around her and get her advice—no matter how Cara felt about Natalie Hartley's choices, she was her mother. And Cara needed her more than ever.

Cara wasn't disappointed. Her mother greeted her with a surprised cry and open arms.

"I waited until Dad left. Nobody saw me come in," Cara said.

Her mother nodded. "He should be gone for a while."

"Good."

"Come sit." Her mother grasped Cara's hand and led her to the same sofa that had been here when Cara was a child, a blue velvet, with faded marks and worn patches.

Much like Natalie, who had once been a beautiful woman, with dark hair like Cara's, and blue eyes, vibrant and full of life, until her husband had beaten her down.

And there was nothing Cara could have done to prevent it. "I'm sorry," Cara whispered. "For not visiting, for cutting you out of my life."

Her mother nodded through tears. "Don't be silly. You have every right to be disappointed in me."

"Not disappointed, exactly. I just wanted you to leave him."

"Oh, honey." Her mother smoothed her hand down Cara's hair, just as she used to do when Cara was a child. "I can't go anywhere. I chose my life. He'd just find me and make things more difficult after. I'm used to how things are. And it's not that bad most of the time."

Cara couldn't meet her mother's gaze and pretend her words were okay. Life was supposed to be so much more than *not that bad most of the time*, she thought, as her tears leaked down her cheeks.

Her mother handed her a tissue from a box on the side table, and they both wiped their eyes.

"Don't cry for me," her mother said. "Just don't make the same mistakes."

Cara opened her mouth to speak, but her mom shook her head. "No. I need to say this. My mistake was in not trusting my gut from the beginning. For going back each time your father promised to never yell or hit me again."

This was the first time Natalie had ever spoken about her life, and Cara listened, wide-eyed and stunned, as her mother admitted things they'd only hidden or pretended didn't exist before.

Her mother sighed. "I wanted so badly to believe him that I closed my eyes to the truth because it would have been so much harder to leave and start over, alone with a child." Her mother's shoulders shook, her eyes damp, but she held Cara's gaze.

"Mom—"

"No, honey. Keep listening. If this is the only chance I get to tell you this, you need to hear me. When you meet a man, don't listen to what he says. Judge him by his actions, past and present. People can change, but they have to prove it to you. Words are just that." Her mother leaned in and kissed Cara's cheek.

"Oh, Mom. There is a man," Cara said through her tears. She told her mother all about Mike, from their one-night stand to the agreed-upon affair with *No hearts involved*. "I knew the score going in, and I tried so hard not to fall in love." But she had, and now she felt his absence even though he was still in Serendipity.

Her mother listened, nodded, and finally held out her arms so Cara could get the much-needed hug and support she'd come for. She wasn't overreacting, either. She could handle his not calling without working herself into a snit, even if he'd promised, knowing he was busy with his life and his job. But he hadn't shown up at Joe's on Wednesday night as they'd agreed, nor had he reached out. At all. Cara didn't appreciate taking the brunt of whatever was bothering him, nor would she let him push her away without an explanation. She had more self-esteem than that, she thought, glancing at her mother, who was the polar opposite. Still, if Cara felt his absence this much now, she couldn't imagine the pain she'd feel when he was finally gone.

Too soon, their time together ended. Cara sensed her mother getting antsy and worried, glancing at the clock, worried her husband would return and find them together.

"I'll go before . . ." Cara didn't want to cause her mother any trouble.

"I love you," her mother said. "And when you're ready to see me again, I'm here. And if not, I understand that too."

So accepting, Cara thought, sadly. Even of the way Cara had decided that she wouldn't enable her mother's dysfunction. What a crock, she realized now. She hadn't abandoned Daniella or the shelter women, had she? Just her own mother, because deep down, Cara was too afraid of turning into her.

No more, Cara thought. Her mother needed her as much as Cara needed her mom. "I'll stay in touch," she promised. "I love you, Mom."

"I love you too." Her mother's eyes were brighter as they said their good-byes.

Cara sneaked back out of the building, relieved to have her mother back in her life. Ironic, that the return of one relationship came as she lost another. And Cara didn't kid herself that Mike was slipping away.

This weekend was Annie and Joe's wedding. Somehow Cara would get through that day surrounded by family and friends. Then she'd call Mike out on his behavior. It was one thing to have a casual affair, another to withdraw completely at his own whim, she thought, her mother's advice fresh in her mind.

Judge a man by his actions.

And Mike's withdrawal, coupled with Simon's remission

and the fact that he'd obviously be returning to work, told Cara everything she needed to know.

Mike's time in Serendipity—and with her—was over.

A Saturday morning meeting with the mayor and then Mike was off to Joe and Annie's wedding. Thank God this past week was almost over. Two more hurdles to get through and then he was gone.

Mike's chest hurt, and he didn't know if it was from the stress of his unresolved family issues, the decision his father was still pressuring him to make, or the fact that he'd basically driven Cara away.

After going silent for four days, he'd texted her Thursday night—*Busy with work. Pick you up at 11 AM for wedding*—since they'd agreed to go together. He got a curt answer back. *Don't bother. I've made other arrangements.* He'd winced even though he deserved it.

Then, last night, while lifting weights at the Y, he'd made the decision to head home after the weekend. He'd called his father and put Simon off, telling him that he couldn't make the decision about the job immediately. He just wasn't ready. Simon pretended to understand, but Mike knew from his subdued tone that he really didn't.

Which was why he needed space from everything and everyone. Once he returned to New York, he'd breathe deep, stand back, and see what it was he really wanted out of life. He couldn't figure that out with pressure at every turn. And though Cara hadn't pressured him—hell, if he didn't call her, she certainly hadn't called him—he felt the weight of responsibility sitting on his chest.

He cared for her more than he'd ever cared for any woman before. He couldn't imagine his life without her bright smile and smart mouth, but he couldn't come to her free and clear of baggage and fear. And she deserved more than that. She deserved a full commitment and Mike couldn't manage one. The only thing he could say in his defense was that he'd never led her on or promised her anything more than what they shared.

So why did he feel lower than pond scum now?

Because he'd hurt her and he'd rather shoot himself with his own gun than cause her pain.

And after the wedding, Mike knew he'd be doing just that.

Joe and Annie's wedding ceremony brought tears to Cara's eyes. She sat in an aisle seat, Alexa on her left, giving Cara a prime view of the beautiful bride as she walked by in a spectacular ivory-colored, body-fitting dress. The color had been chosen in respect for the fact that this was her second marriage, and yet Annie's first husband, Nash, sat with his new wife, Kelly, in the third row. Annie and Kelly had a unique friendship, but both women agreed that making Kelly a bridesmaid would have been a touch awkward. In true Annie form, her blond ringlets hadn't been tamed— because as she'd told Cara at the coffee shop, Joe loved her wild hair. Her eyes sparkled with happiness, as did the groom's; he waited impatiently in a dark suit and tie at the end of the aisle.

Everything about the wedding, from Annie's father walking her down the aisle to the man of her dreams waiting for her at the other end, hit Cara with an emotional pang, reminding her of all she'd never have. Not with Mike, who'd spoiled her for any other man, of that she was certain.

When the couple promised to love and cherish each other, in sickness and in health, in good times and bad, in joy and in sorrow, for as long as they both shall live, Cara nearly fell apart. Only Alexa's strong kick to Cara's ankle, which gave her something else to focus on, prevented her from hiccupping and bawling out loud.

"Ouch!" Cara hissed.

Alexa smiled. "That's what friends are for," she whispered back.

Mike sat two rows behind her, Sam and Erin on either side. She'd caught a glimpse of them as she walked in, forced a smile at her friends, and done her best not to meet Mike's gaze. They'd talk later, she was sure, but all her concentration had been on getting through the ceremony. Whatever he had to say didn't matter. She was finished with the kind of relationship he was willing to give.

She loved him. She knew it. Had known it for a while, even if she'd never allowed the word to surface in her brain. But between the visit to her mother and Annie getting a second chance at real happiness, Cara realized that as much as she loved Mike, she had been settling for whatever crumbs he'd been willing to give. Granted, until the last week they'd been spectacular crumbs, but mere morsels nonetheless.

Too soon, the ceremony ended and the crowd dispersed to . . . where else? Joe's. Despite her mood, Cara couldn't help but enjoy the celebration, which consisted of toasts, some roasting of the groom by his best friends, and a lot of dancing. Through it all, Cara felt the heat of Mike's gaze on her skin. The red dress she'd bought under duress seemed to impress him, if the sizzling look in his eyes was any indication. But he didn't approach her to dance, and talking would have been impossible anyway. The music was too loud, the people too packed and crushed together.

The bride and groom fed each other cake, Joe seductively pulled off the garter, and soon the single women were gathered for the bouquet toss. If asked, Cara couldn't say how it had happened, but somehow, Annie tossed the flowers and Tess, who hadn't yet turned sixteen, ended up in possession of the bouquet.

Ethan, Nash, and Dare looked ready to throttle their bratty sister, but Annie, being Annie, couldn't stop her good-natured laugh, which calmed the brothers down.

The men gathered next for the garter throw, but Cara couldn't bring herself to watch. Instead, she tapped Alexa on the shoulder and asked her friend to say good-bye to the couple for her. She'd had enough happiness shoved at her for the day, and her feet ached like crazy. She'd long since pulled off her high heels, and she held the stilettos in her hand as she made her way to the door. She'd put them on at the exit before she had to head outside.

Reaching the door, she leaned against the wall and was in the process of shoving her hurting feet back into their torture chambers when she felt a hand touch her shoulder.

"Can we talk?" Mike asked.

She turned and looked into his somber brown eyes, and her stomach plummeted toward the floor. She might have been preparing herself to end things with him herself, but his bleak expression told her not to bother. He'd have been doing it anyway.

That quickly, whatever hope lingered from the bubble of happiness she'd let herself live in finally popped, leaving her with the painful reality that was her life. And reality, Cara thought, really sucked.

Cara followed Mike to his apartment, promising herself their talk would be quick and she'd be on her way back to her apartment in no time. Alone.

"Let's sit," Mike said, gesturing toward the couch.

Cara lowered herself onto the sofa. Her new position gave her a perfect view of the bedroom corner of the apartment, where a suitcase sat open on the bed.

Her stomach cramped but she said nothing. He'd asked to talk, and she'd let him begin. She'd focus on getting through this without falling apart.

He settled in beside her, careful not to touch her. The cool distance between them was reminiscent of the early days when he'd come back to Serendipity, and her heart hurt at the distance between them. For all they'd had and suddenly lost.

She couldn't help it. She had to ask. "What happened?" Last time she'd seen him, he'd kissed her in his office, told her he needed her after everything that had gone on within his family. Next thing she knew . . . dead silence.

"Simon's retiring," Mike said.

Of everything, she hadn't expected that.

"And he asked me to take the job. For good."

She blinked. "That must have thrown you. When did he tell you this?"

He looked away, unable to meet her gaze. "Saturday afternoon."

With his answer, a yawning, cavernous pit opened inside her. "And that's why I haven't heard from you."

He had the good grace to at least look embarrassed.

Cara sighed. "I take it you turned him down?"

"I told him I'd think about it." He shrugged out of his suit jacket and laid it over a chair, then undid his tie so it hung loose around his neck. His top button followed, leaving him with an extremely sexy, rumpled look that tugged at her heart.

Hardening herself toward him was hard, but she couldn't afford to feel bad because he looked so torn. "Why didn't you just tell him the truth? That you don't want to stay here? You never wanted to be here in the first place."

"Because I don't know if that's true!" He spun away and walked to the window.

She'd never seen Mike look so torn, so unsure. Unable to help herself, she rose and joined him, placing a hand on his shoulder. "You told me yourself, you were here while Simon needed you. He's in remission. He's retiring. You can go back to the life you love and leave this small town and all of us behind. Like before."

Cara was proud that her voice didn't crack.

"I didn't count on you," he said quietly.

"What?"

He placed a hand on hers and turned. "You heard me. I didn't count on you. And when I tell you I'm not sure what

I want to do, I mean it. I can't imagine my life without you in it."

His hands slipped to her waist, burning her with his touch. "Yes, you can," Cara told him. "Or that suitcase wouldn't be packed." She stepped out of reach, knowing she was close to shattering.

"I just need time," he said, his voice pleading with her to understand.

"You've been nothing but honest with me, so let's not start sugarcoating things now. Actions speak louder than words, but together? They send a potent message." Her shoulders shook, but she continued. "You're leaving just like you always said you would. This was short term and I knew it. Shame on me for falling harder and hoping for more." She turned away, unable to believe she'd admitted her feelings. "Take care," she said, almost running for the door.

"Cara, wait."

She paused without turning to face him.

"I'm suffocating. I just need time and space to sort things out."

She shook her head. "If you needed time, I'd have given it to you. All you had to do was ask. Instead you did what you always do—you packed up and you ran."

She wasn't just referring to his going back to New York, but to his disappearing act this past week. He wasn't dumb enough not to know what she meant.

"Bye, Mike." It took everything she had, but Cara walked out the door without looking back.

Seventeen

Cara's doorbell rang. And rang. And rang. Then the pounding started. She'd taken the week off from work to pull herself together . . . and yes, maybe wallow a little. She had the sick time owed to her and figured she deserved to indulge herself, so here it was Thursday, and someone was banging on her door. At eight in the morning.

She grabbed her fuzzy robe, pulled it on over the tank top she slept in, and stormed to her front door. She whipped it open, prepared to give whoever was there a piece of her mind.

She found Sam, who had been calling her twice daily to make sure she was okay. "Can't a girl take time off without you checking on me constantly?" she snapped at him, leaving her door open for him to follow her inside.

"You're not sick, you're depressed, and though you have good reason to be, it's enough. He may be my brother, but he's an ass. He doesn't deserve you, and he sure as hell doesn't deserve for you to be sitting around sulking over him, so let's go. Shower and get dressed. We're going shopping."

Cara wrinkled her nose. Neither one of them loved hitting a mall. "For what?"

"It's my mother's birthday this weekend and I need to buy her a present."

"Fine. For Ella, I'll pull myself together. Besides, I want to buy Daniella a little motivational gift. She's signed up for paralegal courses online, and she's interviewing with some firms who are willing to wait until she can work. Belinda's got some great contacts," Cara said of Havensbridge's founder.

Sam smiled. "That's great. One less person to worry about," he said. "Has her ex gotten a court date yet?"

Cara shrugged. "I'm not sure. Daniella said he's been quiet, but sometimes she gets that eerie feeling she's being followed. I reminded her not to go out alone, and she said she knows."

"That's all you can do. Now go. Get ready." He prodded her on the back.

Cara headed for the stairs. Pausing, she turned to her partner. "Thanks, Sam."

"That's what friends are for. Hey, have I told you that you look like hell?"

She frowned at him. "Gee, thanks."

"Just calling it like I see it." He tipped his head toward the stairs.

"I'm going." But she paused. "Sam, have you . . ." She trailed off, wanting to ask how his brother was doing.

Had Sam spoken to him? Was he suffering like she was? Or had he gone back to his lifestyle, and women like Lauren, as if the interlude in Serendipity and with Cara had never happened?

"I haven't spoken to him," Sam said, reading her mind. Because that was what a good partner did. And really, what else would Cara possibly want to know? "He's not answering when I call. I'm sorry."

Cara nodded, the lump in her throat that she'd been fighting all week returning as big as ever.

"He spoke to the mayor before he left town," Sam said, surprising her. "He laid out everything about the cold case and the money in the evidence room."

Cara stared, stunned. She'd been so wrapped up in her personal drama, she'd completely forgotten about the case. "What did she say?"

"According to my father, because I didn't hear it from Mike, the mayor uttered a few choice words that her voters wouldn't be too happy to hear. Especially when she found out the extent of the people involved."

"Is Simon in trouble?" Cara asked.

"I've gotta hand it to my brother. He managed to make it a burden for the mayor if she went public with the information."

"How?"

"By reminding her that many of those who were mentioned in that black book, who'd visited the Winkler place, and who had been involved in the cover-up, were also her biggest campaign supporters," Sam said with a grin.

Cara pulled her robe tighter, unable to hold back a smile of her own. "Brilliant."

Sam nodded. "Added to that, the Winkler place had been shut down for years, so there was no point in bringing that up again. Everyone who was once involved appeared to be clean now, and the only person still in public office was retiring." Sam spread his hands wide. "So really, what good would it do to air the dirty laundry except to tarnish her loyal supporters?"

Cara leaned on the banister. "Case closed, huh?"

"Appears that way."

"What about Rex?" Cara hadn't seen him or heard about him since his near arrest. "Did he go back to Vegas?"

"He checked out of the hotel he was staying in after Mike

made sure he knew his presence wouldn't be tolerated anywhere in Serendipity."

Cara exhaled slowly, surprised Mike had a one-on-one
confrontation with his father. "At least he had closure," she
said, knowing how much Mike needed that to move forward
in his life.

"Do you want some advice?" Sam asked.

Cara shrugged, knowing she couldn't stop him. "Go
for it."

Sam met her gaze, his expression sincere and full of
compassion. "Stop caring about him."

Cara shook her head and laughed. "Do you think I
haven't tried?" she asked, storming up the stairs so she could
shower. And then do her least favorite thing in the world:
shopping.

Could her life get any more exciting than this?

The walls were closing in and this damned apartment
didn't feel a thing like home. Mike's small place over Joe's
was more welcoming, and that was because he had more
waiting for him when he walked outside than he had in New
York City. A week had gone by and he hadn't put out feelers
at his old station or with the feds because he wasn't ready
to think about remaining in Manhattan.

But just a short week ago, he hadn't been able to think
about settling in Serendipity either. So he'd turned to his
same M.O. and done what he did best.

He ran away.

Mike hadn't been able to look himself in the mirror since.
He hadn't answered his brother's or sister's calls. He'd come
back here for breathing space and thinking time, but it hadn't
taken long for him to wonder why the hell he had thought
he needed either one.

Everything he wanted had been staring him in the face
in Serendipity. A woman who understood him, accepted

him, completed him in a way he'd never believed possible. He missed Cara, her smile, her laugh, and most of all, he missed the way she called out his full name when he was deep inside her. Hell, he even missed the dingy office at the station and how he could hear Cara's laugh when his door was left open. But every time he thought about going back, he remembered her face when she realized his suitcase was open and half-packed in his apartment.

Destroyed.

That was the only word he could think of. He'd destroyed—not her, Cara was too strong to let him defeat her—but he'd trashed whatever faith she'd had in him. And though he'd given her no reason and even discouraged it, she'd believed in him enough to invest her heart.

What had he done? He'd thrown that gift away.

His cell rang, and he glanced down. For the first time all week, he answered a call from home. "Hey, Sam."

"I'm on my way up the stairs to your apartment. Open the damned door and let me in. We need to talk."

Mike heard his brother's voice in the hall and opened his door as Sam finished his sentence. "Come on in," Mike muttered.

Sam walked inside and looked Mike over. "Thank God you look like shit too."

Mike drew his shoulders back, Sam's words hitting him hard. "Cara's in bad shape?"

"What do you think, asshole?"

His heart hurt at that, and he expelled a long breath. "I deserved that."

"You're lucky I don't haul off and hit you." Sam headed to his brother's fridge and pulled out a soda. "Are you that damned selfish that you couldn't see what you had? Or are you that stupid that you really don't want her?"

Mike sat on the couch and leaned his head back, staring at the ceiling. "I fucked up. I'm not going to go into all the crap in my past, or why I did it. Suffice it to say that everything was coming at me at once, and when I left, I thought I needed time and space to think."

Sam flung himself into the nearest chair. "And now that you've had it?"

He shook his head, disgusted. "I know how badly I screwed up. Everything I want is what I left behind."

"Then why are we sitting here?" Sam patted the arm of the chair.

He leaned forward and met his brother's gaze. "Because Cara made it clear that with my actions, she can trust me to keep my word, at least when it comes to leaving."

"So you've got some work to do. Since when are you afraid of hard work?"

He was afraid of many things, but work wasn't one of them. "Never. But I've done nothing but prove to her that I don't want commitment. Why the hell would she believe I feel differently now?" He studied his younger brother's serious expression, wondering what words of wisdom Sam could possibly offer.

"Are you coming back?" Sam asked, point-blank.

Mike swallowed hard. "Yeah."

"For good?"

He nodded. "I'm going to get my girl."

"That's what I was afraid of."

Mike stiffened. "What the hell does that mean?"

"It means, what happens if you can't convince Cara to take you back? What if she's too battle-scarred from her mother staying in a relationship that hurts her?"

His gut cramped at the too-real possibility.

Sam leaned in close. "If Cara doesn't come around, are you still taking the job as chief? Will you stay?"

Mike already knew his choices. Remain in Serendipity without Cara beside him, or return to this lonely apartment in a city he couldn't care less about and a job he hadn't checked in on once.

Easy answer.

His family was in Serendipity. The people he loved, even if he didn't always show it.

As his mother had already pointed out to him, Mike had spent the last half dozen or more years in one place. He knew how to stick, he just hadn't wanted to believe it. Panic had been second nature to him. Something expected. Comforting, even. He refused to take the coward's way out by blaming his parentage or Rex. Mike had dug into his own way of thinking and screwed up all on his own.

"I'm staying," Mike muttered. Though losing Cara would kill him, it wouldn't change his plans.

Sam grinned, slapping his hands on his thighs. "All right then."

The relief on his brother's face would have been comical if this weren't Mike's life.

"So here's what you're going to do," Sam said. "Go big or go home. Show the lady you mean business. What happens next may be up to her, but at least you'll know you did everything possible to win her back."

"Thanks," Mike said, looking at his brother in a new light.

With that, Sam leaned back and finished his soda, while Mike gave thought to his brother's advice. Sam was right. He'd have to put it all on the line to win Cara back—and he had to do it knowing there was still a chance he'd end up alone in the end.

He shivered, the chill taking him off guard. He couldn't let that happen. No matter what, he had to convince her that he loved her and wanted her beside him for the rest of their lives. There was no other acceptable alternative.

"Hey, Mike?" Sam asked.

"Yeah?"

"You ready to go home?"

*   *   *

Saturday night at Joe's—minus the owner and his new
bride, who were on their honeymoon. Cara was here under
duress from her friends, her good mood forced. But even
she knew it was time to get back to living, and tonight was
as good a time as any to start. She'd just concentrate on her
friends and pretend she was having a good time. Eventually,
she'd feel the corresponding emotions. She wouldn't feel so
numb.

"I feel like dancing," Alexa said.

Cara nodded, wanting to get moving and maybe stop
thinking so much.

"Liza?" Alexa asked, since she'd also joined them.

Liza smiled, rocking her hips in time to the beat. "Why
not? I could use some letting go."

Katy Perry's music set the tempo, and Cara let go in a
way she hadn't done in way too long. The crowd seemed to
grow, the buzzing in the room grew stronger, and soon the
floor was full.

As the steady beat pulsed through her veins, she closed
her eyes and enjoyed the flow of the music and the camara-
derie of good friends.

As she refocused on the room, she realized that they had
company. Liza had paired up with her husband, Dare, and
to Cara's surprise, both Erin and Alexa were doing some
seductive dancing of their own with two good-looking guys
Cara had never seen before.

For Alexa, a woman who preferred work to even her friends'
company, this was an unusual state of affairs. Cara was curious
and knew she'd be grilling her friend later. As for Erin, Sam
was eyeing his sister's moves with a scowl on his face.

When strong arms slid around Cara's waist, she jolted in
surprise, assuming it was one of her fellow cop friends joining her. Willing to have a partner on the dance floor, she

leaned back into the strong masculine body, allowing him to lead from behind.

Hands on her hips, he pulled her tight against him, until the swell of his erection pressed into her behind.

That was going too far and Cara broke his hold.

"What are you doing?" she asked, spinning around and coming face-to-face with familiar brown eyes. "Mike!?" Her knees went weak and her breath caught.

"Hey, baby."

Everything inside her warmed at the endearment, and what a kick in the ass that was, considering how hard she'd fought against his using it.

She folded her arms across her chest in the most defensive gesture she could think of. Anything to help keep her distance. "What are you doing here?"

After the longest, most painful week of her life, his sudden reappearance was a shock, to say the least. Her heart beat rapidly in her chest, fear warring with panic at seeing him again.

"I'm back." His searing gaze never left hers.

She didn't know if he meant for a visit or what, but she refused to let herself care. "Good for you. And you thought you could wrap your arms around me and pick up where we left off?" she asked, her voice rising.

Alexa tapped her on the shoulder. "Are you okay?" her friend asked.

"Yeah." She set her jaw. Well, she would be once she got herself away from him.

"Can we go somewhere and talk?" Mike asked.

She looked at him in shock. "Seriously?"

After the way he'd sidled up to her on the dance floor, she doubted he had talking in mind. "Let's get something straight. I don't know why you're here or for how long, and I don't care. But I will not be your booty call every time you come back to town."

"That's not what I meant. Just give me a chance to explain," he said, reaching for her.

"No." She shoved at his shoulder and stepped out of reach.

The pain in his eyes reached into her soul, and it took all her restraint not to let him back in.

Alexa moved closer to Cara's side. "Let's go," she whispered in her ear. "I'm going to the ladies' room," she said next, loud enough for Mike to hear. She tipped her head toward the back of the bar.

Mike stepped closer to Cara.

"Stay," his voice rumbled in her ear.

Cara shook her head, and before he could ask again, she turned away and followed Alexa across the room, feeling the heat of his gaze on her back as she walked away.

"God." Cara realized she was trembling and wrapped her arms around herself, waiting for the small powder room area to clear.

Once they had the room to themselves, Alexa touched her shoulder. "Are you okay?"

Cara swallowed hard, shaking her head. She wasn't okay. Not by a long shot. "I can't talk about this without falling apart. So let's discuss you. What was that dancing all about?"

Alexa, cheeks flushed, shrugged and glanced away. "I don't know."

"You don't know?" Cara asked incredulously. "This is *you*. And some stranger. Bodies a little too close, you know?"

Alexa glanced in the mirror and swiped at some liner that had smudged beneath her eyes. "It's just flirting." She bit her bottom lip, unwilling to meet Cara's gaze because they both knew it had looked like more.

"Do you *like* this guy? I mean that way?"

Alexa shook her head. "I don't know him. But he's sexy." She managed a shrug.

"I get that, but are you leading him on? Because a lot of guys don't like that," Cara said pointedly.

"I'm lonely, okay?" Alexa gripped the counter with one hand, her knuckles turning white. "He's cute. He's attentive. When was the last time I took something just for me?"

Cara covered her friend's hand with her own. She couldn't ever remember seeing Dr. Alexa Collins looking vulnerable, and Cara hurt for her. "You know I understand. But he's a stranger, and I can't help worrying."

Alexa's normally bright eyes weren't sparkling. "I know. But I don't have time for a relationship. All I do is work and go home to an empty bed. I can't keep this up. I don't know whether I'm exhausted or in need of companionship or both."

Cara sighed, feeling her friend's pain. She met Alexa's gaze. "It's time to change something in your life."

Alexa's shoulders deflated. "You're right. Something needs to give." She sniffed and reached for a paper towel to blot her eyes. "I just need time to think."

Cara nodded. "Fair enough." She kissed her friend's cheek. "You okay?"

"Yeah. Pathetic but okay."

"You're normal. If anyone's pathetic, it's me." Cara glanced in the mirror and made a face.

Alexa shook her head. "You handled him well. You stood up for yourself, and I was proud of you."

"Thanks." Cara didn't feel all that proud. As much as she'd turned him away, she still wanted him. Not that she'd let herself give in, but she hated the weakness those feelings inspired.

"Are you ready to go back in there?" Alexa asked.

Cara straightened her shoulders. "No, but I'm not going to let him run me off, either." She studied her reflection and sighed. "I would like some lip gloss, first."

"Body armor. I like it," Alexa said with a grin.

"Yeah, but I left my purse in the car. I'll run out and be back in a few minutes. I'll meet you back out by the bar."

"Want me to go with you?" Alexa offered.

"Nah. Why should both of us freeze?" They'd parked their cars out back and left their coats to make things easier once inside the bar.

A group of women practically fell into the ladies' room, giggling and laughing loudly.

Cara and Alexa stepped toward the door. "I'll be back in a few minutes," Cara promised, and headed outside.

The freezing cold air rushed over her skin and chilled her to her bones. Still, she appreciated the reprieve, not ready to deal with Mike again so soon. Shivering, she rushed past the brick wall behind the bar, her car a few feet away, when someone grabbed her around the neck.

"What the hell?"

Cara attempted to pivot, but the big body and surprise attack prevented her from using any means of self-defense, leaving her with one alternative. She screamed loudly before the arm strengthened, cutting off her air.

"Shut up, bitch," a deep male baritone said, too close to her ear.

Cara recognized the voice. Bob Francone, Daniella's ex. Shit. Before she could act, Bob yanked her against him, his beefy arm strong and thick around her neck. The harder she struggled, the tighter he held on.

She coughed and would have driven her fingernails into his arms, but the heavy jacket he wore prevented her from hitting skin. And her gun was in her ankle holster, out of reach.

"You convinced my woman to leave me," he raged, and though Cara couldn't see his face, she'd bet it was red with anger.

He squeezed her neck harder, and Cara desperately pulled at his arm. "Can't breathe." She didn't know if the words came out of her mouth or were merely inside her head. White spots floated in front of her eyes from lack of air.

He eased his hold on her throat, but the pain that remained was excruciating and she hacked out a cough.

"Are you insane, attacking a cop?" she asked.

"You convinced her to leave me. Both times. You screwed up my life, and now you're going to fix it," Bob demanded.

Cara concentrated on inhaling gulps of air and planning on how to reach for her gun.

"Well? Do you hear me?"

She didn't answer. She couldn't.

So he slammed her against the wall, his hands at her throat.

Jesus, could the man not find another way to subdue women? "What do you want?" Again, Cara wasn't sure whether her words came out.

He'd cut off her breath and her ears had begun to ring.

Bob got up close, his cigarette-tinged breath in her face. "You're going to tell Daniella to come home." He enunciated each word as if she were a moron. "Got it?" He loosened his grip so she could answer.

"When should I do that? While she's looking at the bruises on my throat?" Cara asked, her voice gravelly and painful.

Bob slapped her across the face and she blinked hard, her vision fading. Dizziness assaulted her, and she had very little time to break his grip before she blacked out.

Grasping at a last-ditch effort, she rammed her knee into his groin.

"You *bitch*!" he yelled, releasing her as he doubled over, clutching the family jewels.

Cara fell forward, her head hitting the pavement as she landed.

"What the fuck?" Mike's voice drifted toward her.

Gentle hands turned her face up. "Cara?" Mike sounded hoarse and petrified.

She'd have liked to reassure him, but she was barely

breathing, the spots in her vision rushing at her from all sides.

"Cara?"

Alexa's voice, this time. And Alexa's soft hands on her face. Peeling back her eyelids.

The wailing of a siren.

"I hurt." Cara reached for her neck as everything around her went black.

Eighteen

Cara awoke to the sound of Mike's voice and an aching, throbbing pain in her throat and head. She hurt; she was woozy and disoriented.

"Alexa said she's okay," Mike said. "Bruised windpipe, which is going to hurt like hell, and a mild concussion." He paused. "No. They sedated her. Apparently, she attempted to climb off the stretcher to get to Daniella. She was damned near hysterical, not hearing that Francone was in custody. Alexa finally gave her something to knock her out so she wouldn't hurt her throat even more."

Yeah, Cara remembered that now.

Once they'd brought her to the hospital, all she could think about was Bob's big hands around her neck, trying to choke the life out of her. She couldn't let him do the same to Daniella. Dizzy and still in pain, Cara shut her eyes again, thinking jail was a good place for the bastard. She hoped they kept him there this time.

"Can you get word to Daniella for me?" Mike asked. "Let her know what's going on? Cara would want that."

The man was a keeper, she thought, before remembering he didn't want to be kept.

"Thanks, Sam," Mike said.

Aah. So he was talking to his brother.

A sudden spasm hit Cara in the chest and she coughed—or tried to. The pain in her head and throat blindsided her, and she moaned.

"Gotta go." Mike spun around and was by her side in an instant. "You're awake."

"I—"

"Don't talk. Alexa said it'll hurt if you try. They're going to keep you overnight to observe your breathing, and they'll let you go home in the morning. Okay?"

She nodded.

He brushed her hair off her face, his eyes warm and full of emotion. "Cara, baby—"

She turned her head, a tear leaking from the corner of her eye. She didn't want his sympathy or pity any more than she wanted to hear whatever he was going to say. Anything sweet and caring would unravel her. She still wasn't over him and probably never would be. The physical ache in her throat now was bad enough. Adding the emotion of wanting to cry had the pain increasing tenfold. He needed to leave.

Instead his big hand covered hers. "You scared me," he said, so softly she could barely hear. "Thank God you're okay. I don't know what I'd do if I lost you."

Nice words that he couldn't possibly mean. He was merely feeling the shock of her attack, she thought, keeping her head averted and her eyes closed tight. She kept her focus on breathing through her nose.

Soon her limbs grew heavy, and behind her eyelids things began to spin. Maybe she still had the sedative in her system. Or maybe she was on painkillers. Something was making her dizzy.

"Sleep, baby," Mike whispered, his voice gruff. "I'll be here when you wake up."

*   *   *

Mike didn't know how long he'd slept, but a hand shaking his shoulder woke him, and he bolted up from his half-prone position on Cara's bed where he'd laid his head. He rose from the chair, every muscle in his body protesting the night he'd spent there.

"I brought you some coffee," Sam said softly, so as not to wake Cara.

"Thanks." Mike gratefully accepted the cup.

Sam tipped his head, indicating they should step out of the room.

Mike paused to glance at Cara. She lay against the hospital bed, eyes closed, her face pale, and with the white sheets, the bruising on her face and neck stood out even more. It was a good thing Sam had handled booking Bob Francone, because if Mike got his hands on the man, he'd kill him and save the state the cost of a trial.

Mike followed him into the hall.

"Were you here all night?" Sam asked.

Mike nodded. They'd moved Cara to a private room, which was why the sympathetic nurse had let Mike, who wasn't family, stay with her. Then again, Mike had towered over the male nurse, flashed his badge, and made it clear he wasn't leaving.

"Listen," Sam said. "I just came here, one, to check on her, and two, to apologize. If it weren't for me, you'd have gotten to her much sooner." Sam's guilt was palpable.

According to Alexa, Cara had just stepped outside to her car to get her bag and when she'd taken too long to return, Mike's gut, which never steered him wrong, told him to go check on her. But Sam had insisted Mike give her time to cool off. And he'd forced himself to wait another few minutes.

Mike knew how much his brother cared about Cara. "Don't do that to yourself. There's no way either of us could have anticipated she was in danger."

Francone had gone quiet since his release and nobody suspected he'd go after Cara.

"But—" Sam geared up to argue.

"Shut up," Mike muttered to his brother. He might be silently cursing them both for the time he'd wasted, but Sam's guilt wouldn't change anything. "She's going to be fine, and that's what matters."

Sam nodded. "Thanks. I'll go look for Alexa and see when she plans on signing her out." He slapped Mike on the back and walked down the hall.

Mike leaned back and closed his eyes, the events of last night playing out in vivid detail, every second feeling like an eternity as he watched the woman he loved struggling for her life.

If anything happened to her, Mike would be lost.

He'd already taken his brother's advice. Mike's *go big or go home* plan was ready and waiting. He was amazed at how much he had accomplished in the short time since he'd left the city. He'd wanted to share his news with Cara last night, but she'd run from him. Now he had a captive audience and he'd stop at nothing to convince her that *she* was his home.

By the time the doctors signed Cara's release papers and gave her instructions, she was antsy and ready to leave this place for good.

"Soft foods, lots of rest, and little talking," the older female nurse reminded her, handing Cara the paperwork.

"Don't worry," Mike said, wrapping an arm around her waist. "I'll make sure she listens to doctor's orders."

Cara narrowed her gaze, frowning at him. She had tried telling him to get lost, but he wasn't listening and short spurts of sentences were all she could manage.

Alexa had left earlier, so Cara didn't have her as a buffer with Mike. And since Cara understood that she needed someone around because of the concussion, she was stuck with him. At least until she could make other arrangements, which she intended to do, by text, as soon as possible.

The nurse looked over toward the door. "Oh! There's the wheelchair now."

Cara groaned.

"Hospital policy. You leave in our wheels." The older woman patted the seat.

A few minutes later, she was settled in Mike's truck, a place she'd never thought she'd be again. The arousing scent of his cologne permeated her pores, causing an ache in her heart she was beginning to think she'd never be rid of.

Angry at both him and the situation, she folded her arms across her chest and stared out the window, until she realized he wasn't driving toward her house.

She prodded him in the arm and asked, "Where are you going?"

"No talking, Kermit," he said with a laugh.

She scowled at him.

"You'll see, so hush and enjoy the scenery." He settled in for the ride.

Cara wasn't so comfortable, not just because of the pain, which she could handle thanks to a generous dose of medication, but because Mike's return unsettled her as much as the attention he insisted on lavishing on her. She didn't want it, didn't need it, and most of all, she couldn't let herself enjoy it again.

She'd texted Alexa and asked her friend to meet her at Cara's house so she could get rid of Mike, but she wasn't answering. Neither was Sam. And now she knew they weren't going home anyway. Out of options, Cara gave in and shut her eyes.

She didn't realize she'd dozed off until she heard Mike calling her name. She forced her heavy eyelids open.

He cut the motor.

"Where are we?" She pressed her hand to her throat as she tried to speak.

"Shh. Just listen, okay?" He shifted in his seat and faced her, the most serious expression she'd ever seen on his handsome face.

Uh-oh. Her insides churned from nerves, and she wished she were anywhere but here. Mike had her at a serious disadvantage, unable to speak, stuck with him in his car, God knows where, while he prepared to . . . what? Explain that he was back for some ridiculous reason that had nothing to do with her, she wondered, and wrapped her arms around herself for comfort.

"I made a huge mistake," he said, his tone gruff.

She narrowed her gaze.

"I should never have left town. I should have pulled myself together and dealt with everything being thrown at me. Rex, Simon, the case, the resignation, the job offer . . ." He frowned, clearly disgusted with his own actions.

Amazed at his honesty, she listened, waiting to hear more.

"You were right. If I needed time, I should have just said so. And I damned sure shouldn't have pulled away from you." He paused before continuing. "I reverted to my old M.O. and I ran when I should have stuck around and dealt with things here." He cleared his throat, his expression as filled with pain as Cara's heart. "I never meant to hurt you."

She managed to swallow before attempting to speak, the words gut-wrenching to admit. "But you did."

He moved his hand to the back of her seat, but Mike didn't move to touch her, for which she was grateful. A simple stroke of his hand and she'd break down.

She was proud of how well she was holding herself together and hoped she wouldn't have to do it for much longer. "So what now? We're friends?" she asked, wincing at the sound of her own voice.

He was right, she did sound like Kermit. What a way to have this final conversation, Cara thought. Well, at least it would be memorable for him.

Mike stared into her eyes for so long, she didn't know what to think or feel.

Finally he answered her. "Yeah, we're friends."

Her stomach plummeted at his agreement. Even though he'd told her he needed time to think, Cara hadn't believed him. She'd known then he was ending things. He'd left her just as he'd said he would, and she choked back a cry at the painful recollection.

"Hey." He slid his hand from the seat to the back of her neck and gently pulled her close. "We're friends and so much more." He drew a shuddering breath. "*I love you, baby*," he said in that husky tone she'd dreamed about since he'd been gone.

Her heart beat out a rapid rhythm as shock enveloped her. "What?"

"I love you," he said, his eyes warm, his emotions there for her to see.

She'd never seen Mike vulnerable before, but he was now, and despite her misgivings about what this declaration meant, that alone made her want to believe.

"I love you," he said once more, no hesitation, no uncertainty.

She couldn't prevent the happy tears leaking from her eyes. "But you said—"

"Forget everything I said before. I'd never been in love. I never had to change my life for anyone, nor did I want to. Until you. So please just listen to what I have to say now, okay?"

She nodded. They both knew she wasn't going anywhere. He had her mesmerized, hopeful, and scared all at the same time.

He brushed her tears with his thumb. "I'm here, baby. I'm staying in Serendipity. The mayor formally offered me Simon's job permanently, and I accepted."

Cara's mind balked. "But you'll get bored. You'll grow to hate it and me—"

"Never." He kept his hand against her uninjured cheek. "As soon as I walked into my New York apartment, I knew I'd screwed up. It took me a week to do something about it because I didn't think you'd want to see me again. And based on your reaction, I was right." He winced at the memory they both held of how she'd rejected him back at the bar.

Cara ought to feel bad, but she didn't. She was too shocked by his words and by the fact that he'd thought this out so clearly—and he'd taken the job.

He was staying.

"When you left the bar, my gut told me to go after you, but I waited. Then I saw that bastard's hands on your throat and your head hit the pavement." His body trembled. "You scared me to death."

"Sorry," she whispered.

"No, I'm sorry. For leaving, for putting you through the last week."

If it brought them to this point, it was okay, Cara thought, her heart close to exploding from her chest. "You warned me not to get too invested, but despite everything, I fell in love with you too."

As much as it hurt to talk, it was worth the pain to finally express her feelings and know they were reciprocated, she thought, running her finger down his cheek.

"Thank God." He moved closer, and Cara threw herself against him, finding everything she'd ever wanted as his strong arms enveloped her in a tight embrace.

He pushed her away long enough to kiss her, a soul-stealing, all-consuming melding of lips that lit her up from the inside out. His tongue slid against hers and she moaned, seeking closer contact, wanting to rub up against him and never be cold again.

"You're sure about all this?" she asked.

"So sure that I gave up my New York apartment and put a deposit on this house—pending your approval. The real estate agent faxed me pictures and I fell in love, but I wanted us to walk through together."

"I don't understand," she whispered.

His grin transformed his entire face, and Cara fell in love all over again, more so because this time she didn't have to push away the emotions because now they were shared.

"You're my life," he said, the words a balm to her soul. "I want to get married, have a family, raise kids here in Serendipity. I want them to know their grandparents. And I want you to know that I will *never* abandon you again."

Cara was crying for real now, but they were good tears, tears that told her he'd just given her everything she'd never dared to hope for or dream about. She watched in disbelief as he reached into his jacket pocket and pulled out a ring.

Go big or go home, Mike thought, holding out the diamond engagement ring he'd picked out himself. He'd managed a lot in a short time, including this ring, which had called to him as soon as he'd laid eyes on it.

He presented it to her with shaking hands. "So, Cara Hartley, will you marry me?" he asked, as he gazed into the face of the woman he loved more than life itself.

She stared at him with those big, blue, expressive eyes, then glanced down at the ring and nodded. "Yes. Yes!"

She threw her arms around him, nuzzling her face into his neck, and Mike breathed easy for the first time in over a week. Or maybe ever in his life.

He separated them long enough to clasp her hand and slip the ring onto her finger.

"Look at that," she murmured. "It's a perfect fit."

He couldn't help but grin. "Just like us."

He met her gaze, loving that her cheeks now glowed with happiness, a feeling that echoed inside him. "Ready to go check out the house?" he asked.

She nodded.

Hand in hand, they walked up the driveway to the huge Colonial set back on a private street in his small hometown of Serendipity. And Mike thanked his lucky stars that she'd given him a second chance.

Cara was *his* and he was finally home.

And now a special excerpt from Carly Phillips's
next Serendipity's Finest novel . . .

Perfect Fling

Coming soon from Berkley Books!

Erin Marsden had always been Serendipity's good girl. As assistant district attorney, only daughter of the ex-police chief, youngest sibling of two overprotective brothers, both cops, one of whom was the current police chief, Erin always lived up to expectations. She'd never made a misstep, more afraid of disappointing her family than of stepping out of the stereotypical role she'd always, always fulfilled.

Until last night.

She blinked and took stock of her surroundings: a strange bed, walls she didn't recognize, and a warm, nude male body beside her very naked one.

Cole Sanders.

She took in his too-long mess of dark hair and the muscles in his upper back, thought about the way her body ached in all the right places, and she shivered. No doubt about it, when she finally stepped out of the mold she'd created, she'd not only done a one-eighty but made the most un-good-girl-like move she could think of. A one-night stand.

A one-night stand.

The thought made her giddy and also slightly nauseous as she silently traced the path that had led her here. She'd started yesterday at her brother Mike's wedding, surrounded by friends, family, and happy, loving couples everywhere she looked, making Erin the odd woman out. Not wanting to go home alone just yet, she'd stopped by Joe's Bar on the way home. Misstep number one. She'd let Cole Sanders, the man with whom her sixteen-year-old self had shared a long-remembered kiss the night before he left town for good, interrupt her dance with an old friend. Misstep number two. He'd pulled her close against his hard body. She'd looked into his dark blue eyes and seen a world weariness that tore at her heart, then acknowledged the sexual tension they'd both ignored since his return. Misstep number three. Then she'd gone for gold, agreeing to join him upstairs in his room over the bar for an all-night session of marathon sex.

And, oh my God, sex with Cole had been phenomenal. She didn't know two people could generate such heat. It had been *that* fantastic. In fact, Erin thought, she'd stretch and purr in contentment right now if she wasn't afraid of waking the man snoring lightly beside her.

Although their parents were good friends, Erin didn't know him well. Nobody did, not anymore. Not even her brother Mike, who had been one of his closest pals. Cole's father had been her dad's deputy chief of police until last year, but Jed Sanders never spoke of his son. According to Erin's brother, Cole had dropped out of the police academy mere days before their graduation. What Cole did after that was anybody's guess, but rumors ran crazy in their small town. Some said Cole had gotten involved in organized crime in Manhattan, others claimed he ran drug and prostitution rings. Having grown up around Cole, even if she had kept her distance from the rough-and-tumble bad boy he'd been, Erin couldn't bring herself to believe he'd gone so wrong.

Call her naïve, but she'd always seen something deeper in Cole, something good, even when he'd clashed with his tough-as-nails father. Even as the rest of the town basically shunned him since his return, Erin couldn't bring herself to do the same. Not that he'd approached her, but when she'd seen him around, she'd always treated him to a hello or a genuine smile. Those steely eyes always looked her over before boring into hers with an intensity that put her off-kilter, but he'd never acknowledged her friendly overtures.

Until last night.

And good girl that she was, Erin still couldn't dredge up an ounce of regret. She was long overdue for a night like that. Which didn't mean she wouldn't make her escape as cleanly as possible. What Erin didn't know about awkward morning afters could fill a book. The quiet, tepid affairs in her past always ended the same way, with a polite "it's not you it's me," before she'd walk away. She'd never had to slip out of a man's bed undetected before.

She snuck one last glance at his broad shoulders, rising and falling with every breath he took. His arm muscles, sculpted from hard work and marked by ink, caused her to shiver anew.

Breathe, she silently ordered herself.

Think, she commanded next. Her clothes were scattered around the bedroom, if she called her bridesmaid's dress clothing to sneak out in. With a last look at the man who'd made the earth move for her last night, Erin eased out from beneath the warm comforter and rose, searching for her dress. She bent over, stark naked, mortified her butt was in the air as she grabbed for her dress.

"I didn't peg you as the type to sneak out," Cole said in a lazy masculine drawl.

She snagged her dress from the floor and turned to face him, hugging the fabric against her for protection, suddenly feeling every inch the good girl she'd been a mere twenty-four hours ago.

"I've already seen every inch," he reminded her, his heavy lidded gaze never leaving hers.

She flushed. Sometimes her lawyerly skills at deflecting came in handy and she opted to ignore the more humiliating comment, focusing instead on the first. "What type did you peg me for?"

He eased up against the headboard. Sexy, tousled and too handsome, one look had her wanting to crawl back into bed with him. That wasn't happening for a number of reasons, the first being that a one-night stand had a shelf life and she'd used up hers. Second, to her extreme disappointment, he wasn't asking. And third, bad-girl Erin was an aberration. This morning, with no champagne in her system, good-girl Erin had returned, more's the pity.

He stretched his hands behind his head and leaned back, studying her. The sheet slipped below his navel and it took all her strength not to stare.

"You were pretty gutsy last night. I wouldn't have pegged you for a coward." He cocked an eyebrow.

Did the man never smile? "I wouldn't have pegged you as a guy who'd want a woman to stick around . . . after."

Which made her wonder why he hadn't let her slip out unnoticed, even if he had been awake. It would have spared them both the awkwardness of . . . this. Then again, they'd have to play this conversation out some time. Might as well get it over with, she thought.

Then his words came back to her. "I was gutsy?" She straightened her shoulders a bit at that.

Erin was tough at work, she had to be in order to keep up with her boss and hold her own against defense attorneys and their clients, but gutsy with men? That was a first, and she kind of liked hearing it.

"I left the bar with you. That took guts," she said, sounding almost pleased with herself.

He eyed her without cracking a grin, but she'd swear she

saw a hint of amusement in his eyes. Before he banked it, that is.

"I meant you were gutsy in bed."

His words along with the deep rumble of approval in his tone warmed her inside and out and the heat of a blush rose to her cheeks. "Thank you," she said, immediately horrified. Had she really just said that?

That earned her a sexy grin she'd never forget. "But back to my original point. We go way back. So no, I didn't expect you to sneak out."

She nodded.

"Regrets?" he asked, surprising her with the question but not with the suddenly defensive edge to his voice.

She immediately shook her head. "None." It saddened her that he'd think she'd have them.

Not that it surprised her. No one in town had welcomed him with open arms and if anyone found out about last night, they'd think she'd lost her mind. And if her brothers discovered her secret . . . She refused to go there. If regret hadn't kicked in yet, she doubted it would. And she wouldn't want him to think she was embarrassed that she'd slept with him.

"You surprise me," he admitted, studying her intently. "And I didn't think there was much left in this world that could."

He sounded as if he'd seen and done too much in his lifetime. A part of her wanted to reach out and soothe his hidden pain. But before she could dissect her thoughts or heaven forbid act on them, he spoke.

"But your instincts about me were right on. I'm not much for long, drawn-out morning afters."

Disappointment stabbed her in the heart and *that* was too dangerous to even contemplate for long. "Glad to know I'm still on my game," she said, forcing flippancy when she felt anything but.

Now that it was time to say good-bye, it wasn't just

awkward, it hurt a little more than she'd imagined it would. Which was what she got for thinking she could handle a one-night stand with a guy she'd always had somewhat of a thing for. No matter how young she'd been at the time.

"Since it was just a one-night stand, you won't have to worry about a repeat performance." She tossed the words as flippantly as she could manage.

"Pity," he murmured.

She jerked in surprise.

Just as she was wondering if she had the nerve to ask him to turn around so she could get dressed, he flipped the covers off himself and rose from the bed—stark, gloriously naked.

All thoughts fled from her brain. She tried to swallow and choked instead, ending up with another blush as she continued to cough until the spasm passed.

"And that just confirms why it has to be one night only," he muttered low, obviously more to himself than to her.

Erin hated puzzles and enigmas. "What does that mean?" she asked.

"Erin, honey, in a world where nothing and no one is what they seem, you're real." He pulled on his jeans, leaving the top button open and Erin drooling. "And that makes you dangerous."

"More riddles," she told him.

He ignored her. Strolling over to the dresser, he opened a drawer and tossed her a pair of drawstring sweats and a faded gray T-shirt. "Here. You'll be more comfortable—not to mention less conspicuous—leaving in these."

She swallowed hard. "Thank you."

He gestured to the open door in the corner. "Bathroom's there. Towels for the shower are in one of the drawers. Take your time," he said, and padded out of the room, a man comfortable in his own skin.

She shook her head, pushing away all thoughts except the rush to shower, dress, and leave. Any emotions or lingering thoughts or feelings could wait until she was alone. At which point, she'd do her customary internal summarizing of events and tuck this episode away in her memory banks for safekeeping. Never to be revisited again, except on long, lonely nights when it was just her and her vibrator. Because everything inside her knew, despite his brush-off and surly attitude this morning, he'd set the bar way too high for any man who came after him.

And Erin had already set it pretty damned high on her own.

SIX WEEKS LATER . . .

If this case didn't end soon, Erin would either pass out on the desk in front of the judge, the jury, and the entire courtroom or she'd throw up on her brand-new shoes. It was a toss-up which would happen first. Judge White, whose hair matched his name, droned on with jury instructions, while for Erin, the next twenty minutes passed in a blur of nausea and exhaustion. Finally she heard the blessed sound of the gavel adjourning them for the day, and she dropped her head to the table with a thud.

"Don't worry, I took notes on everything the judge said and there wasn't anything we didn't anticipate or I'd have objected," Trina Lewis, Erin's second chair for this trial assured her.

"Thanks," Erin mumbled into the desk.

"Come on. Let's get you out of here. Bathroom before we go home?"

Erin forced her head up. "Yeah. Please."

Trina had already gathered Erin's things and put them into her bag and together they walked out of the courtroom. To her relief, most everyone had already left, so she didn't need to deal with people.

"Erin, umm, can I talk to you?" Trina asked as she pushed open the door to the ladies' room and they stepped inside.

"Of course."

Trina had been working in the D.A.'s office for the last two years, and as the only two female lawyers, she and Erin had become good friends. No professional jealousy or posturing between them, Trina was Erin's escape from the male posturing when she needed one and visa versa.

Before speaking, Trina checked underneath the stall doors to make sure they were empty. Ever since Lyle Gordon, the lazy bastard who just happened to be the defense attorney on their current case, had posted his paralegal in here to overhear anything that could help him win, Erin and Trina were extra careful about where they spoke and in front of whom.

"All clear," Trina said.

"What's up?" Erin turned on the faucet and splashed cold water on her face.

"Don't you think this is the longest stomach virus in the history of the world?" Trina ripped a paper towel from the dispenser and handed it to Erin.

"It's getting better," Erin lied.

"No, it's not. You've been sick for two weeks. So while you were sipping tea in the cafeteria during lunch, I ran out to the pharmacy and bought you this." She held out a brown paper bag.

Erin narrowed her gaze, cautiously accepting the bag. "What's in it?" She didn't wait for Trina to answer, peeking instead. "A pregnancy test?" Erin shrieked before slapping her hand over her own mouth. "Are you kidding me? We've been working twenty-four/seven for I don't know how long. I can't remember the last time I used my battery-operated friend, never mind had a real man."

"Liar," Trina said for the second time.

Erin scowled at her friend. They both knew she remembered the exact last time she'd had a real man. Six and a half weeks ago and Erin recalled every perfect, muscular inch of Cole Sanders and their night together.

Their *safe* night. He'd used protection each time, and there'd been many. Besides, what were the chances the one and only time she'd stepped outside her comfort zone, something life altering had actually happened? Fate wouldn't do that to her after all her years as a good girl. Would it?

Erin regretted having shared vague details with Trina, who now stood next to her pointing to the offending test box that every woman on the planet recognized.

"Take it," Trina ordered.

"I can't be pregnant." Erin's stomach revolted at the very thought and every nerve in her body shouted in denial.

"Good. Then prove me wrong and I'll take you to the doctor to find out why you've been nauseous for two weeks straight." Trina pinned her with a gaze that had potential defendants shaking and crying for mommy.

"Fine." Erin grabbed the box and headed for the private stall. Her hands shook so badly she was barely able to read, let alone follow the instructions. But a few minutes later, she and Trina were waiting in uncomfortable silence for the clichéd pink or blue line.

As the second hand of her watch ticked slowly by, Erin thought about Cole. He'd deliberately steered clear of her in the time since their night together. The most contact she'd had with him was a tip of his head before he'd walked out the door of Cuppa Café. Erin would have been more comfortable with a friendly chat to dispel the lingering tension inside her but Cole made it clear that one night meant just that. They weren't even destined to be friends.

She couldn't pretend his indifference didn't hurt and wished he'd leave their small town so he wouldn't be a permanent reminder of her one step outside the lines.

She *couldn't* be pregnant and *not* with his baby. She could think of no worse, no more awkward scenario and her stomach lurched at the possibility.

"Ding!" Trina's too-cheerful voice shook her out of her painful thoughts.

Erin wrapped both arms around herself, aware she was shaking. "You look."

Trina held out her hand and Erin gratefully accepted her friend's support. She held her breath, her heart pounding so hard in her chest she could swear she heard the sound in her ears while at this point she couldn't tell if the lump in her throat was from nausea or panic.

"Well? Erin asked, unable to stand the silence or the suspense any longer.

"It's positive," Trina whispered, no longer feigning upbeat excitement.

Erin let out a sound she didn't recognize and ran for the nearest stall, no longer able to contain the nausea she'd been holding at bay.

Cole woke up to the sun shining through the window in his small apartment. As he did every morning, he catalogued how he was feeling and today was no different than any other day. He'd had a nightmare that woke him at three A.M. and kept him up until the early hours of the morning, and he still felt like shit about his life. Yep, status quo in his world.

He was back home in Serendipity until he figured out what the hell he wanted to do with his life, and he still hadn't a clue. All Cole knew was that it wasn't undercover work. He'd lived for the job, knowing he was taking down the scum of the earth, not thinking that in doing so, he was becoming just like them. After the way the last job had ended, he wasn't so sure—and until he could look himself in the mirror again, he wouldn't be making any permanent decisions.

Working construction for Nick Mancini, filling in part-time when his old friend had an opening, suited Cole just fine. Today was a day off, which meant he could head over to his father's place.

God help him.

Cole and Jed existed in an armed truce, both of them wary and ready for action with the slightest provocation from the other. Cole reminded himself that his father was aging, losing his ability to do the things he liked and that used to come easily, like repairing the loose board on the front porch steps. The old man's pride prevented him from being grateful his son was now around to help him out. That and the fact that Cole and Jed approached life in very different ways, always had, always would.

Take the career they'd both chosen. Jed started out of high school as a part-time construction worker near Philadelphia, turning to law enforcement after he blamed himself for his younger sister's death. Jed saw the police force and the rules and regulations he turned to enforcing as a means of coping with the senseless, random acts that life threw a man's way. Which was why he never understood or accepted Cole's murky world where rules were shady if nonexistent. He would have preferred his son did his job aboveboard, with a badge. He kept Cole's secret, but he never approved of his choice and wasn't proud, even if Cole had been doing good work—for a while, anyway.

And now?

His father had left his fly-by-night construction job, turning to law enforcement as his salvation. So of course, Jed couldn't accept that while Cole was similarly at loose ends, tormented by his part in an innocent woman's death, he hadn't turned to the Serendipity police force and the values Jed held dear. Instead, Cole was doing soul-searching, working part-time until he could get his shit together. If he could. Sometimes Cole thought he was *this* close to losing his sanity.

Needless to say, the two men didn't see eye to eye. On anything. Jed's wife of more than ten years normally acted as a buffer between the two men, but Rachel's daughter had a new baby and she'd gone to visit for a while. Which meant Cole was on his own when dealing with his father.

He took a hot shower, dressed and headed downstairs. Around the corner from Joe's Bar was Cuppa Café, owned by Joe's sister, Trisha, where every morning, Cole picked up his much-needed coffee, ignoring the fact that most people in town gave him a wide berth. Not everyone, since Trisha treated him to a genuine smile for an old friend. Erin had tried to do the same, but Cole had immediately nixed any friendly overtures the first time he'd run into her after they'd slept together.

Erin.

The only good thing about his return home so far. And for that reason he had to stay far away from her, no matter how tempting she was with her good-girl persona, her creamy soft skin, and the combustible chemistry that had taken him off guard. Not to mention the light laughter that warmed his chilled, dark soul.

She might think he was a bastard, and the hurt look on her face when he froze her out made him feel like one, but she didn't need the aggravation that came with being associated with Cole Sanders.

His father let him know that people in town currently viewed him as an unknown entity, a troublemaker who hadn't grown up, among other choice words. As if to prove the point, anyone in his father's generation scowled when he entered their breathing space. And Nick had mentioned a couple of homeowners who'd preferred Cole wasn't on the crew who worked on their homes. As if he'd steal from anyone, but old neighbors? Friends? Jeez.

Yet Cole had to admit they had their reasons. Considering he'd dropped out of the police academy a few days short of graduation and Mike Marsden, the current police chief and Erin's brother, had been in his class, Cole's status was persona non grata. In Mike's view, Cole had spent the last half dozen years or so working mob-related jobs, construction included, and had been arrested in a raid last year that led to the takedown of one of the biggest bosses around. He'd done his thing and testified but his identity had been kept quiet. Nobody knew his past, and Cole didn't care. But a woman like Erin deserved better than to be associated with the man people thought he'd become.

Hell, Cole figured he'd come pretty damned close to being that man so the good folks of Serendipity weren't far off base in their assessment of him.

Grabbing his drink, he climbed into his old Mustang and headed over to his father's place. He pulled up in front of the house where he grew up, taking it in with a critical eye. Never mind the loose floorboard, which wasn't visible to the naked eye, the paint was peeling, the windows needed cleaning, and if they didn't get the roof fixed by next winter, his father would have his hands full with trouble.

For now, however, he'd focus on the smaller jobs and dealing with his father. Once Rachel came home, he'd try talking to them both about moving into a condo that was smaller, easier to take care of, and where the maintenance was covered. His father had bitten his head off the first time he'd made the suggestion.

He walked up the driveway, surprised to see a sporty royal blue Jeep parked in front of the garage. He knew who owned that car.

Erin.

For as much as he'd tried avoiding her, it appeared he was about to come face-to-face with his one-night stand.

From *New York Times* Bestselling Author
Carly Phillips

The first in a new series about a quaint upstate New York town where love, fate, and fortune are intertwined...

Serendipity

Faith Harrington was the classic girl of privilege—until her father was convicted of running a Ponzi scheme and her marriage crashed and burned.

Now Faith is back in her hometown of Serendipity, New York, for a fresh start. But not everyone is ready to welcome her with open arms. Then she runs into her teenage crush—the dark, brooding Ethan Barron, who is no stranger to scandal himself. Faith is sure that getting involved with the town's notorious bad boy will lead only to trouble. But her heart has other ideas—and so do the townspeople of Serendipity...